DIAM
ON THE
LEVELS

An addictive crime thriller full of twists

DAVID HODGES

Detective Kate Hamblin Mysteries Book 13

JOFFE BOOKS

Joffe Books, London
www.joffebooks.com

First published in Great Britain in 2024

Cover art by Nick Castle

ISBN: 978-1-83526-394-5

This book is dedicated to my wife, Elizabeth, for all her love, patience and support over so many wonderful years and to my late mother and father, whose faith in me to one day achieve my ambition as a writer remained steadfast throughout their lifetimes and whose tragic passing has left a hole in my own life that will never be filled.

AUTHOR'S NOTE

This story is totally fictitious and, although some of the geographical place names quoted are real, the action of the novel and all the characters in it are entirely products of the author's imagination, without any intended connection to real events or persons living or dead. Some poetic licence has also been adopted in relation to local police structures and specific operational police procedures to meet the requirements of the plot. But the novel is primarily a crime thriller and does not profess to be a detailed police procedural, even though the policing background, as depicted, is broadly in accord with the national picture. I trust that these small departures from fact will not spoil the reading enjoyment of serving or retired police officers for whom I have the utmost respect.

David Hodges

BEFORE THE FACT

4 March 1998 was an unremarkable day for most of the general population of London. It was just another day for ordinary people. But for one unremarkable, bespectacled employee of the British government, it was about to become the day which would change his life for ever — and not for the better either.

Johnathon Street found the Turkish coffee shop in the narrow street off the Strand with little difficulty. He had previously worked as a sub-editor in Fleet Street, so he knew the area and its wine bars and cafes well. But he was not here for either pleasure or business this time, but self-preservation. His nerves had been badly shot after receipt of the note with the enclosed photographs in his home mail. Fortunately, the envelope had been marked "Strictly Confidential", guaranteeing the explosive contents were safe from scrutiny by his ever-trusting wife. But that was his only comfort and, unsurprisingly, he found no pleasure in the strong smell of coffee that now greeted him when he stepped through the cafe's low doorway, knowing full well that his whole life and career depended on the outcome of his meeting with the sender.

There were around half a dozen circular tables in the dingy interior of the coffee shop set before a glass counter with a curtain at the back. Just two of the tables were occupied, one by a couple of Asian women wearing headscarves and the other by a man in a neat blue suit, who smiled and waved him over.

'Good of you to come,' the suit said, ordering two coffees when the apron-clad waiter appeared through the curtain and waiting patiently as Street squeezed into the other chair between the table and the corner of the room.

Street studied the man opposite him warily. Tall and thin, with thick black hair that looked as though it had been recently expertly trimmed, his sharp, aquiline features and thin, slightly crooked mouth gave him an almost reptilian look, and the dark penetrating eyes were locked on to Street's with an expression of barely concealed contempt. A smooth, self-assured character, this one, Street mused, and not one to be underestimated.

'So, who are you?' he asked abruptly.

The suit shook his head. 'My name is unimportant, but you can call me Mr Williams if you like. Terrence Williams would be good.'

Street grimaced. It was not his real name obviously, but it was pointless pursuing that fact any further. 'What's this about?' he went on instead, trying to project an image of confidence and self-control.

Williams, as he chose to call himself, sighed. 'I would have thought that was rather obvious from the photographs you were sent,' he said. 'You've been a naughty boy, and we have the evidence to prove just how naughty you've been.'

'So, the whole thing was a setup, start to finish?'

'Let's just say we capitalised on your past inclinations with some skilful photography.'

'Hidden cameras,' Street summarised bitterly.

Williams emitted a soft chuckle. 'The naked lady in the photos is certainly very well-endowed, I have to say, but you could afford to lose some weight.'

Street glanced nervously about him. Then, satisfied that the two women were not within earshot, nor in the least bit interested in the pair of them anyway, he leaned forward across the table.

'How much do you want?' he snapped.

Williams made a dismissive gesture with one hand. 'Not everything is about money, Mr Street,' he said.

'Then what?'

The other paused while the waiter delivered the coffees, then resumed. 'I am acting on behalf of a client who needs you to do him a small favour—'

'What client?'

'You don't expect me to give you his name, do you? Client confidentiality and all that. Suffice it to say, he is a very powerful, well-connected gentleman.'

'So, you're a lawyer?'

'Er, of sorts, yes.'

'I didn't think the Bar went in for blackmail?'

Williams made a face. 'Let's not be indelicate, Mr Street.'

'Well, what else is this?'

'We like to call it a business arrangement. You do a little errand for us and we destroy all the incriminating photographs we have from . . . what was the place called? Ah yes, Susie's Pad.'

Street snorted. 'How do I know you will destroy them when I've done what you ask? They could be used again and again for further extortionate demands.'

'You don't, but we are not interested in a long-term contract with you. Just this one-off arrangement. So, once you have completed your side of things, we will destroy the photographs and negatives in your presence, and you will never hear from us again.'

'And if I tell you to get stuffed and decide to call the police instead?'

Williams shook his head disapprovingly. 'That would be very foolish, Mr Street. I don't think your wife would like to see the photos of your carnal adventures at Susie's, never mind that pretty little daughter of yours when she grows up, and I don't think the parliamentary secretary would be too amused to find out what one of the government's ministers has been up to either. On the rocks can mean more than just a neat whisky, you know. It can be applied to married life and high-flying careers too.'

Street slumped in his seat, his pretend confidence dashed completely. 'What is it I have to do?' he muttered in resignation.

'Drink your coffee,' Williams said gently, 'and I will tell you.'

He sipped his own for a moment, watching Street take several gulps from the large cup in front of him, like a man dying of thirst in the desert.

'You are attending a trade conference in Cape Town next month,' he said.

Street stared at him, a wild look in his eyes. 'How did you know that? The South African trip has not even been announced publicly yet.'

'As I intimated just now, my client has excellent connections. The fact is, we would like you to bring back a package for us in your diplomatic bag.'

Street stared at him aghast. 'A package?' he exclaimed. He inadvertently raised his voice, then cut off abruptly when Williams frowned warningly and continued in a lower tone. 'In *my diplomatic bag*? What sort of package?'

'That's not for you to know. It will be sealed inside a small canvas bag which will be handed to you by a member of the South African security service at an appropriate place after initial contact with you at your hotel, using the name Rubin. Got that? It is all arranged. He will approach *you*, so you don't have to do anything. Just be there and do exactly what he tells you to do.'

Street's mind was working overtime. 'A small canvas bag?' he breathed. 'Diamonds. Blood diamonds. It has to be. That's why you need my diplomatic bag, because you know it won't be checked by the authorities.'

Williams didn't confirm or deny the fact but stared at him levelly.

'Do you know what the penalty is for smuggling blood diamonds?' Street hissed. 'They'd stick me in a South African jail and throw the key away if I were caught.'

'You won't be caught. Not if you keep your head and act naturally. You'll be seen as just another diplomat. Now, do you have a wall safe at home?'

'It's none of your damned business what I have.'

'Which leads me to assume you do. That being so, when you get back from Cape Town with the package, you are to deposit it in that safe, then wait to receive further instructions.'

Street shook his head vigorously. 'I won't bloody do it.'

Williams sighed again and, withdrawing another envelope from an inside pocket, he placed it on the table by Street's coffee cup, nodding at him to open it.

The photographs were even more intimate than the ones posted to Street's home address, and he swayed slightly, gripping the edge of the table for balance as he peeled open the flap and peered at them inside the envelope.

'I suggest you shred or burn them all as quickly as you can,' Williams said, draining his coffee cup and standing up. 'But I take it you now agree to our little business deal?'

Receiving no reply, he smiled again. 'Excellent. Then we'll be in touch when you get back from your trip.' He left some coins on the table to pay for the coffees and turned for the door. 'Oh, and have a nice day, won't you?'

A short distance from the coffee shop, Williams — real name Jeremy Brent, legal adviser and fixer for infamous South London crime boss Charlie Hooper — pulled out his mobile phone and punched in a number. The call was answered almost immediately.

'Well?' a rough nasal voice demanded.

'He's ours,' Brent confirmed. 'All systems go.'

Seated behind the big walnut desk in the smoke-filled back office of his Soho club, the balding, overweight man in the Italian-style blue suit released a long, rasping cough and stubbed out his cigar in the ashtray in front of him. Making no further comment, he ended the call, and poured a stiff measure of Talisker single malt whisky from a bottle standing on the corner of his desk into a lead crystal glass. Then, taking a long pull on the glass, he sucked the spirit backwards and forwards through his gold-capped front teeth for a few moments before sitting back in his leather swivel chair and ringing an international telephone number . . .

At the same moment, Brent pocketed his phone and walked quickly off towards the Aldwych, a noticeable spring in his step and a smile of satisfaction on his lean face.

For Street there was no sense of satisfaction, however. He was between a rock and a hard place, and he sat for a long time at the table in the coffee shop, musing over a cold cup of coffee. Do what the man Williams had instructed, and he risked the prospect of ending up in some notorious South African jail, with violent criminals and terrorists for company. Fail to comply with the instructions he had been given, and he was at the very least a ruined man, with his marriage, career and reputation in tatters; and at the very worst someone facing a death sentence at the hands of ruthless mobsters anxious to seal his lips forever. Suddenly his visits to Susie's Pad had become a lot more expensive than he had anticipated and whether he liked it or not, he had no option but to do as Williams had demanded.

In fact, as it turned out, his fears about being caught in the act proved groundless. The rendezvous with the tall, muscular security policeman in the Cape Town waterfront bar three weeks later went well. The perilous exchange was completed within minutes over beers neither of them drank, and he and his contact were off on their separate ways without anyone being the wiser. As far as he knew, he wasn't followed to the bar and none of his colleagues on the trade delegation evinced the slightest curiosity about his decision to go for that after-dinner stroll following the final presentations at the mini conference. They were far too busy celebrating the success of the negotiations. Furthermore, passage for the whole delegation through Customs was also seamless, both in South Africa and at Heathrow, and his minister raised no objections whatsoever to his request for a few days off after the usual departmental debrief.

Where it all went disastrously wrong for him was a couple of evenings later when, in obedience to a brief telephone call from the man who called himself Terrence Williams, he agreed to meet him with the package in a little-used West London car park. The meeting was as brief as the telephone call and he was hardly aware of the long-bladed knife that penetrated his heart from behind, as he climbed back into his car. Jeremy Brent remained only long enough to steal his Rolex watch and wallet before driving away from the scene of what would be recorded as just another opportunist robbery on London's violent streets.

'All done,' Brent told Charlie Hooper shortly afterwards.

'Good,' Hooper responded without emotion. 'Now bring those little beauties to me.'

* * *

10 April 1998. The Somerset Levels. Charlie Hooper was a self-made man, or so the gangster claimed, but his academic education was sadly lacking and, in particular, he had never been a student of history. If he had, he might have known that African blood diamonds, which have been the cause of bloody conflict throughout the continent for many years, had earned an unenviable reputation for themselves. Some were said to have been cursed and had allegedly brought grave misfortune on anyone associated with the handling, trade and ownership of the magnificent gems. As to whether what he'd referred to as his "little beauties", now nestling in a compartment in Hooper's briefcase, carried a similar curse is unclear, but Charlie's imagination was as sadly lacking as his knowledge of history, so it wouldn't have made any difference to him anyway. Furthermore, right at that precise moment he had more pressing concerns on his mind.

Thick white mist, insidious and clinging, had begun rolling steadily out across the desolate marshland like smoke ever since the big black Mercedes had left the main road. The mist carried with it a damp, cloying smell and among its eddying clouds strange, disembodied shapes formed and reformed like visitants from another world.

The powerful car had been forced to slow to a crawl, as the uniformed chauffeur bent forward to peer closely into the murk in an effort to see the edges of the road, and the thuggish looking man dressed in the ill-fitting dark suit in the front passenger seat, was doing his best to supplement the wiper's sweep by manually trying to demist the inside of the windscreen with the palm of his hand. Twice the nearside wheels had strayed on to the grass verge and both men knew only too well that another miscalculation like that could take them into a rhyne (as the man-made drainage ditches were called in this part of the world) or one of the deep bogs that lurked just yards from the tarmacked surface they were desperately trying to follow.

Hooper knew that too and he peered anxiously between them from his seat in the back, for once no cigar stuck between his fat lips. Hooper didn't like car journeys at the best of times and this one had been long, and looked like getting even longer before they reached his isolated house out on the marsh, near Wells.

'Bleedin' country,' he snarled. 'Don't know why I bought a soddin' place out here. Should have stuck to the Smoke.'

Beside him, the man Street would have recognised as Terrence Williams chuckled. 'Your drum's a good place to do business, though, Charlie,' Jeremy Brent said. 'No filth around to stick their long noses into what we're doing.'

Hooper gave a reluctant nod. 'Yeah, maybe,' he said and patted the locked briefcase on his lap. 'And this little lot should set me up for life once me and our Eyetie friends come to an agreement. Good old South Africa.'

Brent shook his head. 'Nothing to do with South Africa, boss,' he corrected. 'The stones came from Angola. Smuggled in via Botswana to aid the war effort of the UNITA independence movement.'

Hooper snorted. 'What's with the bleedin' politics lesson?' he retorted through a fit of coughing.

Brent shrugged. 'Just thought you might be interested in the background, that's all.'

Hooper lit a cigar, still coughing. 'Well, I ain't, see. I don't give a toss where they comes from. Only thing I'm interested in is how much dosh I'm likely to get from the sale of these sparklers to the right people. Got it?'

Before Brent could reply, the car braked hard, throwing the occupants forward in their seats. The mist was so dense that the flashing yellow light was only just visible, and the chauffeur had only glimpsed the "road closed" diversion sign a few feet from his bumper at the last minute. He swung hard left.

'So, when the hell was this road closed?' Hooper exclaimed. 'It weren't when we come along here last week.'

'Probably subsidence,' Brent replied. 'Most of the roads across the Levels are built on peat and they're always cracking up.' He turned his head towards the driver. 'Just go extra slow, Chris. We must be on some sort of a drove now. You never know where that might lead.'

Not very far as it turned out. The four-way flashers materialised in the gloom ahead even as he spoke. Hooper swore. The big white van had ended up slewed around across the drove at an acute angle, suggesting that its front wheels were probably buried in some invisible rhyne. There seemed to be no one with the vehicle. Unless they were on the other side of it or trapped in the cab. There was no way the Mercedes could squeeze past and turning round was out of the question. How the van had come to leave the road was a mystery. Maybe it had been going too fast. But one fact remained. It was well and truly stuck, which meant so were they.

'So, what now?' Hooper snarled at Brent. 'You gonna whistle up a bleedin' tow truck then?'

'Oh, I don't think that will be necessary, Charlie,' Brent said smoothly as a hooded figure suddenly emerged from the mist beside the front passenger door of their car with what was plainly a sawn-off shotgun in his hands.

Hooper's minder in the front passenger seat reacted immediately, his hand diving inside his jacket for his holstered pistol, but he was dead even as his fingers touched the cold metal, the blast of the shotgun taking half his head off and also peppering the chauffeur in the seat beside him with lead shot.

'Do something!' Hooper screamed at Brent, as the chauffeur slumped sideways within the restraints of his seatbelt, groaning and quivering.

''Course,' Brent said laconically and, producing a small pocket pistol in one black-gloved hand, he pumped two shells into the back of the injured driver's head. Then, turning slowly towards his boss, who had shrunk back in his seat with his mouth gaping open in shock, he treated him to a cold smile.

'This is what's commonly called a blag, Charlie,' he said and shot him twice in the face.

Just then a pulsing red and blue strobe materialised in the mist and a powerful spotlight cut through the gloom to pinpoint the car.

'Armed police,' a voice shouted. 'Stay where you are.'

'Shit!' Brent muttered to himself, hurling his pistol through the open window, out across the marsh. 'Who bloody well invited them?'

* * *

April 10th 2023. It was still dark when Lenny Thompson awoke, and he could hear his cell mate snorting and wheezing in the top bunk as usual. He had only been able to sleep in fits and starts all night. He just couldn't wait for the dawn. Not surprising really, since this was his big day. The day he walked out of this stinking hole a free man after being sent down for the piss-awful blagging and murder of Charlie Hooper and his cohorts all those years before. He'd only been in his twenties then and he was now approaching fifty.

Gerry Barlow, his old mucker from the army, had told him in the boozer that it was just going to be a robbery. Doing over some lowlife for a few kilos of coke. All he had to do was nick a van, drive himself and Gerry to some place on the marshes and block the road. Then it was simply a case of providing a bit of extra muscle as backup. No one was going to get hurt, Gerry had assured him. The sawn-off his old mate would be tooled up with would be only for show. A frightener, nothing more. Thompson had agreed to take part because Gerry had promised him it would be a real earner — money for old rope — and he'd been stupid enough to trust the little shit. What Gerry hadn't told him was that the so-called lowlife target in question was a big-time villain from the Smoke and that the blag was actually going to end in a multiple hit to cancel out witnesses. He only realised he'd been had when Gerry opened up on the car with the sawn-off and by then it was too late. He was in it up to his neck. Thereafter, everything had gone downhill.

Neither of them had expected an armed response police unit — an ARV he thought they called it — to turn up just like that out of nowhere, and it was obviously not down to bad luck. Someone in the know had grassed on them. Fortunately for him, he had hung back behind Gerry as they'd first approached the Merc and he was still hidden within the skeins of drifting mist when the law arrived. He'd had the good sense to retreat even further back and had ended up crouched down by one of the rear wheels of the car, as Gerry chucked away the sawn-off and was promptly jumped on, nicked and cuffed by a couple of heavily armed coppers looking like real-life versions of Darth Vader. He was surprised to see a posh "suit" then climb out of the back of the Merc shouting his innocence and pleading with the police not to shoot as he walked slowly towards the waiting officers with his hands in the air.

It had been Thompson's opportunity to slip away before he was spotted, but he had hesitated. The car door had been left half open and from where he crouched, he could see the briefcase still lying in a dead man's lap. "Once a thief, always a thief" the old maxim goes, and Thompson was certainly no exception to that rule. Despite the risk involved, the temptation to see what was inside the briefcase was too great. Creeping forward on all fours while the police were otherwise engaged, he reached into the car, quickly grabbed it and slid it towards him before ducking back out of sight and vanishing into the mist as completely as if he'd never existed.

Self-congratulations on his miraculous escape, plus the mind-blowing discovery he subsequently made in a concealed pocket of the briefcase, proved premature, however. Unbeknown to him, he had carelessly left a couple of his dabs on the stolen van, which police forensics soon lifted and established a match with those on his criminal record file. Three days later he found himself banged up in a police cell in Bristol on a multiple murder rap.

Gerry had played him like a bloody harp, he knew that now. He should have sussed that there was more to the blagging job than he'd been told. Still, at least his so-called "old mucker" had got his just desserts. He'd croaked from Aids-related hepatitis C a couple of years later after being viciously gang-raped in the joint at the start of his life sentence. It meant that for him the blag, the murders and everything else had all been for nothing, and that couldn't have happened to a more deserving arsehole.

Yeah, but Yours Truly hadn't come out of it all too well either, had he? Grilled for hours by a succession of belligerent, hairy-arsed coppers, he had learned that he had been verballed by the suit in the car for wasting two of the passengers with a handgun before running off. Counting two years spent remanded in custody while the prosecution went through the legal process on his not guilty plea, which had been included in overall time to be served, he had still ended up with a twenty-five-year sentence. Over a third of his life gone, if the Bible's threescore years and ten were to be believed, and so far nothing to show for it. His face suddenly twisted into a humourless grin, as he thought about that. Nothing to show for it *yet* anyway. But he would bloody well make up for that once he got out, he guaranteed it. With the glittering "rocks" from the briefcase he had hidden away all those years ago, the easy life was just waiting for him, and man, was he going to enjoy it. All that was required was a one-way train ticket and a bit of legwork, but first he had to get out and the screws seemed to sense he was champing at the bit and made a point of taking their time coming for him.

'You'll be back,' one said when he was finally released.

'You reckon?' Thompson retorted. 'Only when hell freezes over, mate, I can tell you.'

The crash of the prison's main door closing behind him was like music to his ears. Out. He was actually out. No one to tell him what to do. No rules to obey. No screws watching his every move on camera. He was free. He could do what he wanted, go wherever he fancied. He grinned. Yeah, but there was only one place he intended visiting right now and he had been waiting like forever for this particular moment.

He saw the car as he turned into a narrow side street, heading for the railway station, and the alarm bells clamoured inside his head. It was just an ordinary black BMW parked in a gateway, but he guessed who would be inside it and *he* was far from ordinary.

The car pulled out and drew slowly alongside him on the wrong side of the road. A familiar battered face grinned at him through the open driver's window, displaying broken teeth, but the eyes boring into him were hard and unsmiling. It was a face he recognised from his criminal past in the Smoke. Frank Delaney. A fixer for hire, though he had no idea who he was working for now.

'Hi, Lenny,' the big man greeted him. 'We 'eard you was gettin' out today. Long time, no see, eh?'

He kept walking and the car paced him. 'Shalom, Frank,' he replied. 'Can't stop. Got a life to live.'

'Wanna lift?'

'With you? Not bloody likely.'

'Someone sends their regards and wants to see you for old time's sake.'

'Do they, now? Then they're going to be disappointed, ain't they?'

'They says I should insist.'

Delaney threw his door open, scraping against a wall and effectively blocking Thompson's way at the same time as the rear door opened behind him.

'Get in the back, my son.'

'And if I refuse?'

Delaney spat some gum out of his window. 'Then Billie there will 'ave to help you, won't 'e?'

Thompson was conscious of another heavily built man filling the gap behind him but glanced over the top of the car at another BMW parked on the other side of the road, seemingly unfazed by Delaney's threat. 'I wouldn't advise it.'

'And why's that?'

'I don't think the filth over there would need much more of an excuse to poke their noses.'

Thompson saw Delaney jerk round in his seat to look and had the satisfaction of seeing his grin disappear.

'See you again, Lenny boy,' he said, as both doors slammed shut almost in unison and the car pulled away.

'Not if I can help it,' Thompson muttered, watching it disappear at speed round a bend in the road. Then throwing another glance at the unmarked police car opposite, he gave it a cheeky wave before continuing in the direction of the railway station, wearing the tightest of smiles as he thought about his new-found popularity with both the police and his old underworld associates, all of whom seemed to have really missed him . . .

* * *

Moonlight. Bright. Magical. Touching the flat, lightly frosted marshland with bluish fire and returning the Somerset Levels to the wild, secret place it had always been, a place haunted by centuries of myth and legend, which had often been written in blood.

Lenny Thompson stood for several minutes studying the site of the ancient Benedictine abbey laid out before him. In the foreground, little of the original structure, which dated back to the eighth century, remained. Henry VIII had seen to that. Most of it had been reduced to its foundations, the crumbling grey lines of stone now resembling nothing more than an eccentric architect's isometric plan. Beyond, just the largely roofless shell of the building had survived, which the guidebook would have described as originally housing the chapel and part of the cloister walk. A forlorn testament to the grand Benedictine order that had once worshipped within the hallowed walls, now rising stark and ominous against the veined face of the moon.

Thompson had no idea what purpose this stone-walled remnant had once served, but he didn't care anyway. To him, history was as much a closed book as any other academic subject. He had never seen the point of learning anything that did not have the potential for monetary profit. Consequently, his interest in this holy place lay solely in what was hidden within it, and boy, did *that* have monetary potential — maybe in six figure terms, if he played his cards right.

It had been a long, expensive train journey from London's Paddington to Highbridge in Somerset, with a change at Taunton and delays all the way. Then a local bus had taken him out to the village on the Levels late in the afternoon and he had holed up in an old barn, "dining" on stale sandwiches and a can of Coca Cola bought on the train, until it was dark. His wallet was now seriously depleted. The nice wad he had been carrying on his arrest all those years ago, which had been returned to him with his other personal property on his release, might have bought him plenty in the old days, but too many years had passed, and the money had only just covered his outlay now. In fact, the crumpled old-style notes, which should have been returned to the Bank of England and replaced with more up-to-date currency, had raised some eyebrows when he had produced them in payment at the ticket office in Paddington and the clerk had made a point of checking their validity with his supervisor before wrongly agreeing to accept them.

Thompson turned to scan the road he had just driven along through the sleeping village. There wasn't a sound to disturb the heavy silence. Nothing moved on the narrow strip of pot-holed tarmac that seemed to force its way between the grey stone cottages. Even the cold night air seemed to be holding its breath. He nodded his satisfaction. It didn't look as though he had been followed, which was a relief anyway, and it should only take him a few minutes to retrieve what he had come for, then be out of this miserable, creepy place for ever. Ready to embrace the bright lights and fleshpots of Europe's southern shores, once he had traded in the dozen or so glittering stones and sorted out a forged passport.

He could still hardly credit that the last time he had stood on this very spot, enshrouded in a clinging white mist and totally exhausted, he had been on the run from the police with a fortune burning a hole in his pocket. A fortune from which he had then been deprived of any benefit. Fated instead to spend twenty-five years banged up with thugs, drug addicts and nonces for a double murder he had not committed, and latterly forced to share a six by eight-foot cell and a single stinking toilet with a vicious old lag who was on his second lengthy stretch of porridge for violently enforcing the demands of a South London protection racketeer.

Considered in a philosophical sense, twenty-five years — or a quarter of a century — was not actually that significant in the grand scale of things and it would have been just a blip in time for the thousand-year-old abbey hunkered down in the moonlight just yards away. But Lenny Thompson was not into philosophy or anything else of a cerebral nature. His horizons were strictly limited to the physical here and now. Money, booze, gambling, fast cars and women. Being deprived of those key elements in his life for such a long period had therefore been particularly difficult for him. He could, of course, have got a shorter sentence by cooperating with the police, but turning a "grass" was not his style and as the old maxim ran, "if you can't do the time, don't do the crime". His one consolation was that the little package tucked away among the abbey ruins would at least amount to a substantial recompense for the years he had lost, but that was provided it was still there . . .

After one more visual check round to ensure the coast was clear, he climbed over the locked gate in the abbey's perimeter fence and headed across the green swathe beyond, staying wide of the dissecting grey walls of the original foundations, and making for the ruined building on the far side.

He was totally unaware of the ultra-quiet EV saloon which had pulled up in the shadow of a big willow tree at the corner of the perimeter fence, or the cold analytical gaze which followed his progress across the site. Only when he had disappeared into the abbey ruins did the driver, a tall, thin man dressed in a hooded coat, reveal himself and climb out on to the road. Moments later he too was over the gate and walking quickly and purposefully in the direction taken by Lenny Thompson.

* * *

The cloister walk was eerily quiet. Not even the suggestion of a breeze stirred the leaves scattered across the stone-flagged floor and the moon's cold face peeping through the archways, which had once looked inwards to the abbey's central quadrangle, or garth, seemed to be watching Thompson's progress, as he made his way along the route so many sandal-shod feet had followed before him a thousand years before. He found the doorway he was looking for easily enough and felt the tension grip him as he stepped inside, wondering if the package that had cost so many lives already would still be where he had hidden it while on the run.

He well remembered his panic the day he had accidentally stumbled upon the abbey, still traumatised from the murders he had witnessed just half an hour before and expecting the police to be hot on his trail. Then there had been that frantic search up and down the cloister for somewhere — anywhere — to hide the package before it was too late. What had made him check out the chamber in which he was now standing was anyone's guess, but he had been immediately drawn to the battered stone statue of a bearded old man in flowing robes standing in a corner. He'd had no idea that the statue was meant to represent St Benedict, founder of the Benedictine order, and he wouldn't have cared anyway. But

17

he'd gone straight to it and felt behind the figure to see if there was a space between it and the wall in which he could lodge the package. Almost immediately he had found the narrow crevice between two of the stone blocks with which the external wall was constructed and, inserting his hand, discovered quite a decent sized cavity there. It was simplicity itself to push the package into the cavity far enough to be invisible to anyone, but not so far in as to be non-retrievable, and he had quit the abbey soon afterwards, intending to return in a few days, confident that his future investment was safe.

Yeah, but was that confidence justified? At least he could see in the moonlight streaming through the single arched window that "Father Christmas", as he liked to think of the statue, was still standing in the corner, despite the passage of the years. But that didn't mean a lot, did it? What if someone had accidentally stumbled on to his hiding place while carrying out restoration work and had found the package? They might have handed the diamonds in or even fenced them for a big lump sum once they'd found out their worth. Like most professional criminals, Thompson had little faith in human nature and believed everyone was as bent as himself. The scenario he had just dreamed up was pretty unlikely, though, wasn't it? And there was only one way to find out. Rubbing his perspiring hands down his trousers, he crossed the room to the statue and trained the torch he had brought with him on the wall behind it. His heart lurched with excitement. The crevice between the two blocks was still there.

He was about to reach forward to insert his fingers into it when he suddenly froze, straightening up and quickly turning off his torch, listening intently. He thought he had heard something, like the scrape of leather shoes on a gritty floor, coming from the direction of the cloisters outside. He waited, the perspiration now running down his back between his shoulder blades. Several minutes passed as he stood there, motionless. Surely no one could have followed him? He had been so careful. But it was always a possibility. There had been enough visits from cold case detectives and so-called "friends" during his time inside to appreciate that memories had not dimmed and a lot of people were still interested in the whereabouts of the diamonds — particularly, he thought, the surviving posh guy in the car the filth had shown so much interest in during the grilling he had been given and who had falsely fingered him for two of the shootings.

Several minutes passed as he stood there, motionless, but the sounds he thought he had heard were not repeated and he shook his head dismissively. Probably a rat scurrying about among the leaves or bats returning to their lairs high up in the vaulted roof. He was getting paranoid in his old age. Switching his torch back on, he slid two fingers into the crevice and carefully felt around. He touched something and a thrill, like a surge of electric current, went through him. He managed to grip what he had found between his two fingers and slowly pull it out. It was the package, intact and still in its plastic wrapping.

Thompson could hardly breathe. He had it! After all these years, he had finally come up trumps. The future was his at last. Then he turned and found himself staring at the large automatic pistol gripped in the black-gloved hand of the man who had crept into the room behind him.

'Hello, Lenny?' the man said softly. 'You've led me a merry dance, haven't you?'

The other black-gloved hand beckoned to him. 'Okay, now toss the package over, but carefully.'

Thompson swallowed hard. Suddenly his twenty-five years of wasted life and the diamonds he had fantasised about for so long seemed unimportant. Standing in the shaft of moonlight streaming into that small, bare room, he saw death in the gunman's cold gaze and did exactly as he was told.

The gloved hand expertly caught the package and he smiled. 'Thank you, Lenny,' he said, and shot him twice in the head.

CHAPTER 1

Kate Lewis was in heaven. It was just three months into the twelve-month break she and her husband, Hayden, had negotiated in their careers as detectives with the Avon and Somerset Police and she could still hardly believe that she had walked away from a job she had always loved so much. Now wearing the briefest of bikinis instead of a smart work trouser suit, things seemed even more surreal to her as she emerged from the sea and stood there for a moment scanning the beach, the creamy surf foaming around her ankles and the sun gleaming on her slim, oiled body, which, due to her long auburn hair and pale, freckled skin, no amount of sun would ever tan. She spotted her sun-hating husband lying in the shadow of the cliffs in his outsized, knee-length shorts and long-sleeved shirt. He didn't wave back and she gave a crooked grin. He was probably fast asleep after their heavy picnic and anyway, she knew he was angry with her for the scantiness of her bikini. As a man with an old-fashioned, narrow-minded attitude towards such things, something which she had always found incredible, given his recent background as a police detective, this was not the first time he had adopted such a stance where she was concerned, whether it was his aversion to her exposing too much flesh or her other sin of using quite colourful expletives in conversation from time to time.

Shaking her head in resignation as she thought about it, she started back up the beach towards him, ready for yet another lecture on moral behaviour — only to stop short when a shadow suddenly cut across her path and the next instant she found herself confronted by a tall, muscular man in black swimming trunks who, from the look of him, had just been in for a swim like herself.

'Sorry,' she said and made to move round him, thinking that, busy with her thoughts, she hadn't looked where she was going. But to her surprise, he appeared to step back in front of her again, blocking her way.

'No apology necessary,' he said in a cultured, drawling tone. 'It was my fault entirely. I just had to tell you what a superb vision you presented emerging from the sea like that.'

Completely taken aback by the comment, she simply stood there staring at him, unable to find the words to respond.

Probably in his early fifties, and very tanned, with sharp, aquiline features, and a lean, muscular body suggesting a high level of fitness, despite his age, he had thick black hair, greying at the temples, which appeared to have been perfectly coiffed prior to his swim but had now come adrift in places. Dark, piercing eyes met her stare with a slight mocking twist to the thin lips, imbuing him with a rather cruel, raptor like look that was as fascinating as it was unsettling, and, though Kate hated to admit it even to herself, there was an almost magnetic quality to him that she found instantly attractive.

There was no hint of this in the reply she finally threw back at him, however, and she certainly didn't hold back.

'That was the worst pick-up line I have ever heard,' she snapped. 'Maybe you need to practise a bit more.'

He didn't flinch, but seemed even more amused by her reaction, as if he had expected it. 'It was not intended as a pick-up line,' he said. 'No offence was meant either. But what I saw in that brief moment was so evocative.'

Kate snorted. 'Evocative? What the hell are you talking about?'

'The James Bond movie, *Dr No*,' he explained smoothly. 'You know, when Ursula Andress emerged from the sea, carrying a large shell. What I glimpsed was the perfect evocation of that famous scene.'

'I was not carrying a bloody shell,' she retorted, 'and I happen to be auburn-haired, not blonde.'

He shrugged. 'No matter. The sun on your body, the way you walked, it was a sight to behold and, as an artist, I was enthralled.'

'Artist? And what sort of artist is that? Piss-artist?'

His smile vanished and he looked irritated by her crude response. 'I sketch and paint actually. Very therapeutic and it earns me a crust at local exhibitions. What do you do?'

Kate suddenly felt annoyed with herself. Her remark had been uncalled for. He may have been trying to chat her up, but she should have taken that as a compliment. He wasn't to know she was married and, hell, he was devilishly attractive.

'I, er, write,' she replied without thinking, for some inexplicable reason reluctant to reveal that she was a former police detective who had taken a break from her job.

'A writer? Oh, that *is* interesting. We're both artists then. What do you write?'

She mentally kicked herself for choosing something in which she had only dabbled unsuccessfully months and months ago. 'Well, I'm, er, trying to write a crime novel. Came here for the peace and quiet.'

'You live in Freshwater East then?'

She nodded. 'Up there. Overlooking the beach.'

'Good lord,' he exclaimed, 'I live a little way outside the village myself.'

'Do you?' she said drily, unable to help herself, adding without meaning it, 'How interesting.'

'So you could say we're near neighbours?' he continued, seemingly missing the sarcasm in her response.

She gave a brief nod. 'If you stretch things a bit maybe. Now look, I must be going. My husband will be wondering where I've got to.'

Out of the corner of her eye she could see from the motionless lump at the bottom of the cliffs that Hayden wouldn't be wondering any such thing, but it was a good way of extricating herself from what was an uncomfortable conversation.

'We must get together,' he went on enthusiastically, as if he hadn't heard her. 'You know, maybe drinks or afternoon tea at my place.'

She couldn't resist a parting snipe. 'What, you mean so you can show me your etchings?'

He laughed outright. 'Touché,' he replied, flashing even, white teeth. But she was disturbed to see that his smile failed to reach those dark, piercing eyes. For some reason she shivered, sensing danger in this handsome, captivating man, whose very aura had set her heart racing with guilty excitement.

'I must get dressed,' she blurted, turning away from him. 'I'm getting cold.'

'See you again shortly then,' he called after her. 'I'm Graham, by the way, Graham Lutterall. And you are . . . ?'

'Kate,' she threw back over her shoulder hastily, wondering why she had bothered to say anything at all, and feeling strangely hyped up, yet uneasy over the encounter as she quickly returned to her husband.

'So, who was that fellow?' Hayden demanded as he suddenly sat up with a frown, squinting at her in the sunlight from behind his large, square sunglasses.

'Just someone who spoke to me as I was walking back here. Turns out he lives locally — a chap called Graham Lutterall. Why?'

'Is that so? And the guy standing nearby, ogling you, who was *he*?'

She frowned, obviously puzzled. 'What guy? I never noticed any other guy.'

'Thirties, blond, in shorts and a T-shirt. He seemed very interested in the pair of you. Couldn't take his eyes off you, though.'

'Well, bully for him,' she retorted, but half turned to stare curiously back along the beach. She was in time to see the man who called himself Lutterall, now with a coat of some sort draped over his shoulders, walking towards the path which connected with the car park, talking to a blond-haired man dressed exactly as Hayden had described.

'I have no idea who he is,' she replied, drying her legs with a towel. 'But you seem to have been keeping a pretty close eye on me to see all this. I thought you were asleep.'

'Plainly.'

'What's that supposed to mean?'

He snorted. 'Well, you appeared to be having quite a nice, long chat with this Lutterall fellow. Taken with those minute strips of cloth you're nearly wearing, was he?'

Inwardly Kate groaned. *Here we go again*, she mused. Back to the same subject.

She stared at him defiantly. 'It's called a bikini, Hayd, and he was, as a matter of fact. Said I reminded him of Ursula Andress emerging from the sea in the James Bond film, *Doctor No.*'

He gaped. 'He said that to a perfect stranger? Darned impertinence. I told you that walking around half naked, like you are, would wind up the locals.'

'I am not half naked, you narrow-minded arsehole.'

'There you go, back to foul language again.'

'What do you expect? You are such a dickhead, Hayden, do you know that? We were supposed to come to Freshwater East to unwind. Yes, do up the cottage as an investment, but also to have fun, away from crime scenes, corpses and late-night callouts while we made up our minds about the future. But you seem incapable of enjoying yourself. When we first met all those years ago, you were so different, so broad-minded and easy-going. Since then you've become nothing more than a pompous, boring, stuck-up prick!'

'Well, thank you!'

'You're very welcome.'

Then she donned her shorts, slammed her feet into her sandals and stormed back up the steep path leading to their cottage, pulling on her T-shirt as she went.

She was in the shower when he got back from the beach and she could hear him bumbling around in the kitchen-diner as she stepped out and walked down the hallway to their bedroom with a big fluffy towel wrapped around her.

He appeared in the doorway as she was drying herself off, clearly embarrassed after their altercation. With his long-sleeved shirt, extra-long, baggy shorts and knee-length grey socks, his appearance had a distinct, clownish look, which in spite of her anger towards him, threatened to make her giggle.

'Sorry,' he muttered. 'I shouldn't have said what I said just now.'

She tried not to look at him again, determined to stay angry, despite the laughter almost bubbling over inside her. 'No, you bloody well shouldn't,' she replied, her voice faltering.

He hesitated, then asked casually, 'So, er, who was the guy you were talking to?'

She pulled the towel over her head and began vigorously drying her hair, hoping he couldn't see her shoulders twitching under it. 'Why?' she said in a strangely constricted voice. 'Worried I might have my eye on a more attractive, athletic model than the one I'm lumbered with?'

He gulped. 'No, not-not at all. I-I just didn't want you to be unwittingly sending out the wrong message.'

'Wrong message?' she choked inside her towel. 'He approached *me*, not the other way about.'

Before he could follow up on that, she caught another glimpse of him through a gap in the folds of the towel and that was it. Unable to control the laughter, which had been building up inside her, any longer, she was incapable of saying anything for a few moments and was doubled up over the edge of the bed, convulsed with hysterical mirth as he looked on in pink-faced astonishment.

'So, what's so funny?' he snapped.

When she still didn't reply, this only served to irritate him even more. 'Go on, I asked you a question,' he almost shouted. 'What's so darned funny?'

She dropped her towel, tears streaming down her face, as she strode across the room and threw her arms around his neck, hugging him tightly. 'Nothing, at all, Hayd,' she said, still chortling. 'Absolutely nothing at all.'

* * *

Kate heard the noise just a couple of hours after she and Hayden had gone to bed. Frowning, she raised her head off the pillow and listened, her gaze travelling slowly around the bedroom. For a change, Hayden was not snoring, though otherwise still out for the count, and the night was deathly still. Moonlight flooded the room through the half-open Venetian blind partially masking the single window, creating a pattern across the opposite wall, which shivered as the plastic slats stirred in a slight breeze. All appeared perfectly normal.

Thinking that she had probably imagined whatever it was she thought she had heard, or had simply woken from a bad dream, she sank back on to her pillow and turned over on to her side to try and get back to sleep. But even as she closed her eyes and relaxed, she heard the sound again and this time she recognised it for what it was. She had heard it once before. A long time ago when, as a probationary police constable, she had picked up the same sound, as she'd stood in a moonlit high street on a cold winter's night. There had been a low wind at the time, but beat-craft had taught her during her foot patrols to periodically turn her head away from the wind to shut it out, then close her eyes so that by cutting out the key sense of sight, her brain could concentrate its focus on the other key sense, of hearing. It was then that she had picked up the sound she was hearing again: the irregular "chink, chink, chink" of someone forcing a window.

Now fully alert, she swung her legs over the edge of the bed and padded barefoot to the window. Raising one slat of the Venetian blind, she peered out into the small gravel car park at the side of the cottage. Hayden's prize Jaguar Mk II was still parked there and the wooden gates leading on to the country lane beyond were closed.

She glanced briefly in the direction of the bed and the hump beneath the duvet, which had now begun to emit a series of grunts she knew would soon break out into loud snores. But with a rueful smile, she made no effort to wake her husband. She knew from past experience that trying to do so was like trying to wake the dead. Once he was asleep, it was next to impossible to wake him up without a lot of effort and the certainty of a very noisy, protesting response. That was the last thing she needed at that critical moment. Instead, crossing the room to the bedroom door, she eased it open and peered round the frame beyond the dining area into the kitchen. The blinds had not been closed across the French doors and the large room, split by just a line of units beneath a tiled worktop, was flooded with moonlight. There was no one there.

She crossed swiftly to the French doors and studied the decking outside. It ran the whole length of the cottage and was fully enclosed by a wooden guard rail. There was a drop of some seven feet beneath to the expansive lawn, which sloped away to a copse close to the boundary fence at the far end of the garden. The only point of external access to it was via a small, padlocked gate to her right, where a flight of steps led down to the car park and the parked Jaguar, and she could see at a glance that the decking was deserted and the gate was closed.

Frowning, she retraced her steps and made for the hallway to the left of the dining area. There was no one lurking outside the glass-panelled porch and front door to her left, and a quick check of the main bathroom, which was the first room along the hallway in front of her, proved negative. Then quite suddenly, on her way to the two back bedrooms, she heard a sharp "crack" and knew exactly where her intruder was. The second bathroom at the end of the corridor.

Finding the bathroom door ajar, she gently eased it open and peered through. She saw his silhouette immediately. A hooded figure in black. He was in the narrow passageway which ran down this side of the cottage and he had the bathroom window open and was in the process of levering himself up on to the sill. Her heart was thumping fit to burst as she pulled the door back towards her. To challenge him before he actually got into the room would have been to see him immediately drop back into the passageway and take to his heels and she would have had no prospect of catching him. On the other hand, to allow him to get into the cottage meant she would have no option but to tackle him as he came through the door. But tackle him with what? She had no weapon handy and clad in just a flimsy nightdress, she was asking for trouble of an even worse kind in any physical confrontation.

At which point, the decision was taken right out of her hands as Hayden's bellow erupted from the hallway behind her.

'What the devil are you doing out here, Kate? Got up for a pee and . . .'

She never heard the end of the sentence. Forced by his untimely appearance to act, she threw the bathroom door wide and sprang inside. Just in time to see the hooded intruder disappear from the window as he dropped back on to the path outside — exactly as she had feared.

She knew she was wasting her time even as she raced back down the hallway, barging Hayden aside in the process, but she felt bound to do something. The glass door to the porch was ajar, but the front door was locked. In her panic to get the door open, with Hayden burbling behind her, she jammed the key in the lock and, even as she tried to free it, the hooded figure raced past towards the driveway. She got the door open and streaked after him but was halted at the end of the path by the sharp gravel biting into the soles of her bare feet. Almost at the same moment, she heard a car door slam and an engine splutter into life. But she was afforded only a glimpse of the dark-coloured saloon car with a sloping back that then flew past the gates with no lights, disappearing into the night, heading for the village of Lamphey.

'Gordon Bennett,' Hayden exclaimed, as she limped back to the front door, 'what the devil's going on?'

'Just an attempted burglary, Hayden,' she snapped over her shoulder, as she returned to the bathroom to stare at the broken window catch. 'Nothing for you to worry about!'

* * *

The local police constable turned up an hour after Kate's phone call. A huge man, about six foot in height, with a fit, muscular physique despite the fact that he had to be well into middle age, he scratched his thick mop of grey hair with a big calloused hand that might have belonged to a farmer.

'Don't often get break-ins around here,' PC Geraint Rheon said in his lilting Welsh accent, staring closely at the broken window catch. 'None reported recently, far as I know, and certainly no others tonight so far. Pretty quiet, well-behaved place this is normally.'

Kate nodded, handing him the mug of coffee she had just brewed. 'I can't think why he picked our cottage,' she remarked. 'We only moved here a couple of months ago.'

The policeman took a noisy slurp of the hot coffee Kate had made for him, which might have scalded the lips of a lesser man.

'Somerset, you said you were from, didn't you now?' he asked. 'What brought you to Pembrokeshire?'

'I'm, er, a crime novelist,' Kate replied, glaring at Hayden when he choked on his coffee. 'Well, an amateur one really. Still have to make the grade. I thought this place would be ideal for a bit of inspiration.'

'And you, Mr Lewis, are you a writer too?'

Hayden quickly shook his head but stayed with the party line. 'No, I've just retired from, um, teaching. History actually. Ill-health, you know.'

'Ah,' Geraint Rheon went on. 'Comes to us all in the end.' He turned back to Kate. 'Now, I'm afraid we're unlikely to be able to catch your intruder. You've no idea what he looked like and unfortunately we don't even have a car registration number to go on.'

He finished his coffee. 'I doubt whether one of our forensic officers will attend under the circumstances. You said, Mrs Lewis, that you thought your intruder was wearing gloves, so it's unlikely there'll be any prints on the window. All I can promise you is passing attention, I'm afraid.'

Kate smiled slightly. How many times, she mused, had she said exactly the same thing to a burgled householder. In a way, it seemed like poetic justice.

'I understand perfectly, Officer,' she acknowledged. 'Thanks for coming.'

'Crime novelist?' Hayden snorted after the policeman had gone.

'Can you think of anything better?' Kate replied. 'We agreed to keep our previous occupations to ourselves so we wouldn't attract unwelcome local attention.'

'Surprised then you rang the police at all.'

'I wanted to establish whether there had been other similar burglaries in the area, that's all. I knew, as you did, that the local Bill couldn't do anything. I just can't fathom why our intruder picked our place out of all the others. It was obviously a planned job, the way he was kitted up.'

Hayden yawned, then shrugged. 'Well, nothing we can do about it now, except keep a weather eye open in future.'

'You think he might come back?'

'It's possible. Depends on what he was after. He obviously didn't get it this time.'

He grunted and nodded towards her bare leg projecting through a gap in the dressing gown she had put on before the arrival of PC Rheon.

'He might have got something else, though, if I hadn't appeared at the crucial time. After all, you were flaunting it a bit, weren't you?'

'I was wearing my nightdress,' she retorted tightly. 'What do you expect me to wear in bed? A bloody overcoat?' She smirked. 'Maybe I should have resorted to being *au naturel*, as I have in the past. Then he might have stayed for a quick one instead of running away.'

He scowled. 'You really are the limit sometimes.'

She chuckled. 'You're wrong there, Hayd,' she mocked. 'There are *no* limits where I'm concerned.'

CHAPTER 2

Hayden's mobile rang at just after eleven the following morning while he and Kate were sitting in the sunshine on their decking, having coffee.

'You're joking,' Kate heard him exclaim angrily from his recliner a couple of feet away. 'And you're only telling me this now? That's just not on.'

He listened for another few seconds, then ended the call and threw his mobile halfway across the decking.

'I don't believe it,' he raged. 'CPS need me at Bristol Crown Court this Friday.'

She stared at him. 'Bristol Crown Court? Whatever for? I thought all that was over when we quit the force?'

He drained his mug of coffee, shaking his head. 'Apparently not. Some low life I helped the plods nick nine months ago in a street brawl in Bridgwater has just been sent up the steps and is pleading not guilty to GBH. Originally CPS didn't think I would be required to give evidence, as I was only attending the incident on a "shout" and I wasn't directly involved. But now, halfway through the case, the defence have been given permission to produce another witness who is alleged to have been known to the prosecution but whose details were not passed to the defence under the disclosure rules. As a result, it seems, there's a chance I could be needed to corroborate what the arresting officer said to the little toerag when he felt his collar. Blessed legal team are panicking and want me there just in case. Could be a two- to three-day job too.'

Kate swore. 'So much for the quiet life. Well, you'll have to go. You don't have a choice even if you are no longer in the force.'

He calmed down and nodded glumly. 'There's evidently a witness summons on its way to me anyway by express delivery. That call was just a heads-up.'

She glanced at her watch. 'Bit naughty this, but as it's Wednesday today, you'd best be heading off first thing tomorrow so you're there in plenty of time.'

He looked even more miserable. 'I'll have to go this afternoon, Kate. Counsel want to have words with me tomorrow at ten thirty. Something to do with their strategy.'

He climbed to his feet and scooped his mobile back off the floor. 'I'm afraid it will mean you won't have a car, as I'll have to take the Jag. Pity we got rid of your Mazda when we came up here.'

She shrugged. 'We had no choice. We agreed to conserve our cash until we decided whether we would be re-applying to rejoin the force in twelve months or trying something else. The car was on the way out anyway.'

'But you could be a bit stuck here without wheels.'

'Oh, I'll manage. There are buses into Pembroke and a train service to Tenby and Carmarthen.' She smiled mischievously. 'And of course, there's always the lovely beach just down there.'

His eyes narrowed. 'You trying to wind me up?'

She feigned shock. 'Now, would I ever do that to you, Hayd?' she replied.

* * *

Hayden drove away two hours later after booking a hotel room in the city. She watched the sleek, red MKII Jaguar disappear round a bend in the lane towards Lamphey village for several minutes after it had gone, almost as if she expected Hayden to turn right round and come back.

She wandered indoors feeling suddenly very downbeat and suffering a strong sense of guilt over laughing at him the day before. She hadn't meant it in a malicious way. His pompous, holier-than-thou attitude annoyed her intensely, but she loved him to bits and the fact that he was likely to be gone for a minimum of three days, leaving her totally alone in the bungalow, hit her hard. It wasn't that she was worried that their burglar might return while he was away. After so many years on CID dealing with the dregs of society, some of whom had been really vicious criminals who wouldn't have thought twice about slitting a woman's throat, she was quite confident about tackling a local housebreaker and if there was to be a next time, she would make sure she had something with her that would give him cause to regret his return visit. But although she had desperately wanted a rejuvenating break in a quiet backwater like Freshwater East so she could collect her thoughts and enjoy a bit of sustained "me" time, the thought of doing that on her own, even for a short period, was not something she relished.

Walking out on to the decking, she stared down the garden at the breakers rolling into Freshwater East Bay, just visible through the trees that formed the small copse close to the rear boundary. The sounds of the sea and the scream of the gulls wheeling overhead drifted up to her and she could smell the rich salty odour in the air, which as a child she had always recognised as the seaside. The place was idyllic, but its isolation could also prove to be nerve-racking over time; as nerve-racking as the gloomy silence of the mist-shrouded Somerset Levels where she had spent most of her police career probing its infamous secrets.

Dropping on to one of a pair of recliners, she let her mind wander along its own erratic course, conjuring up so many memories, some good, some bad, and smiling sadly as she remembered colleagues she had once worked with, like the irascible DI Ted Roscoe, who had been the bane of her life, but whose violent, tragic death had shaken her to the core. Then there was her last boss, Acting Detective Inspector Charlie Woo, who had declared quite confidently at the leaving do of her and her husband that they would soon be back to the "coalface". And all the others who had been on her team: Jamie Foster, Danny Ferris, Indrani Purewall and the rest. Deep down, did she miss them, she asked herself? And did she miss all the stress and aggro of the job itself? Or was she just glad to be rid of it all? There were no answers to those questions and only time would tell where the truth lay.

She climbed to her feet again and was about to go back indoors when something caught her attention. Something that glittered briefly in the mix of trees and bushes bordering the garden to her right as it was caught by the sunlight. At first, she thought it was just a discarded bottle or a foil top from something thrown there by a local yob or ignorant tourist using the adjacent footpath down to the beach. But it was too high for that. Then, as she looked again, it seemed to flick sideways as if it had a life of its own. Puzzled, she shielded her eyes against the glare of the sun and immediately froze as realisation dawned. A dark figure was just discernible crouched down in the undergrowth there and she guessed that the glitter had come from the lens of a monocular or binocular lens, trained on the cottage. It seemed their burglar was back and this time she was going to make sure he didn't do a runner before she got to him.

Her heart thumping again, just like the previous night, she turned towards the French doors and took her time going back inside so as not to alarm the watcher. Then, closing the doors again and noting that the figure was still there, she donned a pair of shoes and raced to the front door, grabbing one of Hayden's walking sticks from the corner of the porch on the way. She was out through the front gates and at the entrance to the footpath in record time. There was a dark-blue saloon car with a sloping back parked just past the footpath — an old Honda Accord — and she started, remembering the car she had glimpsed driving off the previous night. She paused long enough to memorise the registration number, then crept into the gloomy tunnel beside her, estimating just how far along the boundary of the cottage her watcher had to be.

She had a grim smile on her face when she reached the spot, her feet making hardly any sound on the soft ground. He was still there. She could just see him almost hidden among a clump of mature bushes. Grasping the walking stick in the middle for a better grip, she stepped off the path and approached to within a couple of feet of the man.

He was dressed in a short, brown, hooded coat, with the hood hanging loose down his back, and she gained the impression, even from behind, that he was quite slim and youthful, with long, blond hair that curled back over the hood in untidy strands. He was evidently well tuned into what was going on around him too, for although she was confident that she had made no sound as she crept up on him, he turned suddenly, and promptly climbed to his feet.

Blue-eyed and wearing a full, neatly trimmed beard, plus three or four gold-coloured rings in his right ear, she judged him to be in his mid-twenties. He had a camera in a case slung around his neck and was also holding a small black tube — a monocular, as she'd suspected — in one hand, which he abruptly slipped into a side pocket of his coat. Despite his obvious surprise at her appearance, his moves were smooth and professional and his smile was turned on with practised ease, though his gaze remained wary, flicking from her face to the walking stick in her hand. For some strange reason, he seemed vaguely familiar, but she was positive she had never met him before.

'Hi,' he said in a soft voice, 'you gave me quite a start there.'

'What the hell do you think you are doing here?' she demanded tightly.

He looked mortified. 'Oh, sorry, this must look really bad. I assure you I wasn't peeping on you. I'm what I think folk would call a "twitcher". Birdwatching, you know?' He half turned back towards the wire fence of her property and waved a hand vaguely in the same direction. 'Thought I'd spotted a kestrel fly in here, as I was walking down to the beach, and thought it might be nesting nearby.'

'Bollocks!' she said politely, her gaze fixed on him. 'More likely looking for another way into my garden for a second crack at the cottage tonight.'

He frowned, his puzzled expression almost convincing. 'A second crack . . .' His voice tailed off and then he added, 'Good heavens, you mean you've been broken into?'

'You know damned well I have. How stupid do you think I am? I spotted you from my decking and the monocular you've just slipped into your pocket wasn't searching for bloody birds.'

'I assure you I'm no burglar. Now, it's been nice meeting you, but

I . . .'

He made to push past her, but she stood her ground and he made a face. 'Would you mind letting me by? I wasn't on your property and this is a public right of way. You have no business obstructing me.'

Kate felt the anger rise in her and her fingers tightened on the walking stick. Then she sensed someone behind her and out of the corner of her eye saw a couple of women she vaguely recognised from the village, with terrier dogs on leads, walking past her on the footpath and staring curiously in her direction. She relaxed and, after waiting for them to disappear down the slope in the direction of the beach, she resumed her verbal attack on her intruder. 'I demand an explanation as to why you were so interested in my cottage.'

He shook his head. 'You can demand away, but I think I've already explained to you what I was doing here. Now please let me past — unless you're going to smack me over the head with that thing?'

Kate hesitated, feeling her anger dissipate, as common sense prevailed. She was out of order and she knew it. Undoubtedly this character was up to something, but she had no proof that he had done anything wrong. His "twitcher" explanation was laughable, but it would sound feasible to others, and she was no longer in the job anyway, so had no power whatsoever to detain him. Reluctantly she stepped back on to the path and, with an even broader smile, he followed her.

'Thank you,' he said politely, heading off down the path towards the beach, 'and good afternoon to you.'

She watched him go with a feeling of frustration. She had handled things badly, just like an amateur. She hadn't asked him his name, though he would probably have refused to give it anyway, and she had nothing more than a picture of him in her mind, which was easily forgotten. Okay, she could still remember the car number, but he hadn't got into it, but had gone the other way, so she couldn't even connect him to that. If it was his, he would no doubt come back to collect it later, but she couldn't wait around for hours to see if he did, and there was no satisfactory place to hide anyway.

Furious with herself, she traipsed back to the cottage and slammed the front door shut behind her with a resounding bang that shook the windows in the porch. She almost trod on the piece of paper on the tiled floor, which someone had apparently slipped through her letterbox while she had been confronting her suspected burglar.

She read the short note as she poured herself a glass of red wine at the breakfast bar between the kitchen and the dining area.

It was only short and written in neat, flowing handwriting.

Hi Kate,

Sorry you were out. Just called to invite you and your hubby for afternoon tea — to see those 'etchings' we talked about! Okay? I'll send a car round to pick you both up at three tomorrow, Thursday. Sorry, but declinations not accepted.

Graham Lutterall.

'You're bloody sure of yourself, Lutterall,' Kate muttered to herself and her first thought was to ignore the invitation.

After all, she knew nothing about him and Hayden was no longer there to act as her chaperone. Yes, but that was the whole point, wasn't it? Lutterall had assumed Hayden would be attending as well. He didn't know her husband was on his way to Bristol, so he couldn't have had any funny business in mind.

She flicked the top of her empty wine glass with her tongue and smiled. *Why not just go, girl?* she mused. *It could be fun and he really is devilishly attractive . . .*

CHAPTER 3

The black Mercedes was on time. It pulled up outside Kate's cottage dead on three the following day. She had spent the morning on the beach, wondering how the afternoon invitation would play out and feeling a little nervous as to what was in store for her. She had not told Hayden about where she was going and, to avoid worrying him, had not even mentioned her confrontation with the man she had caught watching their place the previous afternoon. She had said nothing about that to the local police either. What was the point? She had no evidence that the character was their burglar and she couldn't even connect him to the car she had seen parked in the lane. Okay, so she had the car number and the police could have got hold of the registered owner easily enough, but to what purpose? Furthermore, she doubted whether they would have passed his identity on to her anyway. She was no longer "job", so she had no special privileges.

Grabbing a light cardigan to slip over her shoulders in the short-sleeved cotton dress, she walked smartly to the front door and threw it wide before her newly arrived "chauffeur" had time to get there.

He was dressed in a creased grey uniform and cap, aping the traditional idea of a chauffeur none too well, and there was definitely nothing traditional about the man who stood in front of her. Hard piggy eyes studied her from a brutish, pockmarked face, boasting a nose that looked as though it had been rebuilt after contact with a sledgehammer, and no uniform could conceal the barrel chest and the muscular arms that had doubtless once powered knock-out punches in the ring.

For a moment she was completely taken aback by his appearance and couldn't think of anything to say, but he must have been used to the effect he had on people, because the next instant he treated her to a slow grin, exposing a graveyard of broken headstones, and touched the peak of his cap.

'Mrs Kate Lewis?' he said in a deep, halting voice, his attempt at hiding his rough London East End accent failing dismally. 'Mr Lutterall asked me to collect yer at free. 'Usband not wiv yer then?'

She shook her head. 'Sorry. Had to go away on, er, family business at the last minute.'

He nodded politely. 'Mr Lutterall *will* be disappointed.'

Liar, Kate mused, but gave him a brief smile as she followed him down the path to the double gates of the driveway, only to step back quickly when he reached past her to open the rear door of the Merc for her. She was obviously being given the full treatment, she thought, as she sank into the plush, leather seat, but it occurred to her that it was rather OTT sending a chauffeur-driven car to collect someone living what could be no more than a mile away at the most, if her host was indeed local. The mysterious Mr Lutterall was clearly trying to impress and she couldn't help wondering what he might be expecting from her in return. Well, whatever it was, he was going to find he was out of luck!

It transpired that Lutterall's home was at the end of a narrow lane, which burrowed into woodland on the outskirts of Freshwater East. The chauffeur stopped before a pair of wrought-iron gates, which had to be at least seven-foot high and carried the name *Smuggler's Reach* on a big brass plate.

They juddered open, as if by magic, almost immediately and when the car drove through, a burly man in a tight-fitting, dark suit waved at them from the porch of a small bungalow to their left. Beyond, a long driveway snaked away from them. To the right, it was bordered by tall trees and tangled undergrowth, through which Kate glimpsed high wire fencing along the boundary of the property. On the other side, through another line of trees, she saw what looked like tennis courts and an ornamental garden of some sort, maybe belonging to the bungalow. She also saw a number of cameras on long stalks in evidence at various points along the route, all but two outward facing and angled downwards to cover the immediate perimeter. Obviously Mr Lutterall valued his privacy. That was his prerogative, of course, but something was bugging her about her host and this elaborate security setup, particularly after her brief acquaintance with the brutish looking chauffeur, who could not have been more miscast for the role.

Despite Kate's earlier misgivings, Lutterall was charm itself when he met her at the door of his home, though there was a noticeable gleam in his eyes, which Kate took as satisfaction, when she gave the same explanation she had given to the chauffeur as to why Hayden could not be with her. Dressed casually in fawn chinos, an open-necked, light-green shirt and sockless suede shoes and boasting a gold Rolex watch on his wrist, her host bent slightly to brush the back of her hand with his lips, murmuring a word of welcome to what was an enormous ultra-modern house.

Smuggler's Reach seemed to be composed almost entirely of steel and glass, with a pitched, tiled roof and a detached, triple-garage block, with what looked like living quarters above, adjacent to it. Lutterall showed her across the hallway into a thickly carpeted living room, luxuriously furnished with an expensive looking leather three-piece suite, several fully upholstered chairs, an oak sideboard and an ornate cocktail cabinet. An oil painting, depicting a typical

Welsh mountain scene, occupied one of the walls and a gilt-framed mirror another. Directly opposite, beyond a pair of open French doors, a stone-slabbed terrace was visible.

'I thought we would have our afternoon tea in the fresh air,' Lutterall said and waved her towards the French doors.

A steel table, set with delicate bone china crockery, what appeared to be silver-plated cutlery and a bottle of champagne, partially submerged in a silver ice bucket, stood in the middle of the terrace. Lutterall courteously pulled back a chair for Kate to sit down.

From where she sat, Kate had a perfect view of the rear garden, which was at a much lower level than the front, with steps leading down to an expansive lawn. The lawn itself sloped down to a high bank at the bottom, topped by dwarf shrubs, and was flanked on either side by tall hedges. There was a swimming pool on the left-hand side and in the bottom right-hand corner she noticed a rather attractive looking wooden outhouse or potting shed. Beyond the garden, the terrace provided impressive, unrestricted views across a patchwork of fields to a thin line of pale blue ocean.

Kate stared at it all, momentarily spellbound. Lutterall, on the other hand, seemed unaware of the effect it had had on her.

'What did you think of Frank?' he asked abruptly.

'Frank?'

'Yes, my chauffeur.'

She started. It was as if he had read her mind.

'Well, he was different, I'll say that,' she replied in a slightly dry tone.

He laughed. 'Frank Delaney is not everyone's cup of tea,' he agreed. 'But he's a good sort and very loyal to me. Ex-boxer, you know. I rescued him from an East End doss house and he's worked for me ever since. There is a self-contained apartment above the garage, and he shares that with my chef and another of my retainers. I always believe in looking after those who work for me, you see. Treat your staff well and they will repay you in kind.'

'That is very charitable of you,' she said, 'and it appears that Frank has fallen on his feet here. You have a truly magnificent house.'

'Thank you. I had the place built originally as a holiday home some years ago when I was a lawyer in London with my own legal practice. But now I've decided to get out of the rat race altogether and move here permanently.'

'Well, it's very impressive. And you have certainly gone into your security in a big way. The electronic gates, the gateman, the cameras and all that.'

'Ah, you noticed. Just a precaution really. I am a very private person. Almost reclusive actually. I like to be left alone. Also, I have some expensive pieces of artwork here and so I suppose I'm a bit paranoid about burglars. Jack, the man you will have seen on the gate, makes sure I know who's welcome here and who's not. He monitors the cameras from inside his bungalow and his partner, Amanda, does the cleaning for me. It's a very convenient setup.'

'I'm sure it is,' she acknowledged. 'But why not go the whole hog with razor wire instead of just the normal stuff, and what about an alarm system too?'

He looked at her keenly. 'You sound like some sort of security expert, Kate,' he replied. 'Maybe I should have employed you to do the crime prevention survey in the first place?'

You and your big mouth, a voice in her head castigated. If she didn't want Lutterall to know she was ex-Bill, she was saying precisely the wrong things. She shut up immediately and tried to avoid Lutterall's half-amused gaze.

'The thing is,' he went on, 'razor wire is quite lethal and not only could my neighbour or his animals become seriously injured by contact with it, but I don't think the local authority would be too impressed if I tried to install it. As for an alarm, I have cameras, so why would I want an alarm as well? Bit overkill, don't you think?'

'Oh, just one of my silly thoughts,' she replied with a brief smile, then quickly changed the subject. 'But . . . but tell me, what is it you actually do — apart from all those "etchings", of course?'

Another laugh. 'What a sharp tongue you have, Kate Lewis,' he retorted. 'I shall have to watch out for that in future.'

With practised ease, he opened the bottle of champagne, resulting in a soft "plop" and poured her a glass. 'Fact is, I made a lot of money from a business venture a few years ago and invested it wisely.' He waved his other arm around him. 'It enabled me to, as I've already said, quit the rat race and embrace a new life here.'

'No Mrs Lutterall then?'

Just for a moment, his face seemed to freeze and she thought she had put her foot in it, but then his smile was back. 'Sadly, I've never been able to find the right one,' he said, and he held her gaze for a second. 'So these days I prefer to appreciate the opposite sex from a distance, without commitment.'

She gave a discreet cough. 'Well, you have really done well for yourself,' she responded, feeling uncomfortable at his choice of words.

To her relief, a shadow fell across the table, preventing further discussion on the issue. She glimpsed a hand appear at her elbow holding a two-tier, glass cake stand laden with what seemed to be various kinds of cream cake. She glanced up and smiled at the man as he placed the cake stand in the middle of the table. He was tall, lean and blond, dressed in the black waistcoat, white shirt and bowtie and neatly creased black trousers traditionally associated with high-class hotel waiters. But she couldn't help allowing a frown to momentarily darken her expression.

Lutterall picked up on it straightaway. 'You don't like cream cakes?' he queried.

'No, yes, no, I mean it's nothing like that,' she replied, 'I'm just amazed that you have gone to so much trouble on my behalf.'

'I promised you afternoon tea,' he said smoothly, 'and that's exactly what you are going to have. I hope you enjoy it. Please help yourself to what Adam's offering.'

Kate nodded, absently selecting the nearest cake to hand and cutting into it with the pastry fork provided. But the uneasy feeling that had already begun to stir inside her had become even more acute. It had suddenly dawned on her that she had seen the immaculately turned-out waiter he had called Adam before. It was the same man she had spotted leaving the beach at Freshwater East Bay with her host the previous day — the man Hayden had described as "standing nearby, ogling her" — and seeing him close up, she was now pretty sure he had not been ogling her at all. In her job as a police detective, she had seen many men like him, usually wearing the ubiquitous sunglasses, escorting film stars and other celebrities. His physique may not have been quite so noticeable as Frank's, but the short, thick neck and muscular shoulders, which the thin white shirt and waistcoat had no chance of concealing, together with the manner in which he carried himself, gave the game away. He was as much a waiter as Frank was a chauffeur, she decided, and rather than ogling her on the beach, she suspected he had actually been keeping an eye on Lutterall. The person he was paid to protect as his personal bodyguard.

Why on earth Lutterall needed a bodyguard at all in a Pembrokeshire backwater like this, was unclear. But he was plainly very well-off, no doubt a multi-millionaire going by the look of his house, although she had never heard of him before. As with many of his kind, it was possible he saw himself as vulnerable to physical attack and extortion by professional criminals. Another possibility was that he was a recluse and a jealous guardian of his privacy. Or even that he needed to shout out his status to the local community to establish his bona fides as a very important resident, in much the same way as moneyed people often did. But there was yet another possibility too, one which her policing background had inevitably steered her towards and which had created her present sense of unease. In short, that Graham Lutterall was not her host's real name and that his security measures, including the electric gates, the character waving them in from the bungalow, the cameras, the high, barbed-wire fencing, and the pair of heavies he employed for apparent protection were there because he was a big-time criminal himself and was under threat from his villainous contemporaries.

Oh come on, Kate, the voice in her head mocked, *get a life. You're getting paranoid, girl. Give it a rest, you are not a police detective anymore, so don't try and read intrigue into everything. Just take things as they appear to be and enjoy your afternoon tea.*

Then Lutterall abruptly cut in on her deliberations. 'You're not drinking your champagne, Kate. Not to your taste? I have an excellent wine cellar here if you would like something else?'

She recovered in time and shook her head, forcing another smile before taking a sip from her glass.

'No, honestly, it's lovely. But it's so peaceful here, I'm afraid I was away with the fairies for a moment or two. You must think me very rude.'

'I think nothing of the sort,' he replied graciously. 'Now, what about another cake — unless you are worried about that superb figure of yours?'

'No, I've had enough, thank you, really.'

He gave a soft, taunting laugh. 'Then I must show you those notorious etchings we talked about,' he said.

The building he took her to turned out to be a fully equipped artist's studio, complete with easels and finished and unfinished canvasses, in the far corner of the property, close to the rear boundary. Kate was astonished by the quality of some of the framed paintings lining the walls.

A variety of media had been used and though Kate was by no means an expert on art, she had a reasonable appreciation of it from her school and college days. She could see that oils, watercolour and acrylics were all represented. There were also pencilled sketches and a few charcoal drawings. The subjects were equally varied. Landscapes, still life, animals and birds, abstracts and female nudes in various poses.

'I said I would show you my etchings,' he said with another short laugh, 'so feel free to browse.'

47

Kate was plainly over-awed. 'I never thought you were as talented as this,' she said. 'And they're a bit more than etchings.'

He bowed his head slightly to acknowledge the compliment. 'I like to experiment,' he said. 'For me, art is like a doorway to another world and the female form is what fascinates me the most.'

His dark eyes seemed to bore into her skull. Then quite abruptly he said, 'Would you be willing to model for me?'

Though Kate had earlier suspected he would be coming out with something — maybe asking her to dinner — this was the last thing she had expected and for a few seconds she simply stood there, gaping at him.

He gave one of his thin smiles. 'Well, what do you think?' He waved an arm towards a couple of the nude poses. 'I usually use professional models, but when I saw you on the beach, I knew you would make the most fantastic subject I have ever worked with. Your superb figure, the sun on your delicate, almost ivory skin, the way you moved. All that an artist could possibly wish for.'

She was acutely conscious of the embarrassed flush creeping up her neck and face. She started to say something but was so taken aback that she couldn't get the words out. Finally she released a slightly uneasy laugh in response.

His smile was immediately replaced by a frown. 'I am talking about a purely professional arrangement,' he said. 'Nothing sordid. Just a few sittings here in my studio for which I will of course pay you well.'

She recovered her composure and met his stare with a cold one of her own. 'Thank you for the tea, Mr Lutterall, but the answer is no. Absolutely not. I am a married woman and posing naked is not something I would ever entertain. Now, I would like to go home, if you don't mind.'

To her surprise, he showed no obvious chagrin at the blunt refusal and gave a little shrug, 'Of course, I understand, but if ever you change your mind . . .'

'I won't.'

'Fine. Then I will get Frank to run you back.'

'I can easily walk. It's just down the road.'

His reply was firm and polite, but she read just a hint of mockery in those dark eyes. 'I wouldn't hear of it.'

* * *

Kate was still trying to process what Lutterall had suggested when Frank Delaney dropped her at her front door and drove off and she was furious with herself for the way she had reacted to his cheeky proposal. She had always prided herself on being a tough, unshockable, modern woman, with a totally liberal, open-minded outlook towards nudity and sex. Yet instead of simply taking what he'd said in her stride and dismissing it with an offhand laugh, she had behaved like some prudish, shrinking violet from the Victorian era. Absolutely ridiculous in the twenty-first century. After all, on a solo holiday break to Cancun in Mexico a while ago, she had been happy enough to shed her bikini top on the beach and to hurl scorn at Hayden when he found out later and lambasted her for it. So, what was the problem here?

But then she asked herself, was there another reason for her indignant response to Lutterall's proposal? Was it out of a perverse sense of guilt? Had she allowed his flattery about her body to get to her, to the extent that, deep down, a desire to pose for him naked had actually been awakened within her, after touching a critical nerve? Hayden was not exactly a Don Juan and his narrow-minded attitude towards nudity and anything of a sexual nature had been a bone of contention between the two of them ever since they had been married. Though she loved her loyal, supportive partner she affectionately called "fat man" more than anything else in the world, could it be that their dangerously attractive near neighbour had stirred up feelings in her that she had been forced to suppress for so long?

Shaking herself fiercely to clear her head she muttered, 'Get thee behind me, Satan,' and went for a cold shower.

CHAPTER 4

Hayden rang at just after ten in the morning and Kate's response was more than a tad impolite.

'What time do you call this?' she shouted into the phone. 'I was fast asleep.'

She heard his heavy sigh. 'It *is* after ten. I'm at the Crown Court.'

'Well, good for you. I was having a lie in.'

He grunted. 'I thought I ought to let you know,' he went on. 'The case looks like going on into Monday. I'm unlikely to be called today, but I have to stay anyway to be available in the event that I am required at a later stage.'

'So, you went all that way on Wednesday for nothing?'

'Looks like it.'

'Can't you come back for the weekend and return Sunday night?'

He emitted a cough. 'There's something else.'

She groaned. 'Go on.'

'Popped over to Burtle to check on our cottage yesterday afternoon. Seems there's a problem with the boiler. Tenants aren't happy. I managed to get hold of our usual engineer and he's meeting me there tomorrow morning — Saturday — so I'll have to stay on here anyway.'

Kate swore. 'Never rains, but it bloody well pours, does it? Well, you'll have to do what you've got to do.'

Concern crept into his tone. 'What do you mean it never rains but it pours? Do you have another problem there? Our burglar hasn't been back, has he?'

She was quick to allay his fears. 'No, it's all good here. I'm just bored, that's all.'

She could hear the relief in his voice now. 'You could always finish painting the decking. Half of it's been done already.'

She snorted. 'Yeah, right. I'm more likely to spend the day sitting on it with a book.'

'Er, not going to the beach then?'

She grinned, sensing what he was thinking. 'I might. I've bought this new topless, bottomless bikini which I might try out.'

'Very funny!'

'*I* thought so. Enjoy your court case.'

She cut off and returned the phone to the bedside cabinet, sinking back into the soft mattress and closing her eyes. Just ten more minutes, she mused. But it was not to be.

The phone rang again almost immediately.

'Constable Geraint Rheon, Mrs Lewis,' announced the gruff voice at the other end. 'Sorry to bother you so early, but it's possible we have found your burglar.'

Kate shot up in bed this time. 'You have? Where?'

'We're attending the scene of a burned-out caravan in a field just beyond Lamphey village. Sadly there's the remains of a body in the wreckage too. Man, by the look of it.'

'That's awful, but what makes you think he's our burglar?'

'If you could pop over here, I'll explain. I'll give you the address—'

'No point, Officer,' she cut in. 'I don't have a car.'

'I'll pick you up,' he replied. 'Give me ten minutes.'

The liveried police car was old and creaky, with a nice collection of rust on the door sills and an ashtray choked with cigarette butts. Kate smiled to herself. Typical rural run-around, she thought, probably well beyond its service date. Rheon's nicotine-stained fingers on the steering wheel suggested he might be the culprit and she guessed that out here in the sticks, the rules prohibiting police officers from smoking in cars and police stations received scant attention.

The caravan was standing in something like a four-acre field. It had been parked behind a tall hedge off an unclassified road known as the Ridgeway. Little remained of it or the hedge now, apart from a pile of blackened wreckage on a twisted steel chassis. Evidence that the fire service had recently been in attendance was indicated by the two- to three-inch deep lake extending out across the hard, sun-baked earth for some ten to fifteen yards.

'I won't be asking you to look at the body,' Rheon said. 'It's not a very pleasant sight and anyway there's not a lot of him left to see.'

Kate was tempted to say that she was well aware of what burned bodies looked like from her previous life, but she bit her tongue and simply nodded.

'Any idea how the fire started?' she asked.

He shook his head. 'Not at this stage. Fire service thought it might have been a faulty cooker, or something. Those butane gas bottles can go up just like that, you know. Then caravans like this become deathtraps.'

'Dreadful,' she agreed, anxious not to dwell on the issue, but curious as to what he had to tell her. 'Now why have you brought me here?'

'Follow me,' he instructed and led the way past the scene of the fire to an open-fronted stone barn some twenty yards away. Inside, dripping with water, was an old, dark-blue Honda Accord.

'Look like the car you saw?' Rheon asked her, studying her intently.

She nodded, feeling her legs go a little weak at the knees with shock as her gaze focused on the number plate. It did look like the car she had spotted on the night of the burglary all right, and it was definitely the same car she had seen parked in the lane the following day, once Hayden had left for Bristol, when she had challenged the so-called bird-watcher. But for some peculiar reason she was reluctant to pass that information on to Rheon.

Instead, she said, 'Yes, it does look very much like the car I saw driving away.'

He grunted. 'We're waiting for CID at the moment, so I can't open the car up in case they decide our scenes of crime team should take a look at it. But I thought you might be interested to see what I saw inside through the window here. Take a look, but don't touch the car, okay?'

Kate nodded and peered through the front passenger window. She stiffened immediately. A monocular like the so-called twitcher had been using when she had confronted him was lying on the front passenger seat, together with a book entitled *Birds of Britain*. But more significantly, there was a scrappy piece of paper projecting from under the book with an address scribbled on it — an address which read: *Kate Lewis, Willow Cottage, Freshwater East.*

'Willow Cottage is your place, if I'm not mistaken,' Rheon said. 'Seems he had it staked out before he broke in.' His voice changed and there was a more inquiring note to it now. 'So, why do you suppose he had your name and address written down like that?'

Kate was as surprised as the constable. 'I haven't the faintest idea,' she said truthfully.

'You sure?' he asked.

Kate emitted a short, unamused laugh. 'Of course I'm sure. My husband and I have only been here a couple of months, as I told you before. We don't know anyone, and we understand that the cottage was previously owned by a lady who died in an old people's home, suffering from dementia. We found the cottage in a property ad on the internet and the sale was swift and uncomplicated.'

'So why would a housebreaker make a note of your name? The address perhaps, if he was acting on the instructions of someone else, but why your name? That wouldn't help him to find the place, would it?'

Kate was beginning to lose her patience. 'Listen to me, Officer,' she said sharply, 'I have no idea why this man noted my name, I also have no idea why he selected my cottage out of all the other properties in the area. It's a complete mystery to me.'

'And to us, ma'am,' he said. 'Bit worrying too if there's a chance he was targeting you rather than your home. You'd best keep your wits about you from now on, just in case someone else was behind your burglary and has singled you out for some reason.'

Thanks a lot, Kate said to herself, *that really is reassuring.*

* * *

Once Geraint Rheon had dropped her off at home, Kate stretched herself out on her deck recliner and did some deep soul-searching, a cup of black coffee on the little table beside her to aid her thought processes. She was suffering from another wave of guilt on top of that arising from her earlier carnal stirrings in relation to Graham Lutterall; this time for holding back on the local policeman regarding the so-called birdwatcher she had confronted the two days before. Why she hadn't told Rheon about the encounter, she had no idea. It was certainly relevant information and if a witness had withheld material like that from her on a case, she would have been none too pleased. But at the time something inside her, she didn't know what, had frozen her tongue and made her keep her own counsel, and the trouble was, it would look a bit strange if she were to tell Rheon about that confrontation now. After all, what would she say to him? 'Oh, by the way, I forgot to tell you, I think the man in the burned-out caravan was the same guy I caught watching my cottage two days ago.' She could imagine the policeman's reaction. In the end, she finished her coffee, grabbed a towel and headed for the beach, this time influenced by recent events into wearing a one-piece swimming costume under her clothes.

The sea was very calm and she spent two hours enjoying the sun and the sand, relieved that there was no sign of Graham Lutterall, before returning to her cottage via the usual footpath.

The beautiful bouquet of flowers was propped up against her front door and, guessing instinctively who they were from, she gingerly removed the small card and read the message written on it in a neat, flowing hand.

> *Let's start again. My sincere apologies for embarrassing you yesterday. Come to dinner tonight. Allow me to make amends. Frank will pick you up 7.30 for 8.00. Please don't say 'no'. I would hate to have to drink an expensive Bollinger on my own.*
> *Kind Regards,*
> *Graham*

'Damn and blast!' she muttered. But there was an excited tingling sensation running through her and her mouth had suddenly gone very dry.

* * *

Hayden rang again at the worst possible time. It was just after seven fifteen and Kate was late. She had just had a shower and done her hair, and she picked up the call from the extension phone in her bedroom where she was in the process of selecting a dress for the dinner she had been intending to decline all afternoon. Her husband hadn't much to say, except to break the bad news that the boiler in their Somerset cottage couldn't be fixed until a spare part was delivered on the Monday, which meant that even if he were to be released as a Crown Court witness, he wouldn't be able to return home until the part arrived and the engineer was able to sort out the problem.

'You don't seem too concerned,' he commented, sounding miffed that she simply accepted what he'd told her without protest. 'I thought you'd blow a gasket.'

'Resigned is the word I would use, Hayd,' she said, pulling a little black cocktail dress over her head. 'There's nothing I can do about it, is there?'

'No, I suppose . . . What are you doing tonight?'

She looked at herself in the full-length bedroom mirror and nodded her satisfaction. 'What do you think I am doing? It's not exactly Rave City around here, is it?'

'What are you having for dinner? I hope you're looking after yourself.'

She tried to swallow her guilt and glanced quickly at her wristwatch as she tucked the phone into her neck and bent down to pull on her high-heeled shoes. It was seven twenty-two. Lutterall's ugly chauffeur could be there at any minute . . .

'No, I'll be fine,' she replied.

'You sound strange.'

She bit her lip. 'No, I'm just tired, that's all.'

There was silence for a few moments and his next comment seemed to hang in the air, unspoken, for a second or two.

'Not much to say, though, have you?' he said finally.

'What do you want me to say?'

There was a heavy sigh from the other end of the phone.

'Don't know really. I'm just missing you, that's all.'

There were suddenly tears in her eyes and taking a big gulp, she kicked off her shoes angrily. What the hell was she doing? Going to dinner with another man? She ought to be ashamed of herself. Poor old Hayden. She didn't deserve him.

It was now seven twenty-six. Nearly time for bloody Frank to arrive. She struggled unsuccessfully to pull the cocktail dress back over her head with one hand. She wasn't going to Lutterall's and that was that. She had decided.

'Well, I'd better go,' Hayden said miserably. 'I booked dinner at the hotel for seven thirty.'

Headlights blazed through the glazed front door of the cottage and there was the sound of a car outside. Frank! Shit!

'Okay then. Give me a call in the morning when you know what's happening.'

A double ring on the front doorbell.

'Bye. Love you,' he faltered.

She replied in kind and the phone cut off.

Frank stared down at her bare feet and red-painted toenails, then at her dress, which was noticeably askew. She noticed that he seemed to have left his cap in the car this time and that he was totally bald, which only added to his thuggish appearance.

'Early, am I?' he asked, raising an eyebrow.

She tried to look contrite. 'No, Frank, but I'm afraid I won't be able to come to dinner tonight.' She raised a hand to her head. 'I've got this awful headache developing and I'm feeling quite sick. Will you apologise to Mr Lutterall for me?'

He pondered the point for a second, and frowned, looking even uglier than he had before. Then to her astonishment, he pushed his way into the house, forcing her back through the porch into the hallway.

'Mr Lutterall won't like that, 'cause 'e's gone to a lot o' trouble, like.'

She took a deep, trembling breath, shocked by his behaviour, but stubbornly refusing to be intimidated. 'Well, I'm sorry, but that's the way it is. These things can't be helped. Could you now leave, please?'

The little piggy eyes seemed to get even smaller. 'Why don't yer just be a good gel, and put on yer shoes, straighten that dress and come out to the car?' he said.

She glared at him. 'I've told you, I won't be able to come.'

His intended smile looked more like a leer and there was a sudden air of menace about him. 'Shoes,' he said. 'Now!'

'I beg your pardon?'

He moved closer, towering over her and forcing her back through the hall door into the kitchen-diner.

'Mr Lutterall, 'e don't take bein' stood up, little lady,' he growled, 'and me orders is to pick you up — so, *shoes*!'

Kate was not the sort of person who allowed herself to be bullied by anyone, but she knew she was in a fix. Frank was a big guy and he was plainly not going to take no for an answer. She was quite sure that if she continued to defy him, he would simply pick her up and carry her out to the car over his shoulder as she was. She could scream, of course, but who to? Most of the residents on this stretch of road were either elderly or were second-home owners currently back in London or wherever. Furthermore, a scene, possibly involving the police, was the last thing she wanted after what had happened already over the past few days, as it would mean Hayden being made aware of Lutterall's advances and her own complicity in things.

'I'll be a minute,' she said, smoothing down her dress with hands that were shaking slightly through a mixture of anger and dread. Then, crossing to her bedroom at the far end, she left him standing there for a moment while she collected her shoes and a silk wrap for her bare shoulders.

'Okay, so we'd better go,' she said tightly. 'Mustn't keep the boss waiting, must we?'

* * *

Graham Lutterall looked perplexed.

'Frank tells me you have a rotten headache and feel sick?' he said, more as a question than anything else. 'He said you didn't want to come tonight?'

Seated across from her in a deep armchair in the living room, he was dressed in a white tuxedo, black trousers and wore a clip-on, white bowtie with his wingless black shirt. Behind him, on the terrace, the table was again set for two, gleaming silver cutlery arranged with precision and crystal glasses glittering in the dying sunlight.

'I feel a lot better now, thank you,' Kate replied, but avoided a post-mortem on what had transpired at her cottage by saying nothing about the chauffeur's reprehensible behaviour, which she guessed Lutterall was perfectly aware of anyway.

His thin lips formed into one of his cold smiles, his eyes once more carrying a mocking glint that seemed capable of reading her mind. Despite his physical attractiveness, Kate realised more than ever that he was a very dangerous man.

'Good,' he replied. 'Now I felt really bad about the way I treated you yesterday afternoon and I was very keen to make it up to you. I think you will enjoy the meal my resident chef,

Alfredo, has prepared for us. I hope you are hungry. But first a little aperitif.'

As if summoned by some telepathic instruction, the blond "waiter", Adam, from the previous day appeared and poured a drink into a small wine glass on the circular table beside her chair before crossing the room to serve her host.

'This is one of my favourites, Kate,' Lutterall said. 'Kir, topped with Aligoté, white wine. Try it and see what you think.'

Forcing a smile of her own, Kate took a sip and nodded. 'Very nice,' she agreed as Adam withdrew, adding a crass remark in her attempt to hide her awkwardness, which she regretted as soon as she opened her mouth. 'You certainly know how to impress a girl.'

His laugh this time seemed genuine. 'Hardly just with a mundane cocktail like this,' he said. 'But perhaps with the meal to follow. Shall we go through?'

Feeling small and out of her depth, Kate followed him through the open doorway on to the terrace, where he eased her politely into a cushioned chair at the steel table, facing, as before, the sloping lawn and white-capped ocean beyond. In other circumstances Kate might have found the situation romantic, but not as it was now. She was far too apprehensive about what devious plan her enigmatic host might have hatched for her once dinner was over. As a police officer, she had had to face a whole variety of criminals in her career, including murderers, psychopaths and armed thugs, and she had usually felt tough enough to be able to deal with them, but with Graham Lutterall, if that *was* his real name, it was different. In spite of the neon danger signs flashing in her brain, she couldn't ignore the carnal magnetism of the man. She was like a moth, drawn to a flame even though it will die. Now she knew why so many of the abused women she had come across as a detective had returned to their partners in the end despite the inevitability of worse abuse and sometimes even their own deaths. They just couldn't help themselves. Well, she had to, and that meant getting out of Lutterall's house, away from his influence, as soon as possible and never coming back.

CHAPTER 5

Kate awoke with a blinding headache, thinking that it was probably punishment for initially lying about feeling ill to Frank Delaney the previous evening. Then she remembered the red wine and the spirits she had drunk before, during and after the lavish dinner Graham Lutterall had provided and knew that lies had nothing to do with it. She had promised herself that she would go easy on the alcohol in order to stay sober and remain in control, but it was a promise that she had obviously failed to keep and she had no recollection of what had happened after the dinner. Only a dim memory of being brought home in a car and of Frank Delaney's ugly face close to hers as he had carried her indoors. She was still wearing her black cocktail dress and her knickers, and they were not torn or soiled, so that was a big relief anyway, although she seemed to have lost her shoes and her wrap somewhere along the way. But she had no idea what innermost secrets she had divulged to Lutterall under the influence of alcohol. Had she told him she and Hayden were ex-coppers? Or, heaven forbid, that she found him sexually attractive? Still, like it or not, there was nothing she could do about it now. What was done was done.

Rolling over on to her side, she carefully slid her feet over the edge of the bed, stripped off her clothes and padded to the bathroom, holding on to her head to prevent it falling off.

The hot, steaming water was a godsend and she stood there for a long time with her head leaning against the shower door. Never again, she vowed for the umpteenth time in her life. From now on she was going to stop drinking altogether.

The telephone rang in the middle of her pledges and, cursing the interruption, she padded back to the bedroom, dripping water everywhere.

'Kate?' drawled a familiar voice. She closed her eyes tightly for a moment.

It was Lutterall. What the hell was he going to tell her? That she'd disgraced herself while drunk? That she'd smashed one of his crystal glasses or knocked over a vintage bottle of Bollinger on to a priceless Persian rug? Was he going to say he didn't want to see her again after the way she had behaved and was that okay by her? A host of misgivings blasted through her brain in the space of a couple of seconds.

'How on earth did you get my number?' she asked, playing for time while she prepared herself for what might be coming.

'It wasn't that difficult,' he said. 'Old Frank has sharp eyes. You shouldn't keep that old-style telephone you have in full view on the hall table, at least not with the number written on the dial pad.'

She winced, feeling stupid. 'Oh.'

'By the way, you left your shoes and wrap here,' he said after a long pause. 'How's the head?'

She felt her temple tenderly. 'Pretty messed up at the moment. Listen, I'm — I'm so sorry. I don't usually show myself up like that.'

'You didn't.'

'I didn't?'

'No.' There was a chuckle. 'You flaked out after your second double whisky, which, following several glasses of Bollinger was probably not surprising. What is it they say, "never mix the grape and the grain"?'

She sat down heavily on the edge of the bed, thinking that it was a good job he was on the end of a phone and couldn't actually see her, since he would have got his wish to see her stark naked. But with her long auburn hair stuck to her shoulders by glistening soap suds, she had to admit she was hardly a pretty picture anyway.

'It won't happen again,' she said ruefully.

'I'm glad you said that,' he replied. 'It suggests that I will be able to see you once more.'

She shook her head furiously, her skin crawling as she thought of Hayden. 'Look, no, this will have to stop. I'm sorry but I'm married and I have no intention of betraying my husband.'

'Who said anything about betraying anyone? Bring your husband along with you next time.'

She continued shaking her head. 'No, I'm sorry. Thank you for the lovely dinner and afternoon tea, but there won't be a next time.'

There, she had said it. She felt relieved.

'What about your shoes and wrap? They are still here.'

'Could, er, Frank possibly drop them over next time he's passing?'

'Oh, I think it would be much better if you collected them yourself. You did say before that you could easily walk to my place and it's a lovely day. Just the sort of day for a bracing stroll. See you later.'

Her phone went dead and, staring out of the window into the burning orb of the sun, she swore. 'Bastard!' she said aloud. But she needed the wrap and shoes before Hayden came home and there was only one way she was going to get them.

Vigorously rubbing her hair, then drying the rest of herself off, she pulled on a pair of jeans, a respectable shirt and a pair of stout shoes and headed off along the lane towards Smuggler's Reach.

* * *

Kate spotted the familiar police car within yards of the house and gritted her teeth. PC Rheon was the last person she wanted to see at that precise moment, but he stopped beside her and nodded through the open driver's window.

'Out for a stroll, Mrs Lewis?' he asked, then added, 'I was just coming to see you.'

Kate gave him a brief smile. 'Were you? Is there another problem?'

He shook his head. 'Not for you, but it seems that the caravan fire was probably arson. Further examination of the scene suggests some sort of accelerant, probably petrol, was used, which ignited a couple of drums of butane gas. Fella didn't stand much of a chance.'

Kate was horrified. 'Heavens above, why would anyone have done that?'

He shrugged. 'Maybe someone resented him being there or local kids thought they'd have a laugh and it went too far. Or—' and he gave her a hard stare — 'as I said before, maybe he was working for someone and they weren't too happy about his performance.' He sighed. 'See, what I still can't understand is why he picked on your cottage and didn't try to break in anywhere else. We've had no burglaries reported in Freshwater East since, not so much as a forced shed door.'

Kate felt a worm beginning to twist in her stomach. 'I'm afraid I can't help you there, Constable,' she replied. 'I've told you all I know.'

'Have you, Mrs Lewis?' he said, and the way he said it seemed to indicate that he had doubts about that.

'Well, yes, I have. Now I really must be off. I, er, am meeting someone.'

He gave a slow, reflective smile, then nodded. 'Fine. Let me know if you think of anything new, won't you, ma'am?'

Then he engaged gear and pulled away with a wave, leaving Kate to complete her walk with her head bursting with worries. *Who said "retirement" was the best thing ever?* she mused. It was beginning to feel more stressful than a twelve-hour shift back at Highbridge nick!

* * *

The security gates of Lutterall's house opened even as she got to them and she glared angrily at the television monitor angled towards her on one of the posts, then at the man who came out of the bungalow as she walked through. Obviously she was expected. The long walk to the house had taken around half an hour and she arrived hot, perspiring and even angrier than when she'd set out.

Lutterall met her at the front door. 'How nice of you to pop over so soon,' he said with a humourless smile and held up her shoes by the straps in one hand. Thinking he was giving them to her and she could then about-turn and leave, she made to take them from him, but he quickly jerked his hand away.

'Coffee first, Kate,' he said. 'Then I think we should have a little talk.'

'About what?' she snapped as she followed him along the hallway, and this time she didn't try to disguise how she now felt about him and his reprehensible behaviour.

The silver coffee pot was already on the steel table on the terrace with two cups ready and waiting. It was evident that he had second-guessed her and had known she would turn up at his door very soon after his phone call. The arrogance of the man.

'You don't take milk, do you?' he asked, lifting the coffee pot, which seemed to wink at her in the sunlight.

'Can I have my shoes and wrap, please?' she said, remaining standing.

He sighed. 'I can see you are very annoyed with me,' he acknowledged, 'but really, Kate, I had to see you again to sort out our business arrangement.'

She frowned. 'Business arrangement? What are you talking about?'

He poured the two black coffees and waved her to a chair. 'Let's just have a nice cup of coffee, while I explain, eh?'

She remained standing, her expression defiant as she held out her hand. 'Shoes, please.'

'Twenty minutes,' he said. 'Twenty minutes on this lovely sunny day to hear what I have to say, that's all I ask.'

She hesitated. Then, feeling she was being totally unreasonable in spite of her anger towards him, she reluctantly sat down. The next instant she wished she hadn't.

'I desperately need you to model for me,' he said, holding up his hand as she half rose in her chair. 'As I indicated just now, I'm talking about a business arrangement. That and no more. I will pay you well — five hundred pounds for each sitting, in fact, or more if you feel that is too miserly.'

'I've already given you my answer to that proposition,' she snapped, standing up. 'It's not going to happen. I don't intend discussing it any further.'

He sighed his frustration. 'I have no ulterior motive, Kate, just this burning desire to capture your beauty on canvas, and I must be given that opportunity.'

'Must?' she questioned.

His face had hardened and the dark eyes were like those of a cobra ready to strike. 'I always get what I want, Kate,' he said quietly. 'You should understand that.'

'And I always *do* what I want,' she replied. '*You* should understand that.'

He sat back in his chair. 'I don't think your husband — Hayden, isn't it? — would be too happy about your having both afternoon tea and dinner with me while he was away, and it could be a tad embarrassing for you if Frank were to return your stuff after hubby got back. He could come to the wrong conclusion. *I* would in his position.'

Kate's expression was bleak. 'Are you threatening me?'

The cold smile returned. 'Just think on what I have said,' he replied, without answering her question, 'and it would be in your interests to let me have a positive answer before

Hayden returns. Meanwhile, I think I'll hang on to these nice shoes and the lovely soft wrap while I await your answer.'

* * *

Kate was beside herself with rage and any carnal attraction she may have felt for Graham Lutterall had been killed stone dead. *At least that was one positive outcome*, she mused as she marched home along the lane. In a way, he had done her a favour, the arrogant, self-confident pig. But underneath her fury, there was a dreadful anxiety. As Lutterall had pointed out, that wrap and the shoes could get her into real hot water with Hayden. Her sensitive, prudish husband would never understand why she had visited a male neighbour on two separate occasions for both afternoon tea and evening dinner. He was bound to draw the wrong conclusions and that could destroy their marriage. If she had been a man, she would have said Lutterall "had her by the short and curlies", but though she was a woman, the effect was just the same.

She needed time to think things out and the best place to do that, she decided, was in the calming caress of the ocean. Risking her bikini this time — after all, she had nothing to lose now Lutterall had shown his hand — she was soon floating on her back on low, salty crests of incoming foam, listening to their gentle hiss as they met the pebbly strip lining the shore, and allowing her mind to drift with them. But it was no good. After an hour of reflection, she found herself still without a solution and feeling quite cold. Reluctantly she returned to her beach towel and it was as she was drying herself off that for the first time she noted with a grimace the black cloud bank building up on the horizon. *Maybe that was an omen*, she thought grimly, *and if it was, it certainly wasn't a good one.*

* * *

Hayden telephoned her again later that afternoon and he sounded very low. Complaining about being bored and missing her. But weighed down with guilt over everything, Kate was in no mood for making sympathetic conversation and she ended the call after just a few minutes on the pretext of a splitting headache.

The front doorbell rang at just after six in the evening as she was making herself a sandwich she didn't really want. Licking the butter off her fingers, she went to answer it, but when she walked through the porch and opened the door, there was no one there. Puzzled and not a little apprehensive after the events of the past few days, she was about to turn back into the cottage when she spotted the envelope halfway through the letter box.

Returning to the kitchen-diner with it, she tore the envelope open and found a short note inside. It was from Graham Lutterall and it read:

> *I'm not really the rotten so-and-so you must think. I will return your shoes and wrap quietly and without your husband's knowledge in due course. I merely ask that you change your mind and model for me on a day of your choosing. The sitting will all be above board and I'm happy to start with just a standard fully clothed head-and-shoulders portrait first to see whether you want to go any further after that, which, of course, will be up to you. I will still pay you a generous fee for your time. Give me a bell . . .*
> *Graham.*

Attached to the note was a business card bearing his name, with the words: *Landscape & Portrait Artist — Commissions undertaken* on the front and his name and telephone number on the back.

She stood for a moment in a state of flux, tapping the stiff card against her bared teeth. Relieved that, on the face of it, he seemed to have softened his stance, but dubious about his promise to let her decide how far she was prepared to go at any sitting. He obviously intended hanging on to her shoes and wrap, which was suspicious in itself. Why did he need to do that if he had had a change of heart and his new offer was completely genuine? As it was, it was a bit like a "come into my parlour" invitation. Once she was in his studio, she would be trapped, and it would be so easy for a head and shoulders sitting to turn into a demand for her to take all her clothes off. But if she called his bluff and continued to refuse to sit for him, how far would he go to get his own way? She hadn't the slightest idea. But she was fully aware of the fact that until she had got her "incriminating evidence" back, she faced a very uncertain future on the domestic front.

Returning to the kitchen-diner, suddenly no longer interested in a sandwich, she poured herself a glass of red wine instead and sat on the floor of the living room area with her back against a three-seater settee, slowly sipping her drink and trying to decide what to do next. She was there until the sun was swallowed up in the twilight and the bats started flitting backwards and forwards across the French doors in the decking lights. Then she went to bed and fell asleep, thinking fondly of good, old-fashioned Hayden and how lucky she was to have him. But for how long after all this, she wondered, that was the point?

CHAPTER 6

It rained heavily during the night and, though it was over when Kate got up in the morning, water was still dripping from the overfull gutters and pooling on the saturated decking. Throwing open the French doors, she braved the puddles and went out on to the deck, gnawing at a piece of buttered toast and delighting in the coldness of the water on her bare feet. The sea was angry. She could see the height of the breakers racing into the bay and a keen wind had arisen, which was already stirring the tops of the trees in the copse. There was every chance it would get a lot wilder before the day was out and she had no illusions as to what that would be like in the cottage's exposed, elevated position.

She remembered when she and Hayden had arrived in Pembrokeshire two months ago, in the midst of a violent storm. The wind had slammed into the cottage with such force that they'd thought it would take the roof off; ripping branches off the trees with a maniacal howl as a heavy deluge blotted out the horizon, sending the rain hammering into the windows like hail. An altogether scary experience, which much to Hayden's incredulity, she had found exhilarating.

She swallowed her last mouthful of toast and took a deep breath. The air smelled fresh and sweet, with a salty tang to it that was always present after heavy rain. Despite all the worries that had been crowding her mind, she felt vibrant and alive for a change and decided to go for a walk.

Dressed in jeans and an anorak, with stout walking shoes on her feet, she headed off along the lane outside towards Lamphey, then turned down the steep hill towards Freshwater beach and past the near empty car park — empty, that was, but for a police car. Inwardly she groaned as PC Rheon drove over to her.

'Rough day,' he said through his open window. 'Devil of a wind getting up three miles out, the weather men say.'

She nodded. 'I'd better get back then before it hits here,' she said.

'Your man,' he said suddenly, 'the fella in the caravan? Turns out he was a copper.'

'What?' She stared at him.

'Aye, that surprised me too,' he said. 'They found a badly burned police warrant card on his body. Couldn't read the name, but it was a Met card. They're looking into it now.'

'Why are you telling me this?'

He smiled grimly. 'Just thought you'd like to know. Thing is, why d'ye suppose a police officer would try and burgle your cottage, if that *was* him, and why did he make a note of your name and address. Funny business, don't you think?'

His gaze was fixed on her, as before. It was almost as if he was trying to will her into saying something. Maybe he suspected that the dead man had been back to spy on her and was waiting for a "cough"?

'Funny all round, Constable,' she agreed after a pause. 'Hopefully you'll get to the bottom of it in due course.'

'Nothing to do with me anymore,' he said and there was a touch of bitterness in his tone. 'Taken out of my hands now. Some bigwig detective's been down here to look into it.'

She smiled. 'Then at least you've got rid of the headache.'

He gave a nod, which carried little conviction. 'I don't like dropping things I've been following up. See, I am certain there's more to this case than meets the eye. He was in your cottage for a reason and if it wasn't burglary, then what was it, eh, that's what I'd like to know?'

His last comment came over almost as an accusation and Kate just stared at him for a couple of seconds, without saying anything. Then he nodded to her. 'Well, got to be off. Things to do. Keep away from the water, won't you. Getting pretty rough down there.'

Then he engaged gear and drove off, leaving Kate staring after him with a heavy frown on her face. Rheon should not have passed on the information he had given her. It was bound to have been confidential. In fact, his manner had been like a cop talking to a colleague. It was as if he knew she was ex-Bill. But how? If he'd carried out an RO check on Hayden's Jag, it would only have given him Hayden's Somerset address, nothing else, and it was no secret that she and Hayden had come up from Somerset anyway. Also, why was he so fixated on the whole affair? He would have known that a serious case like a fatal arson would have been handed over to CID to deal with and likely even resulted in the setting up of a major crime investigation. So why was he still chipping away at it? Furthermore, why hadn't she yet received a visit from the CID looking into any connection between the attempted burglary at the cottage and the death of the police officer? It should have been automatic.

Something very peculiar was going on, and, as she and Hayden didn't get a local newspaper and rarely watched any television, she had no idea what had been reported in the local press. But unbeknown to her at that precise moment, enlightenment was just a short walk away and with it was to come the grim realisation that, though knowledge was said to be power, there was a great deal of truth in the old adage that ignorance is bliss.

* * *

There were men in Kate's garden. She spotted three of them on the decking through the French doors when she returned home and walked into the kitchen-diner.

Striding angrily across the room, she unlocked the doors and challenged them.

'So who the devil are you?' she demanded. 'And what the bloody hell are you doing on my property?'

The two men nearest her, both dressed in smart, pressed suits, turned quickly. Both looked as though they were in their late forties or early fifties, one consumptively thin, with short, crisp, fair hair and a military style moustache, and the other, completely bald, with thick lips and a prominent beer belly, who reminded her of the late Telly Savalas from the seventies crime series *Kojak*, and seemed to be noisily chewing gum.

Before either of them could say anything, another dapper "suit", with black hair and the distinctive features of someone who hailed either from China or somewhere else in that part of the world, appeared at her elbow.

'Hi, Kate,' he said quietly, 'just admiring your beautiful garden.'

She gaped. 'Charlie?' she exclaimed. 'Charlie bloody Woo? Well, I'm damned, what are *you* doing here?'

It was only a few months since she had last seen her old detective inspector from Highbridge CID and then it had been at the low-key farewell do the department had arranged for her and Hayden. Woo had once been a serving officer in the Hong Kong Police, who had transferred to Avon and Somerset Police when the territory was in the throes of being taken back by mainland China. He was an old friend of hers as well as her former boss. But he was the last person she expected to find standing there on her decking.

'What a lovely property, Kate,' he replied. 'Thought I'd pop over and see this new pad of yours.'

'Like heck you did,' she retorted suspiciously.

He made a tutting sound. 'Such a distrustful nature,' he said and grinned. 'How's the sabbatical? You certainly seem to have found your ideal spot here. I'm quite envious.'

Kate shook her head wearily. 'Cut the crap, Charlie. What are you here for and who are these two characters?'

'Ah.' Woo extended a hand towards the thin man with the moustache. 'Let me introduce you to John Norris, National Crime Agency.'

Norris inclined his head in polite acknowledgement and gave her a smile.

'And this is Detective Superintendent Harry Cole, seconded from the Met Specialist Crime Command.'

Kate raised her eyebrows. 'And did these gentlemen accompany you here because they wanted to see my new pad too?'

Woo chuckled and extended an arm towards the French doors. 'Perhaps we should talk inside.'

Kate shrugged. 'I suppose I'll have to get some coffee on.'

Twenty minutes later they were all seated in the living room area of the kitchen-diner, with mugs of steaming coffee on incidental tables in front of them; Kate and Charlie Woo occupying the only two armchairs and Norris and Cole sharing the settee opposite.

Kate's impatience to get to the bottom of why her visitors were there was almost tangible. 'Okay, Charlie, so are you going to tell me what's going on?' she asked finally after several minutes' awkward silence.

He nodded and, waving a hand towards Norris, said, 'Mr Norris would be better placed to start the ball rolling, I think.'

'Just *Mr* Norris?' Kate queried sharply. 'No police rank too?'

'I'm not a police officer, Mrs Lewis,' Norris explained. 'I am a senior civil servant working with the police. Though I have been given essential police powers to do my job.'

He leaned forward on the settee and studied Kate for a moment, plainly thinking about what he was going to say.

'What do you know about blood diamonds, Mrs Lewis?' he asked.

Kate shrugged. 'Not a lot, I must admit.' She smiled. 'Apart from what I gleaned from the James Bond film

Diamonds Are Forever, and the film *Blood Diamond*, with Leonardo DiCaprio.'

He returned her smile, but it lacked any real warmth. 'Ah, so you're a bit of a film buff then, are you? Well, at least you will have some understanding of what I am going to tell you. The fact is that for quite a few years these sought-after gems have been the currency of conflict and massive bloodshed worldwide, but particularly on the continent of Africa, hence the origin of the term *blood* diamonds. Up until something called the Kimberley Process, which was implemented in 2003 and introduced a certification scheme for the import and export of rough diamonds, diamond smuggling was a free-for-all in West Africa, costing millions of lives. Smuggling still goes on, of course — it would be naïve of me to suggest it doesn't — but today the Kimberley certification scheme has had some effect on slowing it down.'

He paused a few seconds, as if to collect his thoughts, and took a sip of his coffee.

'Following on from the history lesson, let me tell you a brief crime story,' he said. 'One that goes back to the spring of 1998. A big-time South London villain, named Charlie Hooper, succeeded in making a deal with an international crime syndicate linked to the Mafia, to smuggle a consignment of rare, uncut, pink diamonds, procured illegally from UNITA rebels in Angola, into South Africa, and then on to the United Kingdom. In order to achieve the last leg of the journey to Heathrow, Hooper needed a courier who could successfully evade border security and he found him in a government diplomat, named Johnathon Street. Knowing Street was a married man who liked his bit on the side, Hooper snared him in a honey trap, then forced him to pick up the diamonds from a corrupt member of the South African security service, while attending an official trade conference in Cape Town, and smuggle the consignment into the UK in his diplomatic bag.'

Kate whistled. 'Nice one.'

'Hardly the way I would describe it,' Norris replied without too much enthusiasm, 'and unfortunately it worked a treat. Street got through Customs with the delegation he was part of without a hitch. Apparently, the authorities here only learned of the conspiracy following a belated tip-off to Special Branch from the South African Police. They had apparently arrested their bent security man in the course of an unconnected pre-planned crime operation, and he had volunteered the info as part of a sentencing deal.'

'So, Street got clean away with it then?' Kate put in again.

'Not quite,' Cole said, moving his gum to one side of his mouth as he took over the story. 'A few days later he was found stabbed to death in a car park in West London, where it was assumed he had been meeting up with one of Hooper's goons to hand over the diamonds.'

'No honour among thieves, as they say.'

Cole flicked his eyebrows at her in acknowledgement. 'Naturally Street's debut as a courier was kept out of the press and his death attributed to a bungled random robbery. So the incident eventually died a death, if you'll pardon the pun, although the inevitable follow-up story about the mild-mannered diplomat and family man callously murdered by some no account street thug did run its course. As for the diamonds themselves, it was assumed by the Met's now long gone Regional Crime Squad, who already had Hooper under target surveillance and had a snout inside his organisation, that he had the stones safely stashed away somewhere, awaiting collection by his Mafiosi partners. But until they were able to confirm the fact one way or the other, they were stuffed.'

Charlie Woo came in. 'As it turned out, though, the game was far from over. The following month Charlie Hooper was driving to his country pad on the Somerset Levels when he was the victim of a nasty blagging. His minder and the car's chauffeur were both wasted by a hooded thug tooled up with a shotgun and poor old Charlie got a couple of bullets in the head from a handgun, which, according to the one surviving witness in the car, was produced by a second blagger who then ran off after nicking Hooper's briefcase.'

Kate was ahead of him. 'Containing the diamonds,' she put in.

'Seems pretty likely. But sadly, although our force had apparently been given the whisper by the Met — courtesy of their installed snout — that a blagging was on the cards, no one expected it was to be a triple hit. We had an ARV staked out nearby, but it got to the scene a fraction too late. The team managed to nick the man with the shotgun, a nasty villain with a string of pre-cons called Gerry Barlow, and the second blagger, a drifter named Lenny Thompson, was traced a few days later from a fingerprint he left on a stolen van the pair had been using . . .'

'But no diamonds?'

'Zilch, I'm afraid. Thompson must have hidden them somewhere while on the run, but he wasn't saying where. Both he and Barlow got life terms for the blagging and the murders and Barlow subsequently died in stir of hep C. But Thompson went on to complete a twenty-five-year stretch and was released a couple of weeks ago.'

'And you're still looking for the diamonds?'

'You know what they say, "an elephant never forgets", and, as you know, nor do we. A tail was put on him, of course, and when he caught a train for Taunton, we thought we were in business. But he gave us the slip and the next thing we know is a report of a body being found in the ruins of an old abbey on the Levels, a nice round bullet hole in his head.'

'And still no diamonds?'

'Obviously not. Whoever stiffed him no doubt followed him to his hidey-hole and took them off him either before or after killing him.'

Kate took a deep breath. 'Well, all this is really fascinating, but I do have to ask, what on earth has it got to do with Freshwater East and me?'

'Everything,' Cole responded sharply. 'I'm afraid you have become a kingpin in this business.'

'I don't see how.'

'Then we had better explain,' Norris said quietly.

CHAPTER 7

Norris climbed to his feet and went over to Kate, holding up a photograph in front of her. 'Do you know this man?' he asked quietly.

The photograph was a street shot of a man with thick, black, neatly coiffed hair, sharp aquiline features and dark penetrating eyes. He was wearing what looked like a morning suit and tie and carrying a bundle of documents under one arm, tied with pink ribbon. It was plainly a photograph of Graham Lutterall when he was perhaps in his late twenties or early thirties. That in itself was not so surprising, since he had told her himself that he had once been a lawyer. But what Kate did find surprising was the fact that there was a banner carrying the name Jeremy Brent across the bottom and she didn't need to be told that she was looking at a covert police surveillance photo.

'Well I'm damned,' she breathed, 'he told me his name was Graham Lutterall.'

'He also goes by the name Terrence Williams,' Norris said. 'He was Charlie Hooper's lawyer and is as bent as they come. But though we know he has been directly involved in some of the worst atrocities committed by Hooper and are ninety-nine percent certain he was responsible for the murder of Johnathon Street, acting on Hooper's orders, we haven't been able to prove anything against him. The photograph is a very old one, taken by a surveillance team in the course of a major crime investigation into Charlie Hooper, which unfortunately didn't get anywhere.'

Kate released a low whistle.

'Ironically,' Norris added, 'he was the sole surviving witness in Hooper's car after the blagging and we believe he actually set the job up in the first place, and that he, rather than Thompson, wasted his boss in order to get his hands on the diamonds and to take over Hooper's empire. It is pretty clear that he too was the person who followed Lenny Thompson on his release from prison, after waiting patiently for twenty-five odd years for that very moment, and then put a bullet in Thompson's head once he discovered where he had hidden the diamonds.'

Norris returned to the settee and finished drinking his coffee, which must have been practically cold by then.

'You certainly know how to make the best kind of friends, Kate,' Woo sniped.

Kate glowered at him. 'Not funny, Charlie,' she said. 'I've been in the man's house, had tea and dinner with him . . .'

'We know,' Cole cut in. 'We've had *you* under surveillance since he first approached you on the beach down there.'

She hardly heard him. She was thinking what a fool she had been. Frank Delaney's thuggish appearance and behaviour, the intense security at Smuggler's Reach and the way the man she now knew as Jeremy Brent was accompanied wherever he went by the minder who doubled as his waiter, it all should have alerted her to something dodgy straight away. And there had also been the so obvious pick-up routine Brent had employed to ultimately lure her into his so-called artist's studio. Kate felt sick. She had sensed from the start that something was odd about her near neighbour. Her female intuition had flagged up the fact that he was a dangerous man where women were concerned, and she had always felt uneasy and vulnerable in his presence. Yet at the same time, she had been fascinated by him and the sexual chemistry that radiated from him and she had ignored all the warning signs. Now he had sprung his despicable trap and she could see no way out.

Then suddenly the significance of Cole's last comment about surveillance broke through her uncomfortable musings and she surfaced from her navel-gazing to glare at her three visitors who were sitting there in silence, seemingly waiting for her to say something.

'Surveillance?' she exclaimed. 'You mean you've been watching me?'

Woo quickly shook his head. 'Not you per se,' he corrected. 'But you came into the picture when we set up surveillance on him and since the man we had in the field didn't know who you were, he followed up on you with photographs and inquiries . . .'

'Including trying to break into my house, you mean,' she snapped.

Norris sighed. 'That was going a bit too far,' he said, 'but he was trying to establish in what way you were connected to Brent. He had already carried out an RO check on your husband's Mk II Jaguar, but it simply gave his name and address, nothing about him. He forwarded the information he had to us by email, and then it didn't take us long to establish your bona fides and to approach your chief constable. Detective Inspector Woo was immediately asked to accompany us here to, er, break the ice a bit, if I could put it that way.'

But Kate's mind was already on something else. 'Then the man I caught watching my house with a monocular and who died in the fire in that caravan was . . .'

'An undercover Met police officer,' Norris confirmed. 'He contacted us just before he died to say you had rumbled him. What he didn't realise was that so had Brent. We think he had already blown his cover by getting too close to Brent's house well before you came into the picture, and that when Brent later managed to locate him, he sent one of his thugs round on a nocturnal visit to do the business, possibly Frank Delaney who has previous for this sort of thing.'

'So why on earth plonk him in a caravan in a field? He would have stuck out a mile and I would have thought the owner of the field would have had something to say.'

'His cover was that he was an ornithologist, checking out endangered species and he dressed the part. The farmer who owned the field believed him too and was happy to let him park there for a few quid. The alternative would have been a pub or self-catering place and in a rural area like this, it was thought that his comings and goings at weird hours might have provoked local gossip. In the caravan, he was out of the way and free to come and go as he pleased, without risk of attracting attention.'

'Well, the poor devil is out of the way now, isn't he?'

Woo gritted his teeth for a second. 'There's worse, though, Kate,' he said. 'I've said he was a Met copper. What I didn't say was that his name was Peter Foster.'

'Foster?'

'Yes, he was the younger brother of our own colleague on Highbridge CID, Jamie Foster.'

Kate stared at him in horror. 'I didn't know Jamie had a brother. Are you sure?'

'Oh. I'm sure, all right. He was apparently given the surveillance job because of his brilliant track record in Met undercover operations and Jamie was so proud of his achievements.'

'Is Jamie aware?'

'I have that unpleasant task to perform when I get back. At least Peter was single, so I don't have to break the news to a young wife.'

Kate thought of the tousle-haired detective constable who had once been part of her team on Highbridge CID and shook her head bitterly. Always a smile on his face and ready with a quip or a joke, Jamie was one of the nicest people she had ever worked with and, knowing the sensitive soul as she did, she knew he would be devastated when he heard the news about his brother. No wonder she'd felt that the man spying on her bungalow had seemed so familiar. Now she thought about it, he was the living spit of Jamie, despite the beard. If only it had clicked at the time. But even if it had, what could she have done to prevent what happened to him? Absolutely nothing.

'And meanwhile that slimy scumbag simply carries on as usual?' she grated.

'Not if you are prepared to bring him down and locate the diamonds for us,' Cole said soberly. 'That's why we're here.'

* * *

Mystified by Cole's statement, Kate sat back in her chair and waited for him to elaborate on what he had just said. When he didn't, she said, 'What can *I* do? I'm no longer a copper — at least not until I decide whether I want to come back in or not.'

'Once a copper, always a copper, isn't that what they say?' Norris asked pointedly.

'Maybe they do,' Kate replied, 'but I know when it's time to call it a day.'

'Do you?' Woo put in. 'Do you really? It's not how I see you, Kate. Hayden maybe, but I can't see you staying out of it for long. You would miss the action and the satisfaction of a job well done.'

Kate didn't answer, but said instead, 'Can you just cut the crap and tell me what grubby little job you have in mind for me?'

'Before we do,' Cole went on, 'would you mind telling us how you got involved with Brent?'

Kate frowned. 'I wasn't involved with him. He tried to pick me up on Freshwater East beach a few days ago when I went for a swim . . .'

'From what we've heard, it sounds like he succeeded,' Cole interjected. 'You went to tea with him and then dinner the day after.'

Kate's face reddened. 'I'm a happily married woman,' she said hotly. 'I don't have assignations with other men.

Yes, I did accept his invitation to afternoon tea because I was curious about him, but dinner was a big mistake, I realise that now, and I totally regret it.'

'Why do you regret it? Come on to you, did he?' There was a half sneer on Cole's face now. 'Tell you that you had a beautiful body, did he?'

It seemed as if he were deliberately trying to wind Kate up and she kept her cool with difficulty.

'Something like that,' she admitted.

'And you were flattered by his advances and fell for his charm?'

'I didn't fall for anything,' she lied. 'I just went because I . . .'

'Fancied him, eh?'

'Now just a minute,' she said, raising her voice and leaning forward in her chair, her eyes blazing. 'I don't have to sit here in my own home and put up with your snide remarks.'

Cole ignored her outburst and continued in the same vein. 'Tell you he wanted you to model for him naked, did he? Or hasn't he asked you yet? He usually does. It's all part of his game plan. You know, clothes off, then into bed. He's quite an attractive arsehole too, isn't he? You would probably have enjoyed it.'

Kate froze, staggered by his effrontery and the fact that he had hit the nail right on the head, but desperately anxious not to be inveigled into admitting that she had been naive enough to be so easily deceived by the man that she had walked right into his trap.

'And you can piss right off!' she snarled at him, as usual using an insult to shut down a conversation she knew she couldn't win.

But to her surprise, Cole suddenly broke into a chuckle and both Woo and Norris joined in.

'I told you she was a firebrand,' Woo said. 'Calm down, Kate, Detective Superintendent Cole was just testing you out, that's all.'

'Testing me out? Testing me out for what?'

'We needed to be sure you could handle what we have in mind,' Cole answered for him.

'Jeremy Brent is a past master at seducing pretty young women,' Norris explained. 'He has a reputation for it and has done it many times before. It is his main weakness, and we think we can exploit that weakness to our advantage. He specifically picked you out and he is obviously quite smitten with you at present, smitten enough to invite you into his own home on two separate occasions.'

'There would have been a third if I had not already sussed out what he was after,' Kate waffled, keen to convince her visitors that she had retained the upper hand.

'You mean you turned him down?' Norris exclaimed, looking concerned now.

'When he asked me to model for him, I sort of lost it,' she said, 'and I told him to get stuffed, so I am ceasing any further contact with him and . . .'

'But Kate, you mustn't do that,' Norris cut in earnestly. 'We need you to keep your association with him going. He is plainly infatuated with you and you are the one person who has access to his home right now.'

'You asked us why we were here and what we wanted you to do for us,' Cole said. 'I think you must have cottoned on by now.'

Kate issued a shaky, disbelieving laugh. 'You want me to pose naked for him and then sleep with the bastard, so you can get hold of enough evidence to nail him, is that it? Dream on! What do you think I am? Some cheap scrubber?'

Woo winced and shook his head quickly. 'You've got it all wrong, Kate. The one thing you must not do is to sleep with him. That would compromise any evidence supplied by you and at the very least, render it suspect and possibly inadmissible. I'm sure Detective Superintendent Cole would agree that the Met have been in enough trouble over that sort of thing with undercover officers recently.'

Cole nodded sourly at being reminded of the fact, but before he could say anything further, Norris came in again, the passion in his tone now unmistakable. 'Brent is a ruthless killer and needs to be brought to justice, Kate, not least because he is responsible for the horrific murder of one of our own. But on top of that, he is almost certainly in possession of a fortune in uncut Angolan diamonds, stained with the blood of local villagers, many of whom have been forced by terrorists to dig such stones out of the ground using just their bare hands.

'According to sources the South African authorities have tapped into, these particular stones are not the regular, plain, colourless diamonds for sale by commercial jewellers around the world, but incredibly high value pink diamonds, of superb quality and each over one hundred carats in uncut weight. These are not normally found in Angola, where yellow or colourless diamonds are more common, and they are thought to be worth literally millions of pounds. We need to retrieve them before Brent manages to fence them. And in this respect, there has evidently been a change in focus.

'Brent, it seems, has decided to renege on Hooper's original agreement with the mafia. The original *capo* Charlie had dealings with twenty-five or so years ago is now dead, like Charlie, and Brent doesn't trust the son who has taken over the business. So instead, he has approached someone known in criminal circles as the Collector. We have been after this character for a long time. We know he is a super-rich individual who deals solely in uncut diamonds sourced illegally throughout the world, but we have no idea as to his identity. It would be a real coup to catch both Brent and this character in our net and our information is that the Collector is due to visit Brent in the next few days to examine the merchandise. Subject to the diamonds being kosher, Brent stands to receive what amounts to a king's ransom.'

'I don't expect the mafia will be too pleased when they find out Brent has stuffed them.'

'That's an understatement, and we need to watch points on that in case they are already aware and decide to intervene.'

Kate slowly shook her head. 'And you expect me to single-handedly bring Brent to book by doing what, if not screwing him? You may not know this but his house is like a fortress, with electric gates, barbed-wire fencing and security cameras everywhere, plus some tasty thugs guarding his back . . .'

'Let me guess,' Cole butted in, 'Frank Delaney, ex-boxer and mob enforcer for hire, and Adam Crosby, gay former army helicopter pilot, cashiered for a sexual affair with a fellow male officer.'

'Gay? You're saying Crosby is gay?' Kate exclaimed.

'As the proverbial, which is his life choice and nothing for us to criticise him for, but while it is something that is perfectly acceptable in today's more enlightened society, it was a criminal offence in the armed services at that time and it was a dismissible offence.'

'But that muscle man? I'd never have guessed he was gay.'

'Maybe not, but his sexual orientation is irrelevant to us here. What *is* relevant is his history as a minder, first for Hooper and now for Brent and, with his military training and his undoubted intelligence, he is probably more dangerous than Delaney, and not someone you should cross. Brent moved both Delaney and Crosby up here with him from their natural habitat south of the river when he decided to quit the Smoke, but Crosby hasn't abandoned the old ways and his main criminal operation of drug and human trafficking, prostitution and extortion, is still being run for him in London by his nasty little cousin, Billie.'

'Well, I've already met the delightful Mr Delaney and Brent's shadow, Adam Crosby,' Kate continued, 'but there are no doubt other choice scumbags there. I saw a third one manning the entrance when I first visited the place, a Jack someone or other . . .'

'Jack Ferris, I would think, another nice beauty we know well. He's shacked up with a Mandy Thomas, who used to manage one of Charlie Hooper's brothels and now follows him everywhere. They all seemed to have changed masters quite happily after Hooper was hit.'

'A case of "the king is dead, long live the king",' she observed drily. 'I've no idea how many others there might be at the house, but there's also a resident chef, Alfredo something. I haven't met him yet.'

'Yeah, Alfredo Vitale. A weedy-looking little Sicilian, who looks a bit like TV's *Blackadder*, but don't be fooled by him. He has strong Mafiosi connections and he has pre-cons in Calabria for using his carving expertise on a lot more than roast meat.'

'Well, thanks. What you're telling me is really reassuring! And let me also point out that, aside from Brent's entourage, I couldn't nick him even if I had sufficient evidence to do so. I am no longer a police detective. I resigned, remember? Which means I am bereft of police powers and therefore have no more authority than Joe Bloggs down the street.'

'And you won't be expected to try,' Cole went on. 'You are missing the point of, shall we say your "role", Mrs Lewis. You will not be operating as a police officer. Your function will be as our mole, but a mole with considerable investigative experience as a police officer, which is a bonus for us. In the environment in which you will be operating it would not be possible for you to arrest him anyway. It would also be extremely risky to reinstate you as a police officer. Brent has contacts in the Met and if he were to check up on you and find you are listed as a DS in Avon and Somerset, you would be likely to end up like Peter Foster.'

'If his contacts are any good, it wouldn't be difficult for them to discover that I was *previously* a DS either.'

'Yes, but it's less likely and you will be on a different database now that you have resigned. To sum up, we simply need you to find out where the diamonds are being held, plus when the Collector is due to arrive to seal the deal, then report back to us at base. Our office will be staffed twenty-four hours a day, contactable on an encrypted mobile we'll now supply you with.

'This device has an exceptionally long battery life, so you shouldn't need to charge it during the time that we anticipate the operation will last, although we will supply you with a supercharger, just in case. The device has other modifications, in addition to encryption, courtesy of the NCA's tech unit, that will prevent access by unauthorised users, including a specific access passcode which is already installed.'

He produced a small smartphone in a black case. 'Here, catch,' he said and tossed it across to her. 'It's unlocked with the passcode, which I will give you shortly.'

She caught it easily and studied the screen for a moment, but said nothing.

'Now go to the phone's contacts,' he said, 'and tap in the three digits, six six six.'

'The devil's number?'

'Rather appropriate, don't you think?'

She tapped in the number and felt the phone vibrate briefly.

'That's your connection to us instead of a regular telephone number. It's all you will need as a rule to speak to us.'

'All a bit James Bondish, isn't it? Why not just fit me up with a wire instead? Then you could listen in and know what's going on all the time.'

'A wire would not be appropriate on this sort of job, Kate. Wires are usually used as short-term listening or recording devices and would not be suitable here. And imagine if Brent were to have you searched and the wire were to be discovered? It would not only blow the whole operation, but maybe you as well. No, we believe the mobile is the best option. You simply have to make sure you keep in touch with us on a regular basis. I would suggest once every day at least to keep us up to date.

'Everything is set up for you to start right away. Our tactical teams have been standing by not too far away from here ever since Brent turned up at his so-called country retreat, following the murder of Lenny Thompson, so they are on hand to respond the moment you tell us the meeting between Brent and the Collector is happening.'

'And what if I get into trouble in the meantime and need immediate support? What then?'

'I was coming to that. If that were to happen, you would simply tap the emergency call button on the mobile's home screen. You won't get the normal three nines service and you won't hear any response from us, but we will be all over Smuggler's Reach like shit off a shovel. Pressing the button acts a bit like an electronic pager.'

'I agree all this may indeed seem like something out of a James Bond film,' Norris put in, 'but it's a system that's been in operation ever since we set up surveillance on Brent several months ago in London and it works.'

'It didn't do much for Peter Foster, though, did it?' she retorted.

Cole's mouth tightened, but neither he nor Norris said anything and she added, 'You used the word "simply" when you were telling me what I need to do, Superintendent. But there's nothing simple about this crazy scheme. The chances of my being able to check out the house for the diamonds without being caught are virtually nil. Unless I am actually sharing Brent's bed, I doubt whether I will be allowed anywhere but his art studio, and then only under strict supervision.'

'We have every confidence in you, Kate,' Charlie Woo said. 'You've overcome even tougher obstacles as a detective in the past.'

She stared directly at him. 'From my experience, Charlie, the phrase "every confidence in you" is chief officer speak for "I don't know what the hell to do, so I'm passing the buck to you",' she sniped.

'That's unkind,' he replied with a chuckle, 'and it's sad to see so much cynicism in one so young.'

'Maybe that's because I've been on the receiving end of official setups far too many times,' she threw back at him. 'And I'm on one now, aren't I? For it to be "all systems go" on this job in just a couple of days, from IDing me as a potential undercover operative, you must have moved pretty damned quick and been supremely confident I'd play ball before you even paid me a visit, which shows an unbelievable sense of arrogance.'

Cole shook his head again. 'I can understand why you might see it like that, but that is not the case. Presumptuous we probably have been, but we have had little option but to proceed on the basis that you would help us nail this swine, particularly after the tragic murder of Peter Foster. Events are moving very fast and time is not on our side if we are to prevent Brent slipping through our fingers yet again. We feel that you are in an ideal position to be our eyes and ears and, after speaking to DI Woo here and being assured of your excellent bona fides, we reckon we have a real chance of bringing down Brent and the Collector and recovering the diamonds that have so far cost so many lives.

'As for the organisational side of things, because surveillance has been underway for some while through Foster, only minimal changes have been required to the existing setup, including the top level approvals required for your, shall we say, secondment, and the re-branding of the role from external surveillance to an undercover operation. The structure and administration, together with the backup arrangements remain the same . . .'

'Why do I not find that reassuring?' she said drily, once again thinking of what had happened to Peter Foster. 'But there is another problem closer to home, which you don't seem to have considered, and that is my dear old husband. What am I supposed to tell him? You will probably know that he is at Bristol Crown Court at present, but he is likely to be home within a couple of days.'

Woo nodded. 'We know about Hayden. As a matter of fact, I bumped into him last Friday in Bristol and we had quite a chat.'

'Oh really? And did you tell him you were planning to pop and see me to ask if I would shack up with the man he saw chatting me up on the beach before he left?'

'We're not suggesting you, er, shack up with anyone, Kate. Any more than we're saying you *should* do what we're asking you to do, only asking *would* you do it? But this crazy scheme, as you've called it, is the only chance we have of putting a dangerous target criminal inside. As for Hayden, I'm afraid you will not be able to tell him anything about this operation. The least number of people who know about your involvement the better. A chance word in the wrong place could not only blow the whole thing apart but put you in the most deadly peril. We've lost one police officer already and we don't want to lose another . . .'

Kate cut him off with a snort that was more like an explosion. 'Hell's bells, Charlie, Hayden was a bloody copper, just like me,' she snapped. 'He's not going to blurt something like this out to all and sundry. And anyway, unless it's escaped your notice, I happen to be living with him and I share his bed. How do you propose I keep something like this from him?'

'You just tell him you are having your portrait painted by a local artist and will be going to his house for a few sittings for the next few days.'

Kate released a derisory laugh. 'You have to be joking, Charlie. Have you any idea how Hayden will react to the idea of me posing starkers for a so-called artist? He'll go absolutely ballistic!'

'We're not asking you to do anything that you are uncomfortable with, even if that *is* what Brent wants. Knowing you as I do, I'm sure you are quite capable of standing your ground and insisting on a more formal, traditional sitting, or at least distracting him sufficiently to be able to head his proposal into the long grass. I can't see Hayden objecting to a perfectly respectable portrait. He's always struck me as a laid-back sort of a guy. I remember you telling me once that he was so laid-back he was virtually horizontal.'

'Where work is involved, yes. He's inherently lazy — a free spirit, as he calls himself — but he's a totally different person where I am concerned. He is more old-fashioned and narrow-minded than an orthodox priest when it comes to things like this. He will immediately suspect I am over the side.'

'So what? He doesn't own you.'

'He thinks he does.'

Woo sighed his disappointment. 'So you're saying you can't do this?'

Kate made a face. 'I didn't say that at all. I'll be honest. The last thing I want to do is to go back into that house ever again and I certainly don't want a mammoth row with Hayden over it. But with one of our own on the slab, this business has now become personal.'

There was a perceptible sense of relief in the room.

'So you'll do it?' Cole said.

'I don't have a choice, do I?' she said, 'but I shall have to try to square things with Hayden first, heaven help me. Furthermore, I need someone to have a word with the local bobby, Geraint Rheon, who handled my burglary report and was originally investigating the arson of Peter Foster's caravan. He's an old-school copper who's got his teeth into the case and won't let go. He's already revealed to me that the dead man in the caravan was a copper, which was a bit indiscreet of him, and for some reason I think he suspects me of being less than kosher.'

Norris frowned. 'We'll have words in the right quarters,' he said. 'The facts of that case are only supposed to be known to a select few very senior ranks in the force and Dyfed–Powys are fully cooperating with us in that respect. But I agree, the last thing we need is a well-meaning loose cannon.'

Let's just hope I don't become one too, Kate thought as she saw them to the door, asking herself the question, had she really agreed to this risky escapade solely out of a sense of duty or actually because it gave her the means of covering up the fact that Brent already had a hold over her and it offered her the chance of retrieving the incriminating evidence she had left behind in his house? *The jury's out on that one*, she mused sourly.

* * *

Hayden did not ring Kate that evening and she was relieved she didn't have to try and make small talk with him when she had so much on her mind. He would have been certain to have picked up on her downbeat mood and this could have led to awkward questions she didn't feel bright enough to field effectively.

Jeremy Brent did ring, however, and he sounded quite ebullient, as if he had already taken it for granted that she would be agreeing to model for him. His arrogance was unbelievable.

'Had a long enough think over what I said in the note I sent you?' he asked.

She took a deep breath, turning her head away from the mouthpiece as she did so. 'Yes, I will sit for you,' she confirmed, 'but only for a head and shoulders portrait.'

'Excellent!' he replied. 'I'll look forward to that. Tomorrow, say three? We can then have dinner here afterwards. Salmon suit you?'

'How long will the sitting take?' she asked without answering him.

'Oh, a couple of hours initially, including breaks,' he said.

'Initially?'

'Yes, but probably a few days total, if things go according to plan.'

'*Days*?' she echoed.

'Sorry, but it's quite a long process. I am very particular about getting things right. I carry out a rough sketch, in various poses first, and build on that. Then there is the actual painting, which demands careful composition, while oils can be quite a temperamental medium to work with. But there is a pool here, so why don't you bring your bikini along with you? You can then have a relaxing swim between sittings.'

Kate felt the worm begin wriggling around in her belly again.

'Oh yes,' he added, 'and please wear something light and summery, eh? With bare shoulders, so I can catch your full colouring.'

Before she could say anything else, he was gone.

'Shit!' she said aloud. 'He's at it already!' She would have to be careful, damned careful . . .

CHAPTER 8

Kate had a restless, sleepless night, tossing and turning in the humid atmosphere of the room. Twice she heard suspicious noises outside. But when she went to investigate the first time, it was to see an owl lift off the roof of the front porch and the second, she just avoided stepping on a hedgehog scuttling along the decking by the French doors, which would have been a pretty painful experience in her bare feet.

She must have dozed off around two or three in the morning, until the seagulls scrabbling across the roof awoke her at around five. She lay there then for quite a while, wide awake, stewing over what lay ahead of her, before finally getting up to take a shower and do her hair. It was approaching nine by the time she put the coffee percolator on, still tired and very irritable. The mobile Norris had given her rang as she was munching on a piece of toast.

'Fit for the fray?' Cole said.

'I'm invited to my first sitting at three,' she said.

'That was quick. He's obviously a man in a hurry.'

'That's the last thing I need.'

There was a strained laugh. 'Don't do anything I wouldn't do.'

'Piss off!'

The phone went dead, but it didn't remain silent for long. At just after ten her landline rang and it was Hayden.

'Got to be quick,' he said breathlessly. 'About to be called into court. Thing is, I'm not expected to be needed again after this afternoon, so I should be home sometime tomorrow. Isn't that great? See you then.'

Kate closed her eyes in a tight grimace as he rang off. With her undercover role now underway and her first sitting for Brent that very afternoon, his news couldn't have come at a worse time.

'Thanks, God,' she said, throwing a venomous glance at the ceiling. 'Got any more unwelcome surprises for me?'

The answer came even before she could finish eating her toast, with the triple buzz of the front doorbell.

PC Geraint Rheon was standing on her doorstep and he looked far from happy. His face was hard and slab-like and his eyes blatantly hostile.

'Well, Mrs Lewis,' he growled, 'I've just had a run-in with my superintendent and been told to stay out of the arson case. Your doing, was it?'

Kate felt her hackles rise. 'I beg your pardon, Constable?' she snapped. 'If that is the only reason you are here, I strongly advise you to leave now.'

He ignored her. 'See, I think there's something damned funny going on around here,' he said. 'The attempted break-in at this cottage, the arson of the caravan, the car with your name and address on a bit of paper inside it and the fact that the man who died in the fire was a Met copper. All a funny business.'

'I don't see anything funny about it all, PC Rheon,' she snapped back. 'It's just worrying.'

'Oh, it's worrying all right,' he agreed. 'As is another little bit of info that's come to my notice. A little bird told me that they saw you arguing with a man lurking in the bushes alongside your garden the afternoon after your attempted burglary. A man, I might add, who, once you'd gone, evidently got into a fastback car, which from the description given, matched the one we found parked in the barn next to the burned-out caravan.'

Inwardly, Kate cringed, but she met his searching gaze without flinching.

'What little bird told you that?' she asked.

'Oh, there's lots of little birds around here,' he said. 'Tweeting to me all the time. If you sneeze in Freshwater, someone will hear it. You want to be careful what you say and do in villages like this.'

'I'll bear that in mind,' she said drily, remembering the two women with dogs who had passed by during her altercation with the so-called twitcher.

He didn't take his eyes off her. 'So,' he said, 'what *is* going on, Mrs Lewis?'

'You tell me, PC Rheon,' she replied, determined to brazen things out. 'You're the policeman.' Then she added, 'You're quite right, though, I did have an argument with a man who was trespassing on my property. It seems he'd got caught short and was relieving himself in the bushes. But he apologised for his behaviour and I left it at that. As for the car—' she shrugged — 'I didn't see him get into any car.'

He nodded. 'Just relieving himself, you say?' he said, sounding unconvinced. 'Right, so that explains it then, doesn't it? But there is another thing I'm curious about.'

I thought there might be, Kate mused, dreading what it might be.

'You seem mighty pally with that dodgy crew up at Smuggler's Reach. Getting picked up in that flash car and taken there and back at least a couple of times to my knowledge.'

'So what?' she replied. 'I don't need your permission to visit another near neighbour.'

'Maybe not, but I've had my eye on that place and all the strange comings and goings there for a while now. Some sort of millionaire artist, the owner, isn't he? And that chauffeur—' he shook his head — 'he's no more a chauffeur than Owain Glyndŵr was an Englishman.'

Kate tried to keep her face deadpan. Then rather than resorting to waffling, she went for a more hard-nosed approach to shut him down.

'Have you been spying on me, Mr Rheon?' she demanded. 'I would have thought the police in this area should have been better employed investigating real crime instead of harassing law-abiding residents like myself. I think I shall have to speak to your superiors about this.'

If she expected him to be cowed by the threat, she was disappointed. For reply he released a loud guffaw.

'You do that, Mrs Lewis,' he said. 'But it won't make any difference. I've got just two months short of thirty years in the job before I retire, so there's nothing those so-called superiors can do to me.' His expression hardened again. 'But I tell you this, I've got a nose for things that aren't right and there's definitely something not right about what's been happening round here. Furthermore, I think you know a lot more about the business than you're letting on, and I intend finding out exactly what that is. Good morning, Mrs Lewis.'

Then he turned on his heel and walked back to his parked police car, leaving Kate breathing a huge sigh of relief that her interrogation was over. But she had no illusions as to this being the end of the matter and she fully believed his declared intent to carry on poking his nose into things in the foreseeable future, regardless of what pressures were put on him to butt out. She had worked with old-school types like Geraint Rheon before and in some respects recognised herself in his stubborn determination to get to the bottom of things. But it meant that she now had not only Brent and Hayden to worry about, but a nosy local copper whose interference could unintentionally blow everything apart and put her in serious jeopardy as well.

* * *

The big black Mercedes once more pulled up outside the cottage dead on the hour, but Frank Delaney didn't come to the door this time. Instead, he waited patiently for Kate to join him, treating her to an unpleasant, lewd grin as she eased herself into the seat beside him in the short, off-the-shoulder dress that Brent had demanded.

'Very sexy, darlin',' he said. 'I could fancy yer meself.'

'Funny that I don't share the same feelings for you,' she murmured sarcastically.

He seemed to find that dry riposte particularly funny and it drew a roar of laughter from him, which carried on for most of the way to the house. She couldn't wait to get out of the car and away from him on their arrival and she was almost pleased to see Brent when he greeted her at the door.

He was dressed casually as before in a fawn, open-necked shirt, matching chinos and open sandals without socks. *Perfect as Mr Casual*, Kate mused spitefully, forcing an insincere smile as he devoured her with his eyes, *but we know what you really are, don't we, arsehole?*

For once, Brent didn't seem to pick up on her body language and outwardly, was still charm itself. 'You look absolutely delightful, my dear,' he commented. 'Would you like a cool drink before we go down to the studio? I'm very anxious to make a start.'

Kate nodded. 'That would be nice,' she said and sensed his immediate irritation at the potential delay, despite the polite offer. 'Do you have a Dubonnet?'

She lingered over her drink as long as she could, hoping the bright sunlight might start to fade before they could get going, but in the end she had no choice but to follow him down the lawn to the studio, settling on a comfortable upholstered chair in the middle of the room while he pulled on a white smock over his clothes that was spattered with paint residues.

To her surprise, he made no unwelcome advances to her at this stage but stayed behind his easel for two sessions of one hour each, saying very little and apparently lost in concentration. He allowed her a small break and a glass of wine at the end of each hour and on the second occasion suggested she might like to "stretch her legs" and take a short stroll around the garden.

She made the most of that opportunity to study her surroundings. There wasn't a lot to see, save the tall hedges on each side, which she noticed were reinforced on the left behind the swimming pool by barbed wire, and the high, shrub-topped bank at the far end.

She then noticed a gate in the hedge behind the studio and, investigating further, she discovered it was not locked. A big field, enclosed by similar tall hedging, lay beyond, but this time there was a prominent square of concrete in the middle of it, bearing a huge letter "H" within a large white circle and what looked like integrated lighting around the circumference. She raised an eyebrow. So Brent had a helipad as well, did he? Well, that was very interesting. As was the massive, steel building with a line of small square windows at the top and wide double doors beneath that occupied the centre ground behind it. It was no doubt the helicopter hangar, and there was a big white steel tank with hoses attached to the front, which almost certainly contained AV fuel, a short distance from it. But she didn't get the chance to investigate further. The voice behind her was soft, but it carried a hint of menace.

'Nosy!'

She spun round to find Brent standing there staring at her, his eyes hooded and suspicious.

She swallowed. 'Sorry, I was just curious as to what was behind the gate.'

'Obviously.'

'Well, you did say I could take a stroll.'

Suddenly his thin smile was back, though the eyes remained hard. 'Of course, no harm done. But I'd rather you didn't go wandering about too far. We are not too far from the cliffs here and there are deep fissures in the fields close to the property. I wouldn't want you to have a nasty accident.'

A threat, she wondered?

'I didn't realise you had a helipad,' she went on, knowing it would have been pointless to deny she had seen it.

'I got it as insurance in case I needed urgent medical attention out here in the back of beyond,' he replied. 'The NHS is crap, but I do have quite expensive medical insurance.'

'So you have a helicopter as well?'

'Hardly worth having a helipad without a helicopter, isn't it? I use it off and on if I want to get somewhere quickly or just for a fun jaunt across to the Emerald Isle. I suppose you'd call it my toy.'

'So, you are a pilot as well as an artist?' The awe in her tone was not entirely manufactured. He was a surprising man.

He smiled as he held out his hand. 'No point in having a helicopter either if you can't fly it, is there? Adam is also a qualified chopper pilot. Served in the army before he came to work for me. He keeps an eye on things for me, like basic maintenance.'

'A man of many skills then?'

'You'd be surprised at some of them.'

'Fascinating stuff. I've never actually been this close to a helipad before. What sort of helicopter have you got?'

He smiled indulgently.

'Oh, only a small, four-seater Robinson Raven II.'

'Can I see it?'

He looked slightly irritated but nodded. 'Of course, but then we must get on with your portrait.'

Kate had been an observer in the police helicopter many times and she was well acquainted with the machines, but she pretended to be thrilled when he unlocked a padlocked side door and flicked a switch just inside, flooding the hangar with light. This revealed a massive vault of a room with a concrete floor and rows of strip lights suspended on chains attached to brackets in the roof. A number of workbenches stood against the far wall and there were steel shelves above them stacked with a variety of unfamiliar tools and what looked like light engineering equipment.

The helicopter was, as he had said, a Robinson Raven II, and she made a mental note of the registration painted on the tail.

'Sit inside if you wish,' he said, watching her excited reaction.

He helped her up and she stared around her with the apparent wonder of a little girl.

'How far can you go in this?' she asked.

He frowned. 'Oh, about three hundred nautical miles. Enough for a pleasant trip across the water, refuel just outside Dublin and head back.'

She whistled. 'It's beautiful, but how on earth do you get it out of the hangar? Fly it out?'

He laughed at her apparent naivety. 'No, it's on skids. It doesn't have wheels. We have separate ground-handling wheels that attach to the machine and we then tow her out, using an electric tow-cart. The helicopter is very light, so it's easy to move it out to the helipad in this way, then back into the hangar afterwards.'

He glanced at his watch. 'Now we really should get back to your portrait and I'll show you my first attempt at capturing you on canvas.'

The black and white etching standing on the easel in the studio came as a real shock to Kate, for it had not only captured her likeness completely, but something else she had certainly not expected. In the way it was composed, her face was staring straight back at the artist and the coldness of her eyes and the set of her mouth seemed to convey an expression of what could only have been described as deep hostility. Her hated stepfather, who had caused her so much grief as a child, had always told her that she should never play poker or chess, as she wore her thoughts on her face and she had to admit that the truth of that statement could not have been more clearly illustrated than in that pencilled drawing.

Despite knowing the truly evil man Brent was and how he had cruelly intimidated her into sitting for him, she had to acknowledge the artistic skills the man possessed, and she just couldn't understand how someone with such talent at his fingertips could have sunk to the vile depths he had. Gifted with the perception to recognise the beauty to be found all around him, in landscape, animal life and the human form, and equipped with the ability to transfer this so faithfully to canvas, he had at the same time indulged in the very personification of ugliness, including perversion, extortion and murder, simply to satisfy his own obscene greed. It was as if he had a Jekyll and Hyde personality that enabled him to be two different people wrapped up in the one body. But more importantly to her, his perceptive skill was as worrying as it was astonishing. It suggested, as she had sensed before, that he could actually see into her mind, and if that were even remotely the case, then it meant he would know she was conspiring against him. Was the portrait not just a portrait, but a subtle way of communicating that fact, telling her he was on to her, she wondered? The worms in her stomach seemed to think so, for they were already squirming around in near panic.

Then her unpleasant reverie was interrupted by that drawling voice again.

'I think on reflection that that will be enough sitting for one day,' Brent said, pulling off the smock and tossing it into a corner. 'Perhaps you'd like that relaxing swim now?'

She must have looked startled, for he laughed. 'Thoughts miles away, were they?'

'No, no,' she faltered, 'I was just absorbed by the sketch, that's all. It is so lifelike.'

'Then perhaps in due course you will allow me to see more of you to paint,' he replied, bringing the flush to her cheeks again. 'But in the meantime, I was asking if you'd like a swim before dinner?'

She was caught on the hop. 'Swim? Dinner? I, er, didn't realise you had . . . Thing is, I didn't bring my swimming costume with me.'

He shrugged. 'Then don't bother with a costume at all. We're all grown up here.'

She regained control. 'I think I'll forego the pool, if you don't mind. Maybe another time. As for dinner, I hadn't expected . . .'

'I did say we would have dinner after the sitting and I insist that you join me.'

'It's very good of you.'

'Not at all and we'll have a couple of drinks before we sit down. Now, I'll have Adam fetch that wrap of yours as you are likely to feel the cold on the terrace.'

Kate immediately saw her chance. 'Could I perhaps freshen up a little first?'

He hesitated a second, a frown appearing on his face. Then it was gone and his smile was back. 'Of course. Adam will show you where the bathroom is.'

Adam was there within seconds of Brent pressing a little pager attached to his belt, which Kate hadn't noticed before. The man immediately turned on his heel and led her through the living room and along the hallway, past the front door towards a number of white-panelled doors opening off on both sides. Stopping at the second door on her right, labelled bathroom in gold letters, he reached past her to pull the handle down and pushed the door wide before retreating with a polite nod.

Kate stared about her curiously. The bathroom she found herself in was big and luxurious, with expensive looking blue tiles on the walls and floor that reminded her of the Italian tiles she had seen on display in a specialist shop near Cardiff when she and Hayden had been looking to upgrade the bathroom at Willow Cottage. Everywhere there were gold-coloured fixtures and fittings: the twin wash basin taps in the bathroom itself, the head hose and pipework in the power shower cubicle, the ceiling spotlights, even the surround of the circular wall mirror, all glinting at her as she used the facilities and washed her hands.

'Talk about OTT,' she murmured. 'Someone obviously likes to impress.'

But she wasn't in the bathroom to pass judgement on the décor. Moving back to the door, she opened it a fraction and studied the hallway outside. It was deserted. Opening it further, she stepped out and closed the door gently behind her. She paused to listen, but realised at the same moment that it was a pointless precaution. The hall was thickly carpeted wall-to-wall and she wouldn't have heard anyone approaching anyway.

She turned right, away from the front door and the living room and crept towards a steel-framed staircase with green, glass treads, which ascended to the upper level. The white-panelled doors extended beyond the bathroom past the staircase on both sides until the hall seemed to end before a steel-framed door, marked *Exit*, no doubt a fire door. *This really was a big house*, she mused. Holding her breath, she opened the first door. It was just a bedroom, opulent as she would have expected, but still just a bedroom, with only a couple of small, framed pictures on one wall.

The next room was virtually the same. Another bedroom, with similar small, framed pictures on one wall and nothing else of interest.

She checked two more rooms opposite. Unremarkable bedrooms again. She was about to check a third further along on the same side of the hallway when she heard someone cough. She got back to the bathroom in the nick of time, her heart pumping, and had only just closed the door when there was a discreet knock.

'Mrs Lewis? Everything all right?'

Adam, it had to be, though she had never heard him speak yet.

She flushed the cistern and joined him in the hallway. It was only then that she realised she had left one of the bedroom doors ajar. *Bloody idiot, Kate*, she mused. She saw him look, then frown and step across to close it. For a moment he stared at her. Then he held out his hand to indicate that she should go ahead of him and ushered her back into the living room.

Brent was sitting in one of the armchairs and he rose to greet her.

'I have taken the liberty of selecting a bottle of wine for us from my cellar,' he said. 'I hope you like it. It's a vintage Chablis.'

Showing off again, Kate mused, conscious of the fact that she knew nothing about wine, only enjoyed drinking it. *Do you ever give up trying to impress people, you arsehole?* she mused savagely. But she smiled and sat down in the chair he indicated.

Adam was at her elbow again and poured her a dribble to taste. She took a sip and nodded. 'Tastes nice,' she said, allowing him to fill her glass, 'but I'm afraid I'm no connoisseur.'

'So, is your husband still away?' Brent asked suddenly, watching as Adam filled his own glass and withdrew as usual.

'Back tomorrow,' she said.

'What business is he in?'

His eyes were boring into her again.

She took a longer sip on her wine, relieved that she had a good memory and could remember what she had told him before.

'He's not away on business as such, more family business. Our aunt died and he had some things to clear up.'

He nodded. 'Death comes to us all in the end, doesn't it? More quickly for some than others.'

Kate thought, was she getting paranoid, or was that another threat? Paranoia, she decided, to allow herself to enjoy her dinner.

He stood up and motioned towards the terrace. 'Shall we eat then? Please feel free to bring your glass. I'm sure there is much we can talk about, and we must arrange your next sitting, of course.'

CHAPTER 9

Hayden arrived home at just after two in the afternoon the following day. Out on the decking, Kate heard the distinctive sound of the Jaguar pulling on to the gravel driveway alongside the cottage as she was leaning on the guard rail at the other end of the decking. Quickly straightening up, she downed the rest of the Talisker single malt she had poured herself half an hour before to give her some much-needed courage and, leaving the glass on the deck table, she walked back into the kitchen-diner and met him as he walked in from the front door, dumping his suitcase on the floor.

'Hi gorgeous,' she said and affectionately slipped her arms around his neck to kiss him. 'I've really missed you.'

He returned her display of affection with a disappointing peck and gently pulled her arms free, turning to pick up his suitcase. 'I've missed you too,' he said. 'Anything to eat? I'm starving.'

She stepped back a little, her eyes narrowing. Hayden was not the most demonstrative of men, but he usually responded much better than that, with a squeeze of the hand or the arm. She felt an immediate sense of hurt.

'There's some cold chicken in the fridge,' she said hollowly, 'and I opened a bottle of red for you over there on the breakfast bar.'

He grunted and carried his suitcase into their bedroom, this time dumping it on the end of the bed. She knew from past experience that if he emptied it and put the contents back where they should be, it would be a miracle and she wasn't surprised when he walked past her into the kitchen area and raided the fridge instead before pouring himself a large glass of wine.

She noticed that he didn't look at her but seemed to focus his gaze on his plate or the glass as he propped himself on a stool at the end of the breakfast bar and tucked in, saying nothing for several minutes while she busied herself emptying his suitcase.

'Terrible traffic,' he said at last, casting her a brief sideways glance as she returned to the room. He yawned. 'Very tired. Thought I might take a nap.'

Her frown deepened. What was the matter with him? He was not normally like this. He had sounded so lost and lonely the previous days when he had telephoned her from Bristol. But now he was home, he seemed cold and remote. Almost as if he didn't want to talk to her. There was a familiar spurt of acid in her stomach as a horrible thought struck her. Surely he hadn't found out about her visits to Smuggler's Reach somehow? Maybe all this was a prelude to a scathing verbal attack before he announced he was leaving her? Yet how could he have found out? No one else except Brent and his thugs and PC Rheon, of course, knew about them and they would have had no way of knowing how to contact him even if they'd wanted to. Why would they have tried anyway? Then what the hell was wrong with him?

He burped suddenly, apologised, then got up from his stool to head into the hall.

'Think I'll take a shower first,' he said over his shoulder. 'Then I'll have that nap.'

He had disappeared before she could reply. A second later she heard the bathroom door close.

Kate cleared away his empty plate and glass from the breakfast bar and put them in the sink, still turning his strange behaviour over in her mind. She had expected a massive row soon after he had come home, as she'd planned to tell him about Brent straightaway to ensure he didn't find out from another source. Like the interfering Geraint Rheon, for instance. But now she was completely thrown. How was she going to broach the subject when he was like this? And she needed to, that was a fact. Brent had demanded another sitting the following day, again at three, instructing her to wear a short backless summer dress this time, and one thing was for certain; there was no way she could go there dressed like that without Hayden noticing. It was imperative that she came clean with him at the earliest opportunity to negate the power Brent had over her and to explain to her husband where she was going and why well in advance. Otherwise there was a risk that he would throw a wobbly on the day and do something impetuous and stupid. Like storming over to Smuggler's Reach to have a go at Brent, thereby ruining the whole undercover operation.

She was still pondering the issue when she heard the jazzy note of Hayden's mobile. Crossing to the breakfast bar where he had left it on his return, she stared at the caller's ID and frowned. *Lucybaby@* . . . Who the hell was that? She didn't know any Lucy. Probably a wrong number. Nevertheless, curious, she swiped the screen just in time and a woman's voice asked, 'Hayd, that you? It was great seeing you again, Big Boy.' Then the caller dissolved into gurgling laughter.

'Sorry, love,' Kate grated after a shocked pause. '"Big Boy" is asleep. This is his wife.'

'Oops!' said the voice at the other end and the phone went dead.

Kate stared at it for several seconds, as if the thing had just mouthed a string of obscenities. Then she glanced grimly at the bedroom door from behind which loud snores emanated. 'Big Boy, is it?' she muttered. 'I'll give you Big Boy!'

It was gone five p.m. before Hayden reappeared, with his mop of thick, blond hair uncombed and tangled. He stood there for a moment, yawning and stretching. He was now dressed in baggy, grey tracksuit bottoms and an over-sized blue T-shirt ingrained with unidentifiable stains. *Typical Hayden*, Kate thought, appraising him critically. Free spirit or slob, there wasn't a lot of difference when she thought about it, but she had given up trying to change him long ago.

His bleary eyes focused on her sitting in one of the arm-chairs and on the mug of coffee in her hand, as it rested on the chair arm. He treated her to what looked like a nervous smile. *Or was "guilty" a more appropriate description?* she thought.

'Sorry,' he said, making to walk past her towards the kitchen. 'Slept longer than I had anticipated.'

'No problem, *Big Boy*,' she retorted with emphasis.

He froze and stared at her. 'Uh?'

'Lucy rang on your mobile,' she said. 'But I told her you were asleep.' She stared at him with a sardonic smile. 'So, who's Lucy?'

She saw him squirm and screw up his face. 'Ah, I was going to tell you about that.'

'Oh were you? When would that have been, if she hadn't rung?'

He looked across at the French doors, avoiding her stare.

'Sit!' she snapped. 'We're going to talk about Lucy.'

He propped on the arm of the other chair, looking down at his feet, his face flushed. 'It's not what you think.'

'That's the standard phrase of all two-timers. So, what is it I'm thinking then?'

He finally met her gaze. 'I knew you would read something into it when I told you, but it wasn't like that.'

'So, what was it like?'

He exhibited irritation now. 'Just hear me out, will you?' he snapped. 'Lucy Weller is an old friend of mine from my uni days. We were on the same course . . .'

'What was that — intercourse?'

'Don't be so darned crude. I've never . . . you know . . .'

'Had it off with her?'

'Exactly. We were just friends. I hadn't seen her for ages, and then I ran into her when I went for a breath of fresh air

109

from Bristol Crown Court. She suggested we meet up in the evening to talk over old times, so we did, at a wine bar in town, and the following night I took her out to dinner . . .'

'How generous of you? Then, I suppose, it was early to bed.'

He jumped up, angry now. 'I've told you it wasn't like that. We chatted, that's all, and she's married now anyway.'

'Oh I *see*, that means you couldn't possibly have slept with her. That is *so* reassuring.'

'I knew you would think the worst. I was dreading telling you, but I had intended doing so only because I . . .'

'Felt guilty?'

'If you like, yes, I felt guilty. Satisfied?'

'And "Big Boy"? What was that all about? Because you and I know that is not true, don't we, *lover*?'

'It's got nothing to do with what your dirty little mind has conjured up. They all called me Big Boy at uni because . . . because, well, because I was so fat, and it stuck.'

She said nothing and he paused a moment, plainly uncomfortable in the strained silence. Then, unable to contain himself any longer, he fell back on to the chair arm and blurted, 'Listen, you know I wouldn't cheat on you. I'm not like that. It's not in my nature. I shouldn't have met up with Lucy, I know, but I did and it was perfectly innocent, whether you believe me or not.'

Kate nodded and suddenly smiled. Strangely enough, she couldn't feel more relieved by his admissions and the fact that his had come first. 'Okay, fat man, I'll give you the benefit of the doubt. I trust you, funnily enough, and now that you've revealed your guilty secret, it makes it a whole lot easier for me to reveal mine.'

He looked even more startled now. 'Yours? What do you mean?'

'Pin your ears back, and I'll tell you.'

It took her a good half hour to go through all that had happened since he had left for Bristol, including her confrontation with Peter Foster, the arson of the caravan, Foster's

110

death, and the interference by Geraint Rheon. But she skated over the issues, careful to leave out anything that linked the events to Brent, and she took a chance on withholding Peter Foster's identity or what he was doing in the area, hoping against hope that Rheon would not come back later to upset the applecart.

Hayden had listened without interruption to all that she had said and he seemed relieved, but plainly puzzled, that she had not dumped some major revelation in his lap. 'Obviously the fella who tried to screw our house planned on doing it again,' he summed up, 'but was prevented from doing so when the poor devil got burned to death in that fire. As for your PC Rheon, he might have a bee in his bonnet, but he's only doing his job and we should cooperate with him as much as we can. Do the local police have any idea why the caravan was torched? Some local with a grievance perhaps?'

Kate shrugged. 'Possibly. Who knows?'

His frown. 'So, where's your guilty secret in all of that?' he asked. 'Strikes me you've had quite a rough time of it since I've been away. I'm only sorry I wasn't here to support you. I mean, that chap you confronted, he could have become violent . . .'

'Hayden,' she cut in, 'I'm not done yet. That was just news. What I have to tell you now might not be so palatable for you.' She paused a moment and when she continued, she made no effort to try and soften what she had to say, but after what he had admitted, she felt she could be totally blunt. 'Remember the man who accosted me on the beach? Well, his name is Graham Lutterall and he lives in a big house up the road. While you were away, I accepted an invitation from him to afternoon tea and then evening dinner. Like you, there was nothing untoward in it all. We just chatted.'

There was an abrupt change in his demeanour that she recognised only too well. His face had lost some of its colour and his mouth was gaping at her like a fish out of water.

'You did *what*?' he exclaimed. 'You went to the house of a perfect stranger who had already tried to pick you up on the beach, then-then sat down with him for-for dinner?'

She smiled again, feeling confident and in command of herself now. 'And tea,' she said. 'Don't forget the tea. Like you, there was nothing untoward in it at all. It was very respectable and, as it was with you and Lucy, we just chatted.'

He was back on his feet now, fists clenched by his sides and head thrust forward aggressively. 'Respectable?' he echoed. 'A married woman meeting up with another man — in his house? I don't believe it? What will everyone in the village think?'

She shrugged again. 'Does it matter what anyone thinks, Hayd? And it's no different to your, er, little assignation with Juicy Lucy.'

'That was different. She was an old friend and we were in a restaurant the whole time.'

'That's what you tell me and you are going to have to trust me as I said I trusted you. Oh yes, and there's another thing. He's an accomplished professional artist and he wants to paint my portrait. So I will be popping over to his place over the next few days to sit for him. And before you say anything, I will be keeping my clothes *on*.'

'I-I absolutely forbid it!'

'You what?' Her eyes were glittering now. 'You forbid it? Who do you think you are? I'm not one of your possessions. I will do what I like — especially after your romp in Bristol.'

'It wasn't a bloody romp!' he yelled.

Kate's eyebrows rose. 'Hayden Lewis, you swore. You've actually used bad language. Well, there's a first for someone who regards it as one of the deadly sins — that and sex, of course.'

He shook his head furiously. 'I won't be side-tracked. You are not going to sit for this charlatan and that's all there is to it.'

'Three o'clock tomorrow, Hayd,' she went on. 'I'll be picked up here by Mr Lutterall's chauffeur. I shall be away a couple of hours, maybe longer if he invites me to dinner again. I'm sure you'll be able to manage anyway if he does. There's some corned beef in the fridge. Now I think I'll take a shower and wash my hair.'

Then she finished her coffee and set her mug on the breakfast bar on her way to the bathroom, leaving him standing there shaking with rage.

* * *

Once in the bathroom, she closed the door and sat on the toilet seat for several minutes, letting her body release the trembles she had so far suppressed. She had found the confrontation with Hayden quite painful, though she had done her best to conceal her true feelings. But his own indiscretions had made it a lot less traumatic than it could have been and at least things were more out in the open now — at least relatively so. She would just have to tread carefully around him, because he would be like a bear with a sore head for a while now, watching her every move.

Nevertheless, it had had to be done and her next job was to touch base with her mentors to make her first report. Turning the shower on in true James Bond style, she pulled the mobile they had given her from her pocket and dialled the number. The link process was a lot easier than she had imagined it would be and after initially speaking to a man whose voice she didn't recognise, Harry Cole came on to the phone.

'All okay?' he asked.

She reported her findings so far, which didn't amount to much, apart from her information on the helicopter, and she told him that she would be back at the house the following day.

He grunted. 'Helipad, eh? And his own chopper? That's certainly worth knowing. See what else you can find out.'

'I'll try,' she said. 'But it won't be easy.'

'Nothing in this game is, as you well know.'

'I don't get a lot of time in there. Couple of hours at a sitting. Maybe a couple of short breaks, plus an extra one when I pretend I need the toilet. Otherwise, I'm never left on my own to snoop around.'

Cole was silent for a few moments, obviously thinking, and she waited for him to resume.

'Somehow you'll have to build more time into your visits,' he said. 'Stay longer at the house.'

'And how do you propose I do that? He's the host. I get there when he says and leave, usually after dinner, again when he says.'

'I'm sure you'll think of something.'

She smiled wryly. *Was that another way of saying, "every confidence in you"?* she asked herself. Maybe he'd picked it up as an alternative phrase to use after reading the chief officer's buck-passing manual!

'Anyway, somehow you've got to give yourself more opportunities,' he went on. 'You need to get upstairs. That's where his study will be and I'm willing to bet that's where his safe will be, hopefully with the stones inside.'

'Even if I find the safe, how do you expect me to get into it? I'm not a cracksman — or crackswoman for that matter.'

'No, but at least we'll then know where we need to look when we have to. It will narrow down the field. It's the time thing again, Kate, and I suspect we haven't a lot of it left.'

'I'll do what I can.'

'That's all we ask. How's Hayden?'

'Not exactly cock-a-hoop since we had our little chat. We had a mammoth row.'

'To be expected,' came the terse reply. 'What did you tell him?'

'Strictly what we agreed. Just that I am modelling for one Graham Lutterall. Hopefully he'll cool down eventually. But there's also a problem with the local bobby, Geraint Rheon. He's been at me again and he's not only suspicious of me, but has his jaundiced eye on Smuggler's Reach for some reason.'

'We know. It's been decided just to let him have his head. It will cause more hassle if we attempt to shut him down. He's apparently a very stubborn character. We'll just have to play him along. As long as he doesn't get too close to

114

things, we should be okay. But there is another complication that could be a major problem. Word is that, as we anticipated, there's now a contract out on Brent.'

'The mafia?'

'Has to be. We understand that the Sicilian mob are good and mad over Brent reneging on the deal they originally struck with Charlie Hooper and approaching the Collector instead. But we're pretty sure they'll want to secure the diamonds first. Wasting Brent, though certain to be a priority, will only happen after their hired assassin has got hold of the diamonds. So, it looks like you will have a rival to worry about now.'

'Except that I'm not out to kill Brent, much as I'd like to. Have you any ideas on the ID of this assassin?'

'None whatsoever, but we might have to pull you off before long. Things could be getting a bit naughty and we don't want you in the middle of a firefight or a bloodbath.'

'You can't pull me off now,' she found herself saying. 'We're too close. You'll never get another opportunity like this.'

'You're beginning to sound like you love the job. Anyway, we'll see. Just watch your back and keep in touch.'

The phone went silent. He'd gone.

Stripping off, Kate stepped into the shower through the steam now filling the cubicle and began soaping herself down. She recalled Cole's words. *Things could be getting naughty.* Well, they were beyond naughty already as far as she was concerned. What with Brent, Rheon, Hayden and now a professional assassin to contend with, that comment was like the understatement of the century. She couldn't believe she had actually encouraged Cole to let her carry on when she could have walked away from the whole thing on his say-so. 'You really are a stupid cow,' she said aloud, and that wasn't because she had dropped the soap.

CHAPTER 10

The row between Kate and Hayden continued as soon as they both got up the next morning. Neither had slept well, which had to be another first for Hayden, since he usually slept the sleep of the dead. That meant tempers were frayed to start with. Then Lucy Weller decided to ring his mobile again to apologise for dropping him in it and he failed to turn the speaker off in time. Still furious over the hypocritical stance he had adopted, Kate couldn't hold back.

'Your girlfriend ringing again to make sure I haven't clawed your eyes out?' she asked as soon as Weller had rung off.

'You've got a nerve after the way you've behaved,' Hayden shouted at her. 'At least I'm not warming her bed the way you are with your fancy man.'

For reply Kate slapped him hard across the face. 'You scumbag,' she yelled back. 'It's okay for you to have drinks and dinner with another woman, isn't it? But when I do the same with another man, that's the biggest sin going. Talk about hypocrisy.'

'It isn't about just drinks and dinner,' he retorted, his face red and puffy. 'It's this whole portrait thing. You must think I'm stupid. It's such transparent rubbish and you know it. And it stops right here.'

There was a look of fierce defiance in her gaze now. 'Does it? So speaks a typical "gaslighter". Well, I'm going, whatever you think, and you can like it or lump it.'

His eyes bulged and he held up a pair of keys. 'If you do, that's it. You don't come back into this cottage and I've grabbed the only two keys.'

She issued an incredulous laugh. 'You moron. You can't stop me. This is my home as much as yours.'

He shook his head and there was the suggestion of a triumphant smirk on his face. 'It was my aunt who died and she left me the money that bought this place in her will. Furthermore, my name is on the deeds.'

For a moment she simply stared at him, apparently in shock. Then her mouth tightened into a thin hard line and without another word, she turned and stalked across the room into their bedroom, slamming the door behind her. Once inside, she sat on the bed for a moment or two, breathing heavily and thinking.

Well, you've gone and done it now, girl, she said to herself. You've really got him wound up. She hadn't enjoyed engineering another row, but the idea had come to her in the middle of the night and as luck would have it, Lucy Weller had given her the excuse to stir it all up again. Kate loved Hayden to the depths of her soul, but she knew there was no way he would ever have accepted her further trips to Smuggler's Reach without interfering in things. That would have had disastrous consequences, and she was not prepared to renege on her agreement to continue with her undercover role and betray Peter Foster in the process. A man like Brent needed to be brought to justice and that objective was a lot bigger than trying to keep Hayden sweet. Her husband doted on her, she was fully aware of that, and she was quite sure he would come round again once the dust had settled and he knew the full facts. But for now she had an additional role to play as the spurned wife, which would require all her natural skills to achieve.

You have to build more time into your visits. Stay longer at the house, Cole had told her. Well, if it all worked out according to her last-minute plan, that's exactly what her flaming row with Hayden would achieve. All now depended on just how much Brent wanted her company. Taking a deep breath, she dialled his number on her personal mobile . . .

Twenty minutes later, wearing her anorak and carrying a bulging suitcase, Kate returned to the kitchen-diner. Hayden was sitting brooding on one of the bar stools and he started as his eyes homed in on the suitcase she was carrying.

He jumped to his feet. 'Where-where are you going?'

'A car's being sent to pick me up,' she said. 'So you can keep the keys to your bloody cottage.'

'A car? What car?'

'A Merc.'

'I didn't mean that. I meant who is picking you up?'

'Graham Lutterall's chauffeur.'

'What? But you can't stay with him.'

'Can't?' Kate put on her best glare. 'I can do what I like. Some time apart may be good for both of us anyway. Then we'll have the opportunity to think about what we really want.'

'You already know what I want.'

'I'm not prepared to be dictated to the way you are trying to do, Hayd. So you'd better have a rethink while I'm getting my portrait done. After that, it's up to you.' She walked towards the hall door, then half turned. 'Oh, by the way, I won't be sleeping with him, if that's what you're worried about.'

Then she walked out into the hall and he heard the front door slam shut. Seconds later, there was the sound of a car driving away, leaving him alone and in silence.

Sitting beside Frank Delaney, Kate cried all the way to Smuggler's Reach and her tears were not just for show either.

* * *

Jeremy Brent couldn't have been more understanding. He took her suitcase from her and handed it to the ever-attentive Adam before slipping her anorak off her shoulders and waving her towards the living room.

118

'This is most unfortunate for you,' he said, 'and I feel partially responsible.'

She dried her eyes with a tissue and shook her head. 'It's got nothing to do with you, Graham,' she said, stopping herself in time from saying Jeremy. 'Hayden is very old-fashioned and he has quite a suspicious mind.'

He shrugged. 'I hope you don't share those suspicions of me, Kate,' he said. 'I assure you, my intentions are totally honourable. I see our arrangement as purely business, no more, though I know you think I have behaved rather badly in holding on to your wrap and shoes. But no more. You shall have them back, of course.'

Indeed, of course, she thought grimly. *Now Hayden knows, there is no point in you keeping them anymore, is there?*

'But first a drink,' he went on. 'Then I will have Adam show you to your room before lunch.'

'This is very good of you,' she lied. 'I hate imposing on anyone like this.'

'Not at all,' he said, 'it's the least I can do. My obsession with art seems to have caused this situation, whatever you say.' He smiled again. 'But no matter, now you are here, perhaps we could try a greater variety of poses and I can devote more time to perfecting what I produce.'

Adam delivered a familiar silver champagne bucket, deftly removed the cork and poured two glasses, one of which he handed Kate. Brent saluted her with his own glass.

'Here's to our next few days, Kate,' he said.

She feigned surprise. 'Oh, I can't impose on you that long. Honestly, I didn't expect it.'

'Nonsense,' he replied. 'After all, what are friends for?'

* * *

The room Adam showed Kate to was the first of four on the left of the main hallway, just past a second bathroom with its own neat label. It was the furthest back from the glass staircase, where she had carried out her brief reconnaissance during her previous visit to the house. Like the other bedrooms she had checked out on that first visit, it was beautifully decorated and luxuriously furnished. But it faced the back of the house and it had a second door in the far corner she had not noticed in the other rooms before. It opened out on to a walkway overhung with glossy-leaved climbers sprouting large, delicate, white flowers she thought were hydrangeas. A quick glance after Adam had gone revealed that the walkway extended right the way along the back of the house and all the bedrooms appeared to open on to it. There was an archway at each end. To her left, this accessed the terrace itself, and she could see the familiar steel table through the gap. To her right, beyond three more bedroom doors, the arch appeared to open on to another passageway of some sort separating the house from the garage. Just before it, two wheelie bins stood to one side of a pair of open louvre doors — the kitchen she discovered following a quick peek — and next to that was a much smaller solid door, possibly that of a storeroom of some sort.

Sitting on the edge of the bed as she unpacked from the suitcase beside her, she couldn't help a frown as she thought of poor Hayden back at their cottage. She guessed he would have cooled down by now and would be regretting his outbursts, as he always had after their many previous rows. She just prayed his own pride would prevent him from coming after her and creating a scene outside the electric entrance gates. That would do no one any good. But it was a chance she would have to take. At least she was now in Brent's house on a longer term basis and had built in the opportunity for a more thorough look around, as Cole had suggested. What worried her was whether Brent's generous hospitality would come at a price she didn't intend paying and if it did, what would be the outcome. Only time would tell, but whatever happened, barring the extreme, she knew she had to keep him onside with a little more give, even if that went against the grain for her.

* * *

Kate reported back to Cole after lunch, using the secure phone she had been given. As she did so, she ran the shower in typical spy movie style, in case of hidden listening devices, as she had before at home when the only potential listening device had been Hayden.

'Good work,' Cole said, sounding surprised that she had managed to worm her way into the house after her bust-up with her husband. 'How's Hayden taken it?'

'Not well. I just hope he doesn't turn up here to make a scene. As I said before, he might seem laid-back, but he has a real temper. Also, he broods on things and can be very unpredictable if he feels a sense of injustice.'

'I'm sure you can handle him.'

'You mean like you have "every confidence in me"?'

'Touché,' he responded with a chuckle. 'Anyway, we are hearing from our source that you can expect company within around forty-eight hours now, so you'll need to work fast.'

Never satisfied, that man, she thought ruefully.

'Who are we talking about?'

'We reckon it's the man we mentioned. The Collector. Possibly accompanied by a diamond expert?'

'Coming from where?'

'Word is somewhere in rural Ireland. Travelling by car after disembarking from the Irish ferry at Pembroke Dock.'

'What we still don't know is exactly when they're due, which is why we're relying on you to find out. Forewarned is forearmed, as they say.'

'No pressure then?' she said.

'Just keep us in the loop,' he replied, then cut off and not a moment too soon, as someone called her from outside her door.

'Kate?'

She stiffened. It was Brent.

'Just a minute.'

She pulled off her clothes and slipped on a white, towelling robe hanging on the back of the door, sticking her head under the shower to soak her hair before answering the door.

He was barefoot and also dressed in a robe, and he was holding something behind his back.

'I was about to take a dip in the pool,' he said. 'I thought you might like to join me. Then we can finish that last bottle of Chablis before dinner.'

'Oh I'm sorry, Graham,' she replied, 'I didn't bring my costume with me. The rush and everything . . .'

'No problem,' he said. 'I thought that might be the case.' He produced a black string bikini, which he thrust into her hands. 'I keep a full wardrobe for my guest models and I've become pretty good at judging sizes by now. I think this should fit you okay.'

What there is of it, was her immediate reaction as she fingered the ties of the miniscule two-piece costume. He just didn't give up, did he? Her mind was racing. He'd put her right on the spot and at first she couldn't think of a way out. Then, almost at the same moment she found her excuse.

'Tomorrow maybe, Graham,' she said. 'I'm afraid, after today's upset, I'm in no mood for anything at present. Can you understand that?'

The irritation was back in those dark eyes, but his smile remained as if stuck on with adhesive.

'Of course, my dear,' he replied. 'Perhaps tomorrow then, eh? But keep the bikini anyway.'

Kate felt physically sick as she leaned back against her closed door after he had gone. Round one to her, but heaven knew how many rounds there were going to be before she could escape this beautiful, horrible house altogether.

* * *

Hayden rang Kate on her personal mobile later that afternoon. His voice was strained, practically pleading.

'You're not really going to stay there the night, are you?' he said.

She steeled herself to remain cold and hostile, even though it tore her apart.

'Well, you effectively threw me out,' she said, 'so what choice do I have? I have to sleep somewhere.'

'Look, I was angry. I just lost it.'

'No excuses, Hayden. You said some very unkind things to me and I need time away from you to think things out.'

His voice rose perceptibly. 'But you're married to me. This is all wrong spending the night in another man's house. What do you think it looks like?'

'I don't give a shit what it looks like, Hayd. It's what I'm going to do. Now, I have to go. Dinner will be ready soon and Graham will have poured me my wine.'

'Graham? Wine?' he protested. 'Gordon Bennett, Kate, what is this?'

'It isn't anything,' she said, but couldn't resist one final mischievous dig before ending the call. 'Don't forget that corned beef in the fridge I told you about. Sleep well.'

Then she switched off her mobile completely and sank on to the edge of the bed, shaking with emotion and bitterly regretting her last remark, which had been totally unnecessary. But it had been the devil in her wanting her pound of flesh for the way he had spoken to her and it was too late now for retractions. She just had to stay with the programme and hope it didn't send him over the edge.

* * *

Dinner was a subdued affair. Brent appeared to have something on his mind, although he complimented her on the long slit skirt and thin, skimpy blouse she had deliberately put on to impress him. He excused himself just before coffee after Adam had approached him and whispered something in his ear. Kate felt her stomach start to churn again. She thought he had given her one of his searching glances before rising from the table. Could he have found out about her, she wondered? What if he had decided to check up through his alleged Met contact and had discovered that she was a former police detective? Even worse, that she was a plant for the NCA? How would he react? With his form, she dreaded to think.

And the bikini he had left with her. Was it really from one of his former models or from someone like her who had joined the "disappeared" once he had tired of their company? Her throat was dry and she finished off her glass of wine in a single gulp as Adam reappeared to set the coffee pot in front of her before proceeding to pour some into her cup. Prior to gliding away on his soft-soled shoes that made hardly any sound on the slabs, he offered her more wine, which she refused, then apologised to her on behalf of Brent for his master's absence but said he had had an urgent matter to attend to. Staring down into the garden where the coloured lights surrounding the pool glittered among the velvet shadows, she became more and more convinced that that urgent matter was about her. Suddenly feeling cold, she draped the wrap he had returned to her across her bare shoulders and drank some of her coffee to warm herself up.

Then the next moment Brent was back, with a bottle of whisky in one hand, his polished black shoes tapping their way briskly across the terrace before he sat down opposite her again. 'Sorry, Kate,' he said, pouring a generous measure of whisky into a glass on the table, 'but I had a visitor, a PC Geraint Rheon.'

Kate stared into her coffee with the intensity of someone trying to spot floaters.

'Our local copper apparently,' he went on, taking a sip from his glass. 'Came to introduce himself.' He laughed. 'Bit late, this time in the evening, I would have thought, but there you are. Seemed a nice enough chap, though.'

Suddenly that penetrating gaze was fixed on Kate again. 'Said he knew you. Something about you chasing off a burglar. That was very brave of you?'

Kate couldn't hold back the cough as the acid surged up into her throat. 'Yes,' she said in a part-strangled voice. 'I disturbed someone trying to break in a few days ago, but he ran off.'

He shook his head slowly. 'Lot of bad people about today. Funny, though, you never mentioned the business to me. We're always short of excitement round here and it would have been a good talking point.'

Back in control, she shrugged. 'No need. He didn't get anything anyway.'

'So it was a man?'

'I'm not sure. He was wearing a hood. I just assumed it was a "he".' She gave a short laugh. 'After all, you don't get many women burglars, do you?'

'Oh I don't know,' he said casually, returning to his whisky. 'Female of the species and all that. Anyway, I'll tell the boys to keep their eyes open.'

Damn Rheon, Kate thought. *Increased vigilance around the property is the last thing I need.*

Then abruptly he completely changed the subject. 'Love that outfit on you, Kate. We'll try it at tomorrow's sitting. I thought we'd start early seeing as you are here now. How about eleven, straight after breakfast?'

'Sounds good,' she said, surreptitiously glancing at her wristwatch when the sonorous notes of a clock in the hall sounded eleven p.m. while he was taking another sip of his whisky.

'Excellent. Best you get an early night then, eh? Can't have you falling asleep in the middle of the sitting, can we?'

You may be having an early night, she mused, *but I have other plans.*

CHAPTER 11

Two in the morning. Kate rose from her bed and went to the bedroom door. She opened it slightly and listened. There wasn't a sound. The whole place appeared to be in darkness. Somewhere above her head someone was snoring loudly. Brent? Probably. His henchmen had their quarters above the garage and she couldn't imagine him sharing his private floor with anyone else.

She hadn't retired for the night until after eleven and had left her host sitting on his chair on the terrace, staring, somewhat morosely she thought, down the garden. She had bid him goodnight and he had nodded but made no response. It was as if he were miles away, the remains of the half-empty bottle of Laphroaig single malt, which she had declined sharing with him, tilted at an angle in the heavy crystal glass in his hand.

She thought she had heard him stumbling along the corridor outside her room and clomping up the stairs at just after midnight, but she needed to make sure he had gone to bed. As well as the light-footed Adam, who had a habit of materialising without warning, as if from nowhere.

She had stripped off her evening dress and donned the pyjamas she had brought with her straight after returning to her room, just in case Brent decided to pay her a goodnight visit and became suspicious over the fact that she was still fully dressed. Now, however, she exchanged the pyjamas for a pair of black jeans, a woollen sweater and the only pair of trainers she had in her case. Cautiously opening her bedroom door, she studied the blacked-out hallway and listened. The heavy stillness was broken only by the snoring she had heard before. Grabbing her torch, she crept out through the door, closing it quietly behind her. If anyone clocked her, dressed as she was at this time of the night, it would certainly take some explaining and that was a fact. She was conscious of her heart making the same rapid swishing noises she recognised from her days on the beat in Bristol when carrying out dodgy building searches and she could feel her throat tightening up.

Then the searches had usually been in response to an "intruders on premises" alert, following an automatic alarm activation, which had been picked up by a central monitoring station and routed to the police. More often than not it had turned out to be a false activation, either due to a faulty alarm system, a door or window left insecure on the premises by someone, or a rat gnawing through a cable. But on other occasions she had found a broken window or a forced door and had heard someone moving about inside. This had invariably resulted in a surge of adrenalin, as she played a cat and mouse game with the intruder in pitch darkness, until she either managed to nab him or he got away.

Now was different. Now she was not engaged in a lawful search as a warranted police officer. Now she was effectively a trespasser carrying out the search of part of a premises where she had no right to be. Now the shoe was on the other foot and if detected, instead of being the cat, she would be the mouse, which would mean that, rather than facing a spell in police custody, she was more likely to end up in an early, unmarked grave. A particularly sobering thought, as she followed the masked beam of her little pocket torch along the hallway.

The living room was flooded with moonlight and she could see right through it to the terrace. Her main worry had been that the person she had heard ascending the stairs had not been Brent at all, but someone else, and that she would find him crashed out in one of the armchairs, staring back at her. But her concern was not realised. The room was deserted and it was apparent that there was no one sitting in any of the chairs on the terrace either.

It seemed highly likely that the person stumbling on the stairs had indeed been Brent and if he really was drunk, then it was also likely that he was flat out in bed by now. *Time to take the risk and look for that safe*, she told herself without any real enthusiasm. Turning, she headed back into the hall and walked cautiously towards the stairs, only to pause at the bottom to study them dubiously.

A shaft of moonlight passing through the green glass from a high-level window rendered the treads totally transparent and, seeing the hall floor right beneath her as she began to climb, created the impression that there was nothing under her feet and she was walking on air. Twice she stopped after almost losing her balance and she was relieved when she finally got to the landing, making a face as she remembered that she would have to go back down afterwards.

Before her was another thickly carpeted corridor with similar, white-painted doors opening off on each side. She traced the snoring to the first door on her left, what she assumed to be Brent's bedroom, but bypassed it initially to check out the other rooms. The door opposite accessed a long narrow room, boasting three small windows in one wall. None of the luxury that was on show in the rest of the house was evident here. The carpet on the floor was of the thin, plain, serviceable kind. A long table stood in the centre of it with six chairs arranged on either side, plus a further chair at the far end. Each chair had a closed laptop computer on the table in front of it. A printer stood on another smaller table in one corner and a large coffee machine occupied another. The room was clearly some sort of conference or meeting room. *Maybe, like SMERSH in the James Bond films, it was the place from which Brent directed his empire*, she thought with a twisted, humourless smirk.

The room next door appeared to be nothing more than a storeroom, with shelves laden with stationery: boxes of A4 and A5 paper, pens and envelopes in various sizes, plastic packets of inkjet cartridges, and several unused box files — everything in fact that an efficient office needed. There were also a couple of spare laptops and half a dozen mobile phones, apparently unused and still sealed in their original wrappings. She guessed the phones were destined for use as replacement burners. Why else would Brent need all these extra ones on top of his own personal mobile? But she had no means of confirming that fact one way or the other, so she left them well alone.

Quitting the storeroom, she found that the corridor came to an end before a pair of frosted, glass panel doors, leading to a light gymnasium, equipped with wall bars, weights and a treadmill. Obviously Brent liked to work out on a regular basis, which explained how he maintained the muscular physique he liked to use as a means of impressing his conquests and feeding his vanity. There was a shower room, toilet and dressing room in one corner and another frosted-glass door in the end wall, which turned out to open on to a steel fire escape dropping away to the passage between the house and the triple garage block.

Just one more room opposite the storeroom remained to be checked, but she was in for a disappointment. The door was securely locked. She tried the handle several times, but the door refused to budge. It seemed more than likely that this was Brent's study. After all, why else would he want to lock it? But as there was no sign on the door, saying *Study*, she had no way of knowing anyway. One thing was clear, though. She was not going to find out the answer tonight, which meant she had two options. The first was to return to the safety of her room, which was easy, but the other was much more of a challenge, and the point was, did she think she had the guts for it?

As far as she knew, Brent was out cold. Heavily intoxicated and in a drunken stupor. If she was careful, she should be able to check out his room without risk of disturbing him. But that was the theory. The reality could be a lot different. Yet this was probably the only chance she would ever have of getting in there and looking around. To waste it would be unforgivable, if it were to turn out that the safe she was hunting for was in that room rather than in the study.

She stood there a few moments more, chewing her lip and trying to weigh up the risks against the potential benefits. Then a sudden louder burst of snoring made her mind up for her. It was almost as if some mischievous house spirit was in the room, prodding Brent at exactly the right moment to tempt her inside.

Approaching the door without further hesitation, she saw that it was only ajar rather than closed, which made things much easier. Gritting her teeth, she pushed it open a little way and peered into a huge bedroom, luxuriously furnished and thickly carpeted, with what had to be a super king bed positioned against the right-hand wall. There was an inner door — perhaps to an ensuite bathroom, dressing room, or both — to her left, while a pair of French doors graced the opposite wall, opening on to a balcony, enclosed by steel railings overlooking the garden. A massive, multi-layer ceiling light, composed of several large, square, glass panels, completed the picture of opulence, dominating the room like something from a science fiction film.

So much for the wages of sin, Kate mused, focusing her gaze on the bed. Brent was lying there flat out on his back on top of the sheets, still dressed in the evening shirt and black trousers he had worn at dinner. He was obviously well away, and the fact that he hadn't managed to undress suggested he was destined for the mother of hangovers when he finally woke up, which didn't look like anytime soon. As for his intention to make a start on her portrait at eleven, that looked about as likely now as the Pope contracting him to repaint the Sistine Chapel.

Deciding to take the risk, she removed her shoes and slipped into the room barefoot. Big, gilt-framed oil paintings of naked women in erotic poses — no doubt Brent's own work going by what Kate had seen in his studio so far — adorned two of the walls and tiptoeing round his bed, she carefully examined each one in turn. But it was a waste of time. Both pictures were securely screwed to the walls at each corner and were immovable. The possibility of a safe being located behind either was impossible.

It was as she was in the process of quitting the room that it happened. She hadn't seen the crystal tumbler lying on the floor, where Brent had obviously dropped it when heading for bed, and her heel caught it, as she was backing away towards the door. It was just a touch, but the glass must have been lying on its side and this was enough to send it flying. The crash as it hit the metal leg of an incidental table couldn't have been louder and Brent shot up in bed with a loud snort, his rheumy gaze wandering around the room.

Crouched on the floor at the foot of the bed, Kate remained perfectly still, teeth clenched and eyes tightly closed as she inwardly cursed her stupidity. If Brent decided to get up and investigate further, he couldn't fail to see her. Then she would have just two options. Either admit to the fact that she was snooping and end up with a bullet in the head, or pretend she was feeling randy and had come looking for him, which would mean hopping into bed with him. Neither option particularly appealed to her, but she waited for several tense minutes to see if his face would suddenly appear over the end of the bed, where she was hiding, to look down at her.

Those minutes passed and nothing happened. Cramp spread up her legs into her back. Downstairs the hall clock chimed three a.m. Out on the main road the faint sound of a car travelling fast was audible. She tried to ease one foot out from under the other and heard the sinews crack. Shit! Now one of her legs was beginning to shake under the pressure of her crouched position. She had to stand up. She couldn't remain like this any longer. She started to straighten, dreading being confronted by those dark penetrating eyes fixed on

131

her like those of a cobra. But the next instant there came loud snorting, grunting sounds, like those of some rutting animal, and she breathed a prayer of thanks. Miraculously, Brent had gone back to sleep.

When she stood up, she saw that he was on his back again, with his arms thrown wide, once more insensible. She stayed only long enough to pick up the tumbler, which for all the noise it had made, was fortunately still intact. She placed it carefully on the little table it had struck. Then she slipped quietly out of the room, leaving the door ajar, exactly as she had found it. Standing motionless in the corridor outside for a few seconds, she waited for her breathing to return to somewhere close to normal.

That had been close, too damned close, and she still hadn't got into the study. Somehow she had to find a way, but that was for another night. Right now, she reckoned it was time to pack in before she suffered any more calamities. It was getting on for three thirty now too and other members of the household, like the chef, could be waking up soon.

Picking her way down the treacherous glass staircase, she returned to her room and was soon climbing back into bed. She was fast asleep within minutes, dreaming fitfully of a face with dark satanic eyes staring at her over the foot of her bed, like some ghoul from a horror film.

* * *

Kate would not have slept at all had she been aware of another pair of eyes, far removed from any dream, that had noted her return to her room from the walkway outside. Eyes that watched her switch on her table lamp through a gap in the blinds, then undress and climb into bed before plunging the room once more into darkness. They were the same eyes that had seen her get dressed in the black jeans and woollen sweater before leaving her room earlier. But they didn't belong to some sick, voyeuristic member of the household, driven by lust. These were the eyes of someone with a more nefarious purpose in mind. Someone not in the least bit interested in whether Kate was clothed or not, but intensely curious as to what she was up to in the middle of the night, and who slipped away into the shadows once her bedroom light was extinguished.

The watcher was dressed entirely in black. Black balaclava with eyeholes cut into it inside a black hooded top, skinny black trousers, black trainers and even black gloves. They carried a black haversack on their back and if anyone had been given the opportunity of looking inside, they would have discovered a number of curious items, including wire cutters, reels of sticky tape, nylon climbing rope and a pair of powerful binoculars fitted with long-range night-sights.

They had used the wire cutters to make a hole in a section of the perimeter fence blind to one of the security cameras so they could slip through, and they had been surprised to find the fence was neither electrified, nor alarmed. Obviously, Brent had thought his reliance on the CCTV cameras was enough, but that was a big mistake.

After seeing Kate return to bed, the intruder made their way along to the terrace and slipped into the living room via the French doors, which had been so carelessly left open. They then followed more or less the same route as Kate, though they sensibly steered clear of Brent's bedroom which was still under his noisy nasal assault. They checked the conference room Kate had just investigated, but like her, found it of little interest. The locked door of the room almost opposite immediately attracted their attention, however, and they allowed themselves a contemptuous smile. The lock was sprung in seconds and, slipping inside, they paused briefly to stare around the room in which they found themselves. Which was obviously Brent's study, as Kate had suspected.

The drawers of a steel-topped desk under the window were all locked. That didn't present a problem for the intruder, but after forcing each one in turn and finding nothing but papers, a bottle of whisky and a cash box containing a few hundred pounds, which they ignored with a sneer, they turned their attention to a large oil painting of the house on the adjoining wall. Removing it from its twin hooks, they found the safe, which had been hidden behind it. *How original*, they thought sarcastically.

The safe was fitted with a circular, rotatable combination dial and was of a type they instantly recognised. What they didn't know was whether it was a three- or a four-wheel combination, which meant that opening it would possibly take longer than they had anticipated. But such was life. Slipping off their haversack, they unzipped it and removed a stethoscope. Climbing on to a chair, they inserted the earpieces on the ends of the rubber tubes into their ears, then bent towards the safe and pressed the diaphragm of the stethoscope against the door, close to the dial. Gripping the dial, they began the complicated process of very slowly rotating it backwards and forwards and listening for the telltale double clicks as the tumblers fell into place.

This took patience and a steady hand, but they had both and after a good fifteen minutes, they were able to press the handle down on the door and pull it open. But their expected reward was not for the taking this time. The safe was completely empty save for a note stuck on the back wall of the two-foot square steel box, and the eyes staring out of the slits in the balaclava glittered when they read the sneering message printed on the piece of paper in block capitals:

WHOEVER YOU ARE, NOT TODAY, DICKHEAD

'So, you want to play games with me, do you?' the intruder breathed. 'Well, that's fine by me.'

A few minutes later they were through the hole in the wire fence and had vanished into the night.

CHAPTER 12

Something was up. Roused early by loud voices and the sound of running feet, Kate sat up in bed and stared at her door. Her watch said eight a.m. and she fell back on to her pillow with a groan. She had only had about four hours sleep after the night's escapades and she felt half dead.

Eventually dragging herself out of bed, she forced herself into the shower and emerged drying herself down with the strength of an eighty-year-old.

It was nearly an hour before she had recovered enough to leave her room and she walked straight into Adam, of all people.

'Mr Lutterall is busy at the moment,' he said briskly. 'He sends his apologies and says he will join you later.'

'Something happened, has it?' she asked.

'Please go through to the terrace, Mrs Lewis,' he said, without answering her. 'I will serve you breakfast shortly.'

With that, he was gone, striding off along the hallway and out through the front door.

Kate's curiosity was now really aroused, but she went through the living room to the terrace as requested and drew up the chair she always used. A jug of fresh orange juice, together with a plate each of toast and croissants had already been set out for her and there was a percolator filled with hot coffee close to her plate. The smell of the coffee was irresistible and she poured herself a full cup straightaway.

As she sipped the drink, her gaze roved around the garden and the next instant she caught sight of Brent, accompanied by the lumbering figure of Delaney, emerging from the gateway leading to the helipad and walking towards the terrace.

Brent waved at her as he approached and nodded to Delaney who broke away from him and headed towards the passageway between the side of the house and the triple garage block.

Brent climbed the steps to the terrace and eased himself into a chair opposite her, immediately going for the coffee. He looked dreadful. Grey-faced, with bleary inflamed eyes and a constant twitch to his right cheek. Inwardly, Kate was delighted. He was obviously suffering from a very bad hangover and she knew from past experience that he would probably feel the effects of his night's overindulgence for the rest of the day.

'Bad night?' she asked innocently, unable to resist rubbing it in.

He scowled, popped a couple of pills in his mouth from the pocket of his dressing gown and swallowed them in a single gulp.

'Don't remember much about it,' he replied. 'You sleep well?'

'Like a top,' she lied. 'But what was wrong this morning? I heard people running about all over the place.'

He threw her a quick glance. 'You didn't hear any noises during the night, did you?' he asked. 'Like, er, someone walking up the stairs or along the walkway outside your room.'

She shook her head. 'I heard what I think must have been you climbing the stairs after I'd gone to bed, but nothing else.'

Immediately she realised she had said the wrong thing.

'Oh?' he said. 'How did you know it was me?'

136

Mentally she fumbled, then tried to recover. 'Well, er, I didn't, but as you were the only one I saw up and about when I turned in, I assumed it was you.' She gave a short laugh and hoped she didn't sound too awkward. 'Also, you were well into your cups when I left you — that bottle of scotch, for instance — and whoever it was on the stairs, they seemed to be having difficulty getting up them.'

To her relief, he returned her smile and it had a rueful quality. 'That obvious, was it? I'm certainly paying for that single malt now.'

He poured himself some more coffee, then looked at her again. 'We had a visitor last night.'

'Visitor?' Kate's heart skipped a beat.

'Yes, someone cut through the wire fence — Jack found the hole this morning — and it looks like they had a pretty good look around the house.'

Remembering how she had woken him up in his bedroom, she almost dreaded asking her next question. 'How do you know they got into the house?'

His face tightened. 'Because the door of my study had been forced and left open and the drawers of my desk also forced by someone.'

'Heavens,' she said. 'Anything taken?'

He shook his head. 'Fortunately not, but they must have known their business, as the combination of my wall safe had been cracked and the damned thing was also left open. But they were out of luck there too, as it was empty.'

Bullshit, I wonder? Kate thought. But the way he spoke suggested it wasn't. If he'd lost his precious diamonds, she couldn't believe he would have taken it so calmly. No, she felt sure he was telling the truth, which begged the question, where had he hidden the stones then?

'In fact, I never keep anything really valuable in my safe. It's too obvious a target.'

He seemed to be studying her face quite intently again and she hoped his words were not meant as a subtle insinuation. But it was difficult to read his expression.

'Maybe it was the same person who tried to burgle my cottage?' she blurted.

He nodded slowly. 'Possibly, yes. I hadn't thought of that. Perhaps I should get your PC Rheon on the case, eh? What do you think?'

She met his stare full on, knowing he would have no intention of doing any such thing. 'Maybe you should, but he wasn't very successful with mine, was he?'

The thin smile was back. 'Perhaps you're right. Waste of time, I would think and I haven't lost anything, so it's probably best to put it down to the price of experience.'

He eased his chair back and dabbed his mouth with a napkin. 'Now, I have an apology for you. I said we would start on your new portrait this morning, but—' he raised a hand to his head and winced — 'after my overindulgence last night, I don't feel I could do you justice.'

She tried not to allow her relief to show. 'That really isn't a problem, Graham. I do understand. I'm just happy to be here.'

He seemed to be pleased with her reply. 'Well, you're very welcome, my dear, and there's always tomorrow, isn't there? Meantime, why don't you just relax. Read a book, go for a swim even? It looks like being a nice, hot day.'

'Have you any objections to my taking a walk around the grounds. They look so beautiful and . . .'

He flicked his hand in an "as you wish" gesture. 'But of course. You're not in a prison. Go where you like. I will see you at lunch, hopefully feeling much better.'

He rose from the table and walked past her a little unsteadily back into the house. Kate didn't make any immediate move but sat there finishing her breakfast and thinking over what she had just learned.

So someone had screwed Brent's study, had they? She must have just missed them prowling about the place. A sobering thought considering what they might have done to her in a sudden confrontation. It sounded like the job was the work of a professional too if the safe combination had been cracked. She didn't believe in coincidences, which meant that the culprit must have been after the diamonds, as she had been. She remembered what Cole had told her about the contract that was out on Brent. The nocturnal visitor had to be the assassin hired to find the stones and terminate the man who had stolen them from Charlie Hooper. If that was the case, then a further visit was inevitable very soon. But Brent had been forewarned, so he would be forearmed now too. That could present complications for her as much as for his nemesis. The stage was getting far too crowded.

She was also uneasy about Brent's manner towards her at breakfast, which had seemed slightly hostile. It was as if he was beginning to suspect her of something and couldn't quite make up his mind as to whether she was all she claimed to be. That could put her in real danger. It would only take a phone call to his contact in the Met and a bit of intelligent digging to establish her former occupation and then it would be all over for her. She had to keep her wits about her and not give Brent any cause to doubt her bona fides.

She was put straight through to Cole when she rang the contact number on her encrypted mobile from her bedroom. Conscious of the fact that Brent or Crosby could walk in on her at any moment, as her bedroom door lacked a key, she delivered her information quickly and concisely and with the shower once again running full blast.

Cole was his usual abrupt, hard-nosed self. A typical crime squad detective. 'Bugger it!' he said when she had finished. 'So we're no further forward?'

'Well, the stones are obviously not in Brent's safe, so I'll have to keep looking, but it's difficult to know where to start.'

'You're a woman. Use your intuition.'

'I beg your pardon.'

There was a sharp intake of breath. 'Sorry, I shouldn't have said that. I'm just under a lot of pressure at the moment.'

'You're not the only one. Particularly as I've got this other character to watch out for now, and there's something else too. I'm beginning to think Brent is getting suspicious of me.'

'What makes you think that?'

'It's his manner. It seems to have changed. It's colder and he appears more watchful.'

'Maybe you should try and soften him up. Most men are putty in a woman's hands. They think they're tough, but they're easily won over if the right buttons are pressed. He's obviously obsessed with you. Perhaps you should distract him. Lead him on a bit by giving him a little of what he wants?'

'You mean sleep with him? No bloody way!'

'I'm not suggesting you go that far and, as we've said before, that's one thing you must not do.'

'Then what?'

'I'll leave that to you. But it could mean offering him some sort of incentive to keep him interested in you and overrule any misgivings he could have about you. You might have to bend a little to avoid putting him off. As a woman, the power is with you.'

'Thanks, Dr Freud!'

'You're welcome. The only alternative is we pull you off this thing and shut it all down. It's your call.'

She hesitated. She knew that would make sense. Brent was already responsible for the deaths of six people she knew of, and she realised that, for all his charm and his fixation on her, he wouldn't think twice about making her number seven if he thought she was a threat to him. But the face of the young policeman she had confronted in her home who had later been so horrifically burned to death in his caravan, kept forcing itself in front of her mind's eye. Peter Foster, Jamie's brother, had he died that agonising death in vain? Was his killer now going to get away with his and the other murders just like that? And all because the one person who could have brought down a monster had turned chicken when things got tough?

'No,' she found herself saying. 'I'm not ready for that yet. We can't stop now and let that scumbag get away with everything he's done. I'll carry on as we are.'

'If you're happy with that, then fine. But as I've said before, keep me in the loop.'

The phone cut off.

For a moment she sat there, thinking about what Cole had suggested. Lead him on, he'd said. Give him a little of what he wants. The power is with you. *What power?*, she thought. And not only was it a question of did she have it, but had she the guts to use it? Picking up the bikini Brent had given her, what there was of it, she once more fingered the straps and gave a rueful smile. Perhaps it was nearly time to find out. She was still thinking about that when there was the sound of loud rapid knocking on her bedroom door.

Adam was standing there. 'You had better come, Mrs Lewis,' he said. 'Your husband has turned up and he's thrown all of his toys out of the pram.'

* * *

Kate could hear Hayden's voice even before she was in sight of the entrance. He was shouting angrily, 'She's my wife, damn it!'

Hayden was standing on the other side of the main gate, gripping the wrought-iron bars with both hands. Jack Ferris and Frank Delaney were standing silently inside the gate, arms folded, watching him. As she got closer, she could see that his face was puffed up and beetroot red, his eyes bulging, as if he were having a fit. Hayden rarely got mad. He usually just sulked when he was upset. The few times she had seen him really lose his temper — her recent walk-out from their bungalow being one of them — had been nothing like she was witnessing here. He seemed to have lost it completely this time. He was kicking the gate and shaking, his eyes bulging from their sockets, like someone demented.

As soon as he saw her and the look she gave him, he seemed to calm down a little, releasing his grip on the gate and stepping back, as if embarrassed, but still trembling with barely suppressed rage.

'They won't let me in to see you,' he protested.

'I'm not surprised, the state you're in,' she said sharply. 'You're behaving like a two-year-old.'

'But you're my bloody wife.'

'You don't own me,' she snapped back defensively. 'And it was you who threw me out, remember?'

'I-I didn't mean you to . . . For heaven's sake. Come home. This isn't right.'

She was conscious of the muscles in her stomach twisting with the emotion of the moment. She felt desperately guilty and near to tears and she wanted nothing more than to walk out of those gates and throw her arms around this big bumbling man she loved so much. But she had no choice but to steel herself and bury her feelings.

'I told you I need time to think things out,' she said, her voice quavering slightly, 'and Mr Lutterall has kindly allowed me to stay here while I do that.'

Hayden began to lose it again and shook the gate in his frustration. 'You mean while you pose for him starkers, then join him in his bed?' he snarled. 'I won't have it. I want you out of this place and home with me, or-or . . .'

'Or what, Mr Lewis?' Brent's voice spoke from Kate's elbow, cold and menacing. 'I suggest you turn around and go home before you find yourself in real trouble. Kate is staying here with me until she wants to leave. Is that clear?'

Hayden gaped at him, the menace in Brent's voice slicing through his blind fury.

'So-so you're Lutterall, are you?' he stammered, his tone much more subdued. 'Well, I'll have you know that-that Kate and I were . . .'

Kate froze, to her horror, guessing that Hayden was about to blab about their former occupations as a means of adding weight to his response to Brent's thinly veiled threat.

'Happily married, Hayd,' she blurted before he could finish his sentence. 'Yes, I know, and we could be again. I just want time to think.'

Her distraction paid off. He obviously forgot what he had been about to say and before he could say anything else, there was another more dramatic intervention. The sound of a high, revving engine announced the arrival of a liveried police car, which swung in front of the gates, wheels sliding in the soft earth, and blue light pulsing.

Even as its wheels came to a halt, Geraint Rheon hauled himself out of the car, hatless, closely followed by another younger police constable.

'We got a call . . . ?' Rheon announced, looking questioningly from Hayden to those behind the gate.

To Kate's surprise, Brent said smoothly, '*I* rang you, Mr Rheon. This man is the husband of my house guest, Mrs Lewis, and he's causing a bit of a disturbance.'

'Is he?' Rheon growled, staring directly at Hayden.

'Kate?' Hayden protested, looking at her for support.

Kate ignored him. 'We've had a bit of a domestic, Officer,' she explained. 'I'm now staying here for a few days. I think it would be best if my husband were to leave.'

Rheon gripped Hayden's arm. 'Come on, sir, time to go. We'll run you home.'

The shock betrayed look Hayden gave Kate cut through her like a knife and his stare never left her face, as he was placed in the back of the police car and driven away.

'You okay, my dear?' Brent asked. 'I regret you had to go through that. Quite unpleasant for you.'

'I'm-I'm fine, Graham,' she lied. 'Just a bit shocked, that's all.'

Leaving his cohorts talking by the gate, he began escorting her back up the driveway to the house.

'Well, I don't think he'll be back,' he said. 'At least I hope not. I don't want this sort of hassle on my property and I certainly don't like calling on the police to intervene in domestic disputes like this.'

His displeasure was clear and Kate also picked up the warning hint of: *you're on thin ice at the moment, so for your sake, it better not happen again.* Damn Hayden! He had very nearly scuppered everything. But then that very thought made her feel even more guilty. Poor old Hayden too, she was really putting him through it, and there was no way she could lessen his pain, not even a little. She just hoped he would forgive her when it was all over, one way or the other, and he learned the truth. Somehow she had her doubts and she suspected that the relationship between the two of them would never be the same again. Was what she was doing worth that sacrifice? Whether it was or not, it was too late to do anything about it now, but one thing she needed to ensure was that the sacrifice did not turn out to be in vain. She had to keep things going now at all costs and, whether she liked it or not, that meant keeping Brent sweet and onside — short of sleeping with him.

* * *

Lunch was served on the terrace by Alfredo Vitale, the chef, for a change. A delicious lasagne with fresh salad and a bottle of Emidio Pepe Pecorino white wine. Vitale was a small, thin man with jet-black curly hair, an olive skin and a moustache that would have rivalled that of Agatha Christie's Hercule Poirot. He spoke quickly with a rich Italian accent, and outwardly, he seemed very friendly, but Kate noticed a long thin scar down one side of his face and a deadness in his eyes that she did not like. She remembered Cole's description of him. *Don't be fooled . . . he has pre-cons in Calabria for using his carving expertise on a lot more than roast meat.* Seeing that scar on his face, she guessed that someone had once done the same thing to him. What a delightful little crowd she had for company, she thought cynically . . .

The atmosphere at the table was strained at first and Brent said very little. Apparently more or less recovered from his hangover, he appeared nevertheless to be brooding over something and Kate assumed she was the subject of his thoughts. Hayden's visit seemed to have changed the dynamics of the situation and not for the better either.

In the end, she could not stand the silent treatment any longer and took a big risk.

'Would you rather I left your house?' she asked. 'I don't want to cause you any problems.'

He considered that for a moment, took a sip of his wine and then stared at her, saying nothing.

'Well, I have thought it might be for the best,' he said finally, 'With the break-in and everything, it could be safer for you back home. But you can still visit here to model for me, of course.'

Kate's heart sank and she chose her words carefully. 'If you don't want me to stay anymore because of my husband's behaviour, I can understand that, but you forget, we had an attempted burglary at our cottage, and I'd probably be at more risk there than here.'

'It's got nothing to do with your husband's behaviour,' he said. 'I am thinking solely of you.'

She shrugged. 'That's fine, but I wouldn't be able to go home. Not after all that's happened.' Inwardly feeling a treacherous bitch, she went on to sell Hayden down the river. 'You saw the way my husband was. He's quite a possessive, violent individual and I definitely wouldn't feel safe with him anymore. I would have to find somewhere else to stay.'

He frowned. 'I'm sorry to hear that. It rather complicates things.'

She seized the moment to dangle the carrot. 'Well, I will leave, of course, if that's what you want, but I have to say I will be sorry. It's been such a relaxing experience here and I haven't yet tried out your pool . . .'

His face changed. 'You would like to?'

'Now that I feel up to it, yes, and it's such a nice, hot day. If I'd stayed on, I might even have plucked up the courage to pose for you in the way you wanted eventually. But I do see your point.' She half rose in her chair. 'I'd better get my things packed and order a taxi into Lamphey. I know there are a couple of hotels there.'

He shook his head quickly. 'You'll do no such thing. You'll remain here. I have no intention of doing what your husband did and forcing you to leave. So how about that swim? I'll have Adam bring some champagne to the poolside to celebrate.'

What was it Cole had said, Kate thought. *Men are putty in a woman's hands . . . they're easily won over if the right buttons are pressed.* Well, she had pressed some buttons, but only time would tell whether they were the right or the wrong ones, or whether she had in fact pressed one too many.

CHAPTER 13

Calling the swimming costume a string bikini was a pretty accurate description. It seemed to consist of little else. Kate was not shy about her body, but the costume left very little to the imagination and she hoped the thing would not come off in the water and give Brent an early sight of what he was after.

She made her way to the pool about an hour after lunch to find he was already there, wearing a pair of brief trunks. She could feel his eyes devouring her as they had on the beach that first time as she disrobed and used the pool steps to slip gently into the water. It was quite warm in the sun and she allowed herself to drift on her back for a while before making a more energetic effort with a cautious breaststroke style that did not put too much strain on the bikini. When she finally climbed out half an hour later, he was waiting for her with a large fluffy towel and she tried not to recoil as he slipped it over her shoulders.

'Champagne for the lady?' he quipped and poured her a glass from a bottle resting in an ice bucket on a corner of the pool, shaded by an umbrella.

She drank with the towel self-consciously wrapped around her middle and he laughed, seemingly in good spirits now.

'You are a shy one. You were quite happy flaunting everything on the beach that first day.'

She made a face, remembering that Hayden had used the same word. 'I wasn't flaunting anything. I was having a swim like everyone else, and in a costume nowhere near as revealing as this one.'

'If you pose for me like you've finally agreed to do, you'll be showing the whole goods, so what's the problem?'

"The whole goods"? she mused indignantly. He made it sound as if she would be exhibiting herself at a meat market, and now she was beginning to regret making that desperate offer and wondering whether in the end she would be able to do it. *Too late to say no now, girl,* the voice in her head told her. *You're committed to it.*

She was conscious of the fact that he was speaking to her again. 'I said what about tomorrow morning?'

For a second, she just stared at him, uncomprehendingly. 'Sorry, tomorrow morning for what?'

'Your modelling session.'

Although she knew the question would be coming at some stage, she hadn't expected it so soon, but before she could think of a suitable excuse to say no, she was saved by the bell — or more accurately, the double ring of his mobile lying on the pool walkway by his chair.

Motioning her to stay silent, he picked up the phone, checked the number on the screen, and answered with a crisp, 'Give me a second.'

Mouthing a silent explanation of "business", he climbed to his feet and followed the walkway round to a changing room hut on the far corner of the pool.

Dropping her towel, Kate was up from the chair the moment he disappeared inside, her bare feet making no sound on the stone slabs. Standing just outside the door, she bent her head towards it and closed her eyes to enhance her hearing.

She heard the tail end of the conversation. 'Arriving on the afternoon ferry, Saturday at Pembroke Dock then.

You should get here easily by one thirty. I've given you the address, but your sat nav should get you to us without any problem.'

There was no "goodbye", and she was nearly caught out when the next instant she heard the scuff of his feet on the wooden floor, indicating the conversation was over. There was no time for her to return to her chair, so she did the only thing she could do in the circumstances. She dived straight into the pool.

He stopped a second when he stepped out of the hut and stared at her. She'd had the good sense to turn around towards him in the water immediately to make it look as though she was completing her swim from the other end of the pool, but she thought he looked puzzled about something. Then she realised what it could be. Performing her dive so clumsily, she had splashed water up over the walkway outside the hut. She felt the beginnings of a spasm start in her stomach and, as she swam to the side of the pool, she waited for him to say something. He did too, but it wasn't what she'd expected and it was now apparent that his expression had been one of delighted surprise rather than puzzlement.

'Very nice too, Kate,' he said, laughing his head off.

At first she didn't cotton on. Then, looking down at herself, she realised what he was laughing at. Unbeknown to her, diving into the pool had not just cascaded water up over the walkway but had also been too much for the flimsy bikini top she was wearing, which had come right off and was floating away behind her even as she stood there staring up at him.

Any embarrassment she might otherwise have felt was overcome by a sense of absolute relief. Flashing her bare breasts was a lot less problematic than having to explain to him what she had been doing on the walkway outside the hut, listening to his private conversation. But almost at the same moment, her relief was overshadowed by the arrival of Adam Crosby, who had appeared on the walkway beside Brent's chair to refill the champagne bucket with ice. To get there from the house, he would have had to descend the steps from the terrace and cross the lawn, which meant that he would have had the pool in sight for at least half a minute. Long enough to have seen Kate diving into it from just in front of the changing room hut and then seeing his boss come out through the door with his mobile in his hand.

Okay, so he may not have seen anything in it. He would not have known Brent went into the hut to answer the call, but what if he had taken longer to cross the lawn than she had estimated and he had seen her bent close to the door of the hut in listening mode? It would only take Brent to tell him about the call and he would quickly put two and two together, signing Kate's death warrant. As it was, as she climbed out of the pool again, pulling on the bikini top she had rescued, Crosby threw her what she thought to be a sly, half-amused look, before walking back to the house.

Forced to stay with Brent by the pool for the rest of the afternoon, drinking his champagne while she worried and wondered, the voice in her head constantly urged her to get back to her room as soon as possible to pass on what she had heard to Cole. She could be wrong, but her intuition told her that the call Brent had received was not just any business call, but from the Collector who was coming to look at his diamonds. She had just one more day before they arrived and she still had no idea where he could have hidden those elusive stones.

* * *

Cole was his usual abrasive self when she finally got back to her room and rang him. This time, because she was in a hurry, she didn't bother turning on the shower.

'Saturday, you say,' he said, not even complimenting her on making the discovery. 'Are you positive it was the Collector?'

'No, I'm not,' she retorted, miffed at his attitude. 'How could I be? But it sounded very much like it.'

He grunted. 'I'll set something up in readiness, but you do realise we only get one crack at this. If it isn't the Collector, or it is but he changes the day without you knowing, we've blown it and then you'll need to get the hell out of there while we deal with the aftershocks. Sure as God made little apples, once Brent knows you're the source, he'll want your scalp more than Sitting Bull ever wanted George Custer's at the Battle of the Little Bighorn.'

Kate was not impressed by his apparent knowledge of American history and found his long-winded reference inappropriate in such a dodgy situation. 'Just make sure you can get in here,' she snapped. 'And there's something else.'

'There usually is with you. Hayden, is it?'

'You know he came here?'

'Yep. We've got another bod out there on static surveillance.'

'You might have told me.'

'Best you didn't know, but you do now. Anyway, we've had a word with the local Bill through backdoor channels and they're keeping him in the nick until tomorrow on grounds of preventing further breaches of the peace while he's in the state that he is.'

'He's in a cell?' she exclaimed.

'Novel experience for him,' Cole replied with a chuckle.

Kate closed her eyes tightly for a second. 'Poor old Hayden,' she breathed. 'He'll never forgive me for all this.'

'He will if someone gives you a medal.'

She snorted. 'As long as it's not a posthumous one,' she said grimly, and ended the call.

* * *

Another clear, moonlit night. Kate waited, as before, until she was sure everyone had gone to bed, then dressed in the same sweater, jeans and trainers. Dinner had been a lively affair for a change. Brent was in high spirits, though whether because he could be about to seal the deal on his precious diamonds when the Collector turned up in two days' time, or because Kate was due to pose naked for him in the morning, she had no idea. In any event, the meal of Dover Sole with all the trimmings had been superb and the wine had flowed non-stop. As usual, Brent drank too much and she was not slow in encouraging him, hoping that he would be as unfit for portrait painting in the morning, as he had been that day. But if she was honest, she was now resigned to what she had to do, telling herself it was only one stage further than the afternoon, following her bikini mishap, and

most young women would think nothing of it, these so-called liberal, enlightened days anyway. She dreaded what Hayden's reaction would be when he eventually found out, though — if she was still alive and they ever got together again after all this.

On that depressing note, she left the room via the door to the walkway this time, but without any clear idea as to where she was going. She had lain awake for two hours trying to figure out where the diamonds could be hidden, but she'd got nowhere. All she could think of doing was taking a look at the helicopter in the hangar again. At least that might give her something to pass on to Cole and his team. She had had a good look around the garden area over the past few days and, though she had noted the same sort of external-facing security cameras evenly spaced out along the rear boundaries as she had seen at the front, she had been surprised by the apparent absence of any cameras covering the inside of the property. Maybe there weren't any? Maybe Brent felt secure enough with the external coverage he already had of the approaches to his house, that he didn't consider there was a need for surveillance internally. On the other hand, maybe there were other cameras, but they were hidden from view? If that was so, she was about to drop herself in it big time. She would have no real reason to be out and about in the middle of the night other than to spy. But as she crept along the walkway to the right of her room, heading for the archway at the end, she was already thinking about what she could say if she were caught.

One option was: 'Oh, I couldn't sleep, so I thought I'd go for a walk on such a lovely night.' Another was: 'The trouble is, I do have a tendency to sleepwalk and I had no idea I was out here until you woke me up.' Or even: 'I heard a noise outside my room and glimpsed this hooded figure creeping past, so I thought I'd follow them.' As excuses, they were all about as bad as each other and in the end, she gave up trying. She just had to make sure she didn't run into anyone in the first place.

Passing the louvre doors of the kitchen, she peered through the archway into the passageway separating the house from the garage-cum-apartment block. It was deserted and the moonlight reflected back off the steps and guard rails of the steel fire escape as if it were wreathed in dying fire.

She made the end of the passageway without incident and stood for several minutes in the shadows, studying the sweep of the lawn at the foot of a similar flight of stone steps to those serving the terrace.

She was about to chance her arm and move off when she heard the sharp tap of leather-soled shoes crossing the terrace, which jutted out from the other end of the walkway and was concealed from her view by a large conifer tree. She stopped short.

The shoes seemed to pause and she heard what sounded like the rasp of a match. Seconds later she smelled cigar smoke. Then the shoes were off again a little further away. She guessed from the sound of them that someone was descending the other stone steps to the lawn. She saw him clearly moments later. It was Brent, still fully dressed in the same clothes he had worn at dinner, smoke trailing behind him from the cigar in his mouth, as he crossed the lawn, heading diagonally towards the gap in the hedge leading to the helipad.

Her heart was at it again. She ignored its adrenalin-fuelled thudding and, after waiting a few seconds, she went in the same direction as he had taken, keeping close to the shadows bordering the tall hedge. Her mouth was as dry as a camel's armpit, as Charlie Woo might have put it. If Brent were to come back out through the gateway, she would meet him head-on.

But he didn't. Peering through the gap shortly afterwards, she saw the enclosure on the other side of the hedge was empty and the lights were on in the hangar, though the double doors were still closed. As she stood there, undecided as to whether or not to cross the bare, moonlit enclosure to the hangar, which would put her in full view of the building, the lights set into the helipad came on. They stayed on for a couple of minutes and then were abruptly switched off. It looked as though Brent had decided to test them out, and he had chosen to do it at night to avoid attracting unwanted attention. Notably from his nosy guest, Kate Lewis. But why? Was he preparing to do a bunk after sealing the deal with the Collector or was he just playing safe in case he needed to make a quick exit if something went wrong?

There was no way of knowing the answer to either question and she was still thinking about it all when the small door in the side of the hangar, through which she had entered the building with Brent the previous Monday, opened and Brent and what looked like Adam Crosby came out. Crosby turned to close the door again, bending as if to attach a padlock, then both men walked away from the hangar, striding quickly towards Kate.

She just had time to sprint into a narrow gap between the hedge and the artist's studio in the corner before they emerged through the gateway. They then stood there for a while talking, while Brent puffed on his cigar, gesticulating towards the end of the garden. She saw Crosby nod his head and heard him say something in a louder voice which she couldn't quite catch. Brent immediately silenced him with a quick flick of his hand and glanced around him cautiously before nodding towards the house, which was evidently Crosby's cue to go back there.

Kate expected Brent to go with him, but he didn't. Crouched uncomfortably behind the artist's studio, with bugs from the hedge all over her, she was forced to stay where she was. Brent seemed in no hurry to go anywhere either but stood by the gate, leisurely smoking his cigar and watching

Crosby's progress towards the garage block. Only when his man had disappeared through a side door into the building did he make a move, and then it was swift. Stubbing out his cigar on something in the gateway — Kate presumed one of the gateposts — he pocketed it. Then, swinging round, he strode directly to the door of the studio and Kate heard keys jangle, followed by the crack of a door being opened on stiff hinges.

Anxious to see what he was up to, Kate eased herself up into a standing position and crept very slowly along the rear wall of the building to the end where she remembered seeing a window on her previous modelling session. She found that a vertical blind had been closed across it, but quite carelessly and one corner had fouled against something — possibly a cupboard — which left a small gap through which she could peer.

Brent had switched on a thickly shaded spot-lamp. By its dim light, she could see that he was bent over pulling picture frames out from the far corner of the room and stacking them a few feet away. Why he was doing this in the middle of the night and had been careful to make sure Crosby had gone back to his apartment beforehand, was a mystery, and the answer was not forthcoming. After a time hauling canvasses from one place to another, he suddenly straightened up, glanced quickly around the studio, then left, closing and locking the door behind him. Kate waited a few minutes before peering round the front of the building. She saw him already halfway up the steps accessing the terrace and, as she watched, he stopped briefly to drain a glass left on the metal table before disappearing into the living room. Kate forced herself to stay put a few minutes more in case he re-emerged, but he didn't and her patience was soon rewarded when the light came on in a room upstairs, which she knew was his bedroom.

Stepping out of cover, she checked the door of the studio just to be sure.

But as she had assumed would be the case, it was locked and for the first time she noticed that it was no bog-standard

Yale or mortise lock. It was a no-nonsense, high-end, security cylinder lock. The only way someone could successfully break into the studio was via one of the very small windows, which, even with her slim figure, she would find difficult to manage and which she now suspected might be made of reinforced glass anyway. The only other option would be to literally tear the door off its hinges. Not something anyone could do without making just a "little bit" of noise!

It appeared that Brent was very protective of his artistic creations. Maybe they were worth something in the art world after all and he had paid a visit to his studio to sift through those he was about to put up for sale. She couldn't think of any other reason why he would go through them in the middle of the night, which still seemed a bit extreme, unless he had decided to do it because he was out checking the helipad anyway.

Then, with a dawning sense of shock, something else completely unrelated to his visit to the studio occurred to her. Going by his earlier sketch of her, he was obviously a very skilled artist and able to produce really lifelike portraits of his subjects, which sold well on the open market. That meant that in any portrait he painted of her she would be easily recognisable to anyone who knew her — like Hayden and half the police force in Somerset, for instance. Hell's bells! The portrait she had agreed to model for was to be a full nude study. Somehow she didn't think she was ready for total public exposure and the ridicule and embarrassment that would go with it, and Hayden certainly wouldn't be! If he was in the mood to forgive her when he finally learned the truth about what she had been up to behind his back, he wouldn't be if he had sight of that all-revealing portrait. It would put the kybosh on everything, including their marriage.

'Bloody hell! What have I done?' she breathed. To which question, the voice in her head responded immediately, *Yes, and how the bloody hell are you going to get out of it?*

But even as the torture in her brain magnified the more she dwelled on it, she was suddenly given something much more pressing to think about and she quickly shrank back behind the studio. A hooded figure dressed entirely in black, with a haversack on their back, had appeared from the passageway between the house and the garage block where she had been standing a short time before and was creeping stealthily along the edge of the lawn towards her, using the shadows cast by the tall hedge as cover. She had unexpected company.

CHAPTER 14

Kate pressed her body rigidly against the side of the building, concerned that the intruder may have seen her. But when, after a few minutes, there was no confrontation or challenge from them, she cautiously made her way back round to the front of the building. Only to find that they had disappeared.

She scanned the entire area, hedge to hedge, but there was no sign of anyone and the house was in total darkness. There was only one place they could have gone and she moved quickly to check it out. The gate to the helipad enclosure was wide open and she was just in time to see the figure step away from the big double doors at the front of the hangar and head down the side of the building from where Brent and Crosby had emerged earlier. She waited, focusing her gaze intently on the spot where she could see movement in the shadows. There was a sharp, metallic snapping sound and she saw the side door jerk open, then close. They were into the hangar.

Taking a chance on being spotted, she ran diagonally across the helipad and stopped on the corner of the building. For a moment she stood there, head on one side, eyes closed, listening.

There was a sound of movement inside the big steel shed. Scraping noises, like shoes on a gritty concrete surface.

Then a faint chinking noise, like metal against metal. She moved closer. The side door was ajar. She bent down and her hand brushed against something cold. She pulled out the torch she had brought with her and, risking the narrow, masked beam, she examined what she had found. It was a padlock still attached to a hasp. The whole thing had been ripped or levered off the door post it had been attached to. Someone had come properly equipped, that was plain, and now that same someone was up to something in the hangar. She had to find out what it was, even though her warning senses were screaming at her to "get out now".

The door made one squeak as she gently pulled it open and she became motionless immediately. But whatever the intruder was doing inside, they were obviously too wrapped up in the task to hear. She carefully lifted one foot over the raised sill, then the other, and stepped inside.

Moonlight streamed into the hangar through four large skylights in the roof, banishing the gloom to the extremities and in places just touching on the workbenches and other equipment she had noticed on her previous visit. The helicopter crouching there resembled some giant bug, the half of the split glass windshield that was closest to her reflecting the moonlight like a single malevolent eye. In one brief fantasy moment, she found herself half expecting to see the thing suddenly take off and whizz around the hangar in search of prey.

Silence. The chinking sound she had heard a couple of minutes ago had stopped. She remained perfectly still. Where had the intruder gone? When she had last visited the hangar, she hadn't seen any rooms leading off this one or any other exit doors either. The minutes dragged by and, although she was standing up, she could once more feel cramp stealing up her legs, as it had in Brent's bedroom the night before. She was about to move on, intending to keep close to the wall and the encircling shadows, when she heard a loud "ding" as if some tool or other implement had been dropped on the concrete floor. It came from the other side of the helicopter.

With a deep, trembling breath, she edged round the nose of the helicopter for a closer look, making a point of carefully lifting her feet with each step, a bit like Neil Armstrong on his moon landing all those decades ago. But she never got there. The cold hard object dug into her neck from behind before she had taken more than two or three steps.

'This is a suppressed Glock 17 automatic, sweetheart,' a harsh, rasping voice said close to her ear. 'You have five seconds to tell me why I shouldn't blow your brains out!'

* * *

Fear can do unpleasant things to the human body. Suffice it to say that one of those things is the involuntary release of waste fluids. Kate only just stopped herself from doing just that as she stood there rooted to the spot with shock.

'Nothing to say?' the voice went on, 'Then on your knees, little girl.'

'No!' Kate blurted, suddenly finding her voice. 'I-I'm no threat to you. I'm just Brent's guest.'

'I guess I know that. I saw you parading around the pool with no top on. His slut, are you? Keeping him entertained.'

'He-he asked me here to mod-model for him, that's all.'

Her captor said nothing for a few seconds, then asked, 'So what were you doing checking out the house last night and why are you wandering about out here tonight?'

Kate mentally clawed her mind free of the ice-cold fist that was gripping it and forced it into overdrive. She knew only too well that she was moments away from being sussed as an undercover copper, so it would have to be good.

'Press,' she lied, blurting out her reply. 'I'm doing an exposé on slave trafficking in London for *Time* magazine. This bastard is a key figure in it. I was posing as a model to worm my way into his confidence. I've been trying to find evidence of his involvement ever since.'

There was a hard laugh. 'A reporter, eh? So what evidence did you expect to find in a helicopter hangar?'

'Details of the machine to go with a future article. He-he uses the chopper to meet up with criminal contacts in Europe.'

Another long pause. 'Hm. So tell me, why should I not kill you?'

Kate tried to keep the desperation out of her voice. 'I can't stop you, but what will you gain from that? I haven't seen your face, I don't know who you are and, as I said before, I am no threat to you. I have no idea why you broke in here or what's behind all this, but as far as I'm concerned, you can do whatever you like to Brent. He's a pig and deserves anything that's coming to him.'

'An impassioned speech,' the other said, 'and you're lucky this time. The only reason I won't kill you is because your death, as you rightly say, is of no value to me, and the last thing I need is a police investigation into a murder on Brent's property or a newspaper investigation into your disappearance after Brent has dumped your body in a hole somewhere.'

The gun was removed, allowing Kate to breathe again.

'But keep your mouth shut about our little meeting. Tell Brent anything and I will come back for you. Now, don't turn around and, like the kid's hide and seek game, count very slowly to a hundred before you leave here.'

Kate was seriously shaken and she counted to two hundred before she finally plucked up the courage to walk out the door. She found the enclosure and the garden beyond it completely deserted and she got back to her room without further incident at just after two thirty.

Once there, she literally collapsed on her bed. It had been the night of all nights without a doubt. She was far from being a coward, as her record in the police would have shown, but the experience of having a Glock 17 pressed against her neck with the expectation of a skull-shattering bullet to follow was not something anyone would have found easy to come to terms with afterwards, however brave they were.

Recovery from her ordeal was a little slow in coming too. But with the help of a mug of strong black coffee from the makings provided on an incidental table in the corner of her room, she did get there in the end and it was only after she had undressed and lain back on the bed that she was able to reflect more objectively on all that had happened to her since leaving her room just two hours before. Not that any of it was of much use in helping her to come up with any answers, but instead, simply raised more questions.

Why had Brent decided to check out the helipad in the middle of the night? Why had he chosen to stop by on his way back to the house to sort through his canvasses? Why had the intruder broken into the helicopter hangar? What had they expected to find in there? The diamonds, maybe? But she couldn't see Brent choosing a hangar or a helicopter as a place in which to hide them. It would have been much too risky. In fact, none of it made any sense at all and there was only one thing she did know for certain. Despite the attempt by the intruder to disguise their voice, it was clear that the person holding that gun to Kate's head had been a woman!

* * *

Kate returned to the helicopter hangar. Why, she wasn't sure, but there had to be a reason. She pulled open the side door, as before, and crept back round to the nose of the helicopter. Then the hooded intruder was there again, the Glock in her hand swinging up to take aim, as she screamed at Kate, 'I warned you what I'd do.' Kate threw up her hand in a futile defensive reaction and saw the 9 mm shell leave the barrel in a crimson cloud, travelling at what looked like slow motion, as if something were trying to hold it back. She threw herself to one side to try and dodge the fatal round and fell heavily . . . on to the floor of her bedroom.

She had broken out of the nightmare and was lying there, shaking fitfully, and her pyjamas were soaked in perspiration. Relief that it had all been a dream should have been immediate, but it wasn't, because the sound which had obviously awakened her and become part of her nightmare was now repeated — the loud echoing crack of what she recognised from her early years on the police firearms team as the vicious discharge of a twelve-bore shotgun.

Gripping the edge of the bed and hauling herself up off the floor, she automatically glanced at the luminous dial of the watch on her wrist and saw that she had only been asleep about half an hour. Crossing to the window, she pulled back the blind and stared out into the moon-splashed walkway. It was deserted. But someone had fired that gun and the sound, she was sure, had come from the front of the house.

She was about to turn back into the room when she saw two figures walking slowly along the walkway from the direction of the terrace. One was Frank Delaney. She would have recognised his huge shape anywhere. The other one looked like the man she had seen guarding the gates, Jack Ferris. Delaney was carrying what she was positive was a sawn-off shotgun, held loosely in one hand, while he was using the other to help Ferris drag another person along between them, a person whose body seemed to be limp, with their head hanging down and their feet scraping along the ground behind them.

Kate felt sick. The hood and black clothing were unmistakable. It was the intruder from the helicopter hangar. That she was dead seemed very likely and she was being carried like hunters returning from a shoot in a forest might haul the corpse of a small deer. The sight was as unreal as it was horrifying and Kate half turned towards her bedroom door with the intention of racing out of the house to challenge them on what they had done. But she stopped herself just in time. She was no longer a police officer and was at that moment powerless to do anything about it, plus the fact that she had no illusions as to what Frank Delaney would do with that shotgun if she tried. Despite the enormity of the crime that had been committed, she reasoned that one close encounter with a deadly weapon was enough for one night.

As she came to that conclusion, the two thugs, obviously so absorbed in their task of dumping their "kill" somewhere that they were completely unaware they were being watched, disappeared from view in the direction of the passageway between the house and the garage block. Kate quickly pulled on her jeans and sweater over her pyjamas. It was absolutely essential that she saw where they were putting the body, so that she could lead Cole to it when the police raid finally happened.

But just as she stepped out on to the walkway, she was startled to see a light come on just before the louvre doors accessing the kitchen. She had anticipated that the pair would be carrying the body across the back lawn to bury it somewhere on the scrubland beyond the perimeter fence, but it looked like she was wrong. She could hear gruff voices talking none too quietly not too far away and she saw that the plain wooden door next to the louvre doors of the kitchen was half open and a light was showing inside.

Moving right up to it, she peered through the gap. She spotted a flight of wooden stairs dropping away in front of her and glimpsed part of a rack of what looked like wine bottles to the right of the stairs at the bottom. A cellar. She remembered Brent boasting to her about the collection of good wines he had in his cellar and this was obviously it.

Then she heard the familiar sound of heavy footsteps, and the light went out. The beam of a torch probed the stairs and she heard the clump of feet coming back up.

She just had time to slip through the unlocked louvre doors into the kitchen next to the cellar before Delaney and Ferris re-emerged and she heard the metallic snap of a key being turned in a lock.

Someone coughed up something and spat on the floor. 'Do you have to do that?' a voice she didn't recognise complained. Ferris, she guessed.

'I wouldn't if I didn't 'ave to,' Delaney's voice retorted. 'Nose all busted up inside from the ring, see.'

'We just going to leave her down there then?' Ferris went on, changing the subject.

'Till the boss 'as 'ad a little chat wiv her when she comes round, yeah,' Delaney said. ''E's too pissed at the moment.'

'Then what?'

'Then we find her a nice little plot out on the headland for 'er. She'll 'ave company soon anyways, I bet, when 'is nibs 'as done wiv that ovver bit o' tail too.'

'What if this one bleeds to death in the meantime, though?'

Delaney gave a throaty laugh. 'Like they says, if she dies, she dies, eh?'

He was still laughing at his own joke when he and Ferris walked away, but Kate certainly wasn't. It was clear that the person Delaney had referred to as "that other bit of tail" was her. So darling Jeremy planned to get rid of her once he had no more use for her, did he? Was that what had happened to his other models in the past, or was she favourite for the chop because she had got too close to him and knew too much about his setup? Instead of feeling frightened as a result of what she had learned, she felt angry and more determined than ever to bring him down.

Back in her room, she poured another coffee and thought about her next moves as she considered the latest things she had seen and heard.

So, the intruder had been caught and got herself shot, had she? Ferris had said she was bleeding, so she was obviously injured, but how badly Kate had no way of knowing.

At least she was not dead yet and she had been granted a temporary reprieve until Brent had interrogated her. So there was still time to save her from a bullet in the head. But how, that was the problem? Kate had already checked the cellar door and had found it securely locked after the departure of Delaney and Ferris, and she had no idea where the key was kept.

Then she had a brainwave. She had already deduced that the cellar was where Brent kept his wine and, while Delaney had walked off with the key, it stood to reason that it wouldn't be the only one. Apart from Brent himself, Crosby, in his waiting role, was bound to have a key and since the chef would need to have access to the wine in the cellar when preparing meals, Kate guessed he would have one too. The only question was, where did he keep it? If it was with his other keys on his person, Kate was stumped, but there was just a possibility that it could be hanging up somewhere in the kitchen and there was only one way to find out. She just hoped that this time she wouldn't be sticking her head above the parapet once too often.

CHAPTER 15

Kate found the key without difficulty. It was hanging up on a hook near the electric cooker in the kitchen alongside two others and it was helpfully carrying the label *Wine Cellar*. She was rather surprised that, with all the security Brent had set up around his house, he had been so lax with his keys. Especially with regard to his wine cellar, which from what she had seen and sampled at evening dinner, had to contain some pretty expensive varieties.

As it was, she was able to unlock the cellar door without difficulty, the torch she had brought with her lighting her way down the steep flight of stairs. She had noticed a light switch just inside the door at the top and there was another one at the bottom, but she had avoided switching either on because of the risk of attracting attention, even though she had closed and locked the door after her to be·on the safe side.

Her torch revealed a surprisingly large vault. Tall wall racks filled with red wine on each side, plus what she guessed were wine coolers occupying both corners of the far wall with a further rack of reds between them. A large table stood in the centre of the room with two bar stools on each side and a variety of equipment on top, no doubt there for wine-tasting purposes. The place smelled musty, but it seemed to be dry and well-ventilated, with steel grills fitted to the walls above the racks all the way along. In any other circumstance she would have been tempted to take a long, hard look at Brent's wine stock, but she resisted it. This was no time to hang about down here longer than was absolutely necessary.

In fact, it had already occurred to her that she shouldn't be poking her nose into this latest business at all. She was jeopardising the whole undercover operation and putting herself at greater risk than was required of her — and for what? To check on a dangerous criminal who had twice broken into the grounds of the house and, going by the Glock 17 she had been carrying, could be the professional assassin Cole had referred to, with a mandate to find the diamonds and kill Brent. But whatever the woman had done or was planning to do before she was shot, Kate couldn't simply leave her to her fate. Even though she was no longer a police officer, she had a duty as a human being to prevent someone's death if she could, regardless of other factors.

She found the woman without difficulty. The beam of the torch picked her out immediately. She was sitting on the floor, propped up against one of the steel legs of the table, all four of which were bolted to the floor. Her haversack had been dumped on the table top above her. Its straps had been left undone, some of its contents, including a pair of binoculars and a reel of sticky tape, spilling out on to the polished surface, with a black woollen balaclava lying beside it all. Her feet were thrust out in front of her and her hands tied together behind her back around the leg of the table with some sort of thick cord. She was dressed, as Kate remembered from the hangar, in skinny black trousers and a black hooded top, with the hood now pushed back off her head and trapped between her back and the table leg.

Kate thought she was probably in her mid-thirties with short, black hair, which appeared to have been recently cropped, and thin, well-moulded features. It was apparent that she had suffered a nasty injury to her left thigh from

Delaney's sawn-off. Her trousers were ripped open, exposing her leg, and someone, probably Delaney himself, had tied a piece of dirty looking cloth around the wound, which was already soaked through and leaking blood on to the floor. Kate formed the impression that she had at least escaped the full blast of the shotgun and no arteries had been punctured by the lethal pellets or she would have long since bled out completely. But she was plainly in a lot of pain. Her face was ghastly pale and her teeth were clenched in a tight grimace, the lips slightly parted, as if in a perverse expression of grim humour.

Her eyes, which seemed to glitter in the beam of the torch, followed Kate's approach intently and when Kate bent down to examine her wound, she released a short, grating laugh.

'Florence Nightingale to the rescue, is it?' she said.

'Shut it!' Kate snapped. 'I'm risking my neck here.'

'Then why do it?' the woman said ungratefully. 'I wouldn't if I were in your shoes. You're lucky I didn't blow your head off in that hangar.'

Kate ignored the comments and looked around her. 'I need something to cut those ties on your wrists with.'

'Sorry, I didn't bring my nail scissors with me.'

Kate glared at her. 'Comical cow, aren't you?' she said. 'I hope you're still laughing when they come back here and put a bullet in your head . . .'

At which point she broke off and turned quickly to look towards the stairs, extinguishing her torch at the same time. Footsteps were approaching along the walkway outside. Brent's thugs were returning, as she had dreaded. She stared wildly about her, scanning the walls with her torch, but the beam caught nothing but the glint of wine bottles. She was trapped. It was much too late to try and get out of the cellar before they arrived, yet at first sight, there appeared to be nowhere to hide.

It was then that she spotted the ladder. It was leaning against one of the racks and was obviously used to reach the topmost bottles. Above it she saw that there was a gap between the top of the rack and the roof. Just wide enough for her to climb into — at least she desperately hoped so, or she was dead.

She had reached the ladder when she heard the footsteps stop directly outside the cellar door. She was only a quarter of the way up before there was the loud metallic snap of the key turning in the lock. Halfway, and she heard the door swing open. Even as she reached the top, the cellar was flooded with light as someone pressed the switch. Several pairs of feet were clomping down the stairs as she hoisted herself up over the edge of the rack and wriggled her way in on her belly. A split second later she froze as she found herself looking down on Delaney's bald head.

It was then that Brent appeared, apparently the worse for wear, and wearing a dressing gown. He had obviously been roused from sleep following the shooting and the capture of the young woman. He stumbled a couple of times, then stood there for a moment beside Delaney, swaying slightly and staring down at his prisoner.

'Well, well, well,' he commented, his voice thick and only just coherent. 'So our intruder was nothing more than a stupid bloody woman. I knew someone would be coming after the stones, but I never expected a bit of skirt.'

He moved closer to the table and tipped out some more of the contents of the haversack.

'You certainly came prepared,' he commented. 'No fewer than two mobile phones, binoculars, rope, tape, even wire cutters. Very professional. So, who are you working for then?'

The woman said nothing. She just stared back at him with a sneer on her face.

'Boss asked you a question, bitch,' Delaney said and, moving at surprising speed, stepped past Brent and struck her hard across the face with the back of one hand. Kate had a ringside view and gritted her teeth in fury as the woman's nose burst open and blood spurted down her chest.

'Steady on, Frank,' Brent mocked. 'That's no way to treat a lady, and she's injured too. Can't you see her poor leg?'

He held out his hand and Delaney slapped a pistol into it. 'Glock 17?' Brent said softly, bending down in front of the woman and almost falling over in the process. 'Now that's a nasty weapon for a young filly like you to have in your possession. Meant for me once you found what you were looking for, was it?'

There was still no reply and he sighed.

'Well, I'll tell you what I think, shall I? Though it's only a theory. I think you were hired by the new *capo* on the block in good old Sicily. All fired up because I reneged on the deal Charlie Hooper had with his old man back in the day. But when I put a couple of bullets in Charlie's head as a goodbye present — what was it, twenty-five, twenty-seven years ago? — that deal became null and void and I didn't have the stones then anyway on account of that shitty little blagger, Lenny Thompson, running off with them. Now, having had a nice little chat with Lenny on his release from stir, the stones are back where they should be — with Jeremy — and he reserves the right to sell them to whoever he bloody well pleases. *Capiche?*

'Thing is, I would like to know for certain who hired you and whether there are any more like you in the pipeline. It would help me to sleep easier at night. So what about it?'

There was no answer, merely a look of defiance.

'It's your ticket to a longer life, sweetheart.'

The woman simply smirked at him.

He straightened up with Delaney's help.

'Okay, Frank, we'll leave it there for the moment. Resume again after breakfast tomorrow when I'm more myself, eh?' He studied the woman again with his head on one side, like some predatory bird. 'Enjoy your night's sleep, sweetheart, because tomorrow you'll have a busy day, and I wonder how you will fare when I get Frank here to chop off your fingers one by one until you tell me what I want to know. Think about it.'

Then he turned unsteadily and headed back towards the stairs with Frank in tow.

Shortly afterwards the light was extinguished, the door slammed shut and the key was turned in the lock.

Kate found getting down from the rack a lot more difficult than getting up on to it and she almost fell as she swung round and felt for the top of the ladder. When she got to the woman she saw that her nose was in pretty poor shape and that the blood was still pouring out of one nostril. She did her best to stop the flow by pinching her nostrils together, but she felt her flinch and utter an agonised groan under the pressure. Kate guessed her nose was fractured at the very least. After several minutes the haemorrhage had lessened to just a trickle and Kate was able to clean her up a little with some tissues she had in her own pocket. But she could do no more for her than that. The important thing now was to get her out of the cellar altogether. But how the hell was she going to do that without first having the means to cut the cords off her wrists and second to also avoid giving away the fact that outside help must have been involved in the rescue, which would inevitably mean the finger of suspicion being pointed at Kate Lewis.

The woman then answered the first part of the question for her.

'Check out the zipped pouch in the bottom of my haversack,' she said, sniffing blood back up into her nostril.

Kate did so and found a wicked-looking bowie knife in a sheath inside. It took her seconds to cut through the cords holding her. Then she watched the woman haul herself back on her feet, gripping the edge of the table for leverage, and stand there awkwardly, her teeth gritted against the renewed pain in her leg combined with the returning circulation.

'So, who are you?' Kate asked.

'You can call me Midnight.'

'What sort of a name is that?'

'It's the one my clients use to contact me. Now, cut the chat. I need out of here pronto.'

Kate shook her head, resigned to the fact that she wouldn't get anything else out of her.

'How on earth can you walk with your leg like that?' Kate exclaimed.

'I can walk,' the other replied. 'It's not as bad as it looks. Your man was a poor shot and a sawn-off is no good at a distance. Tried twice too. First blast missed. Second hit a tree. I just caught a few stray pellets.'

'But it's bad enough and you've lost a fair bit of blood. Where will you go?'

'I have somewhere safe not too far away. I just need to get back to the fence where I got in. Now, as you've helped me, I must reciprocate. It will be obvious to Brent and the others that I must have had help getting out of here and you are bound to be their first suspect.'

Kate nodded grimly. 'I've been thinking about that.'

For reply, the woman peeled back the left cuff of her hooded coat with her other hand and produced a razorblade with a triumphant smile, dropping it on the floor by the severed cords. 'Just something I keep for emergencies,' she explained. 'Trouble was, I couldn't get to it this time. Leave it where it is. They will assume I had it hidden somewhere on my person and the ugly bastard who did this to me will get the blame for not searching me properly.'

'They won't swallow that. You'd have to have been a contortionist to be able to use it with your hands bound behind your back.'

She shrugged. 'They will have no idea where I had it hidden, will they? Just a little puzzle for them to try and work out. But we'll have to take the chance. There's no other way.'

She turned and, packing the things back into the haversack that Brent had tipped out on to the table, she secured the straps and slipped the bag over her shoulders.

'As for the door,' she added, smiling weakly at Kate, 'help me up the stairs.'

Kate lent her an arm and together they slowly began the climb, with Kate expecting at every step to hear the sound of the key turning in the door lock as Brent or one of his henchmen returned to check on their prisoner. It didn't happen and at the top the woman pointed at the door. 'Unlock it,' she instructed.

So, this is where you hobble off into the night and leave me to take the rap, Kate thought. But she was wrong.

She made no effort to limp away. Instead, she placed the haversack on the wide top step by her feet, undid one of the straps and reached inside, producing a small pocket torch, masked like Kate's with black tape to reduce the width of the beam.

'Very cheap lock,' she said after peering at it. 'Now lock it again.'

Kate did so and watched her curiously as she delved into her haversack again and came up with a leather pouch, which she opened up in the light of the torch held between her teeth to reveal a set of strange looking steel tools, with black plastic handles and thin shanks fashioned into curious hooks, forks and probes. They were like the instruments used in a dentist's surgery. She smiled grimly, recognising them at once for what they were — lockpicks.

'Don't watch *me*, love,' the woman snapped, half opening the door and nodding Kate through. 'Relock the door and watch for bloody company.'

Kate quickly complied and she stood outside for several tense minutes, anxiously listening for the sound of approaching feet. If Brent or one of his men decided to come back to check on their prisoner, she had nowhere to go and it would all be over.

Sudden rustling and she jumped as an unearthly screech erupted from the climbers above her head. Then she breathed a sigh of relief as a shape as white as a ghost rose with a silent flap of large wings and disappeared into the night.

From inside the door, she heard metallic scraping noises as the woman worked on the lock with her lockpicks, obviously trying to find the best fit. She apparently tried several before she hit on the right one. But she evidently knew what she was doing and very soon afterwards Kate heard a series of clicks and saw the door swing open again.

The woman grinned at her, despite the pain she had to be feeling in her leg, and Kate saw her snap the picklock from one side to the other several times in the inside lock, until it snapped in two, with the top falling on the ground with a soft "ding" leaving the end jammed in the lock.

'That should convince them,' she said, returning her kit to the haversack and pulling it back on. 'Bit daft leaving all my kit in the same room as me anyway, wasn't it? Amateurs!'

She swung round unsteadily towards the archway, then nodded to Kate. 'Don't forget to return that key from wherever you got it before anyone notices,' she said. Then added, 'Thanks, copper, I owe you one.'

Kate started. 'Copper? What do you mean?'

A short unamused laugh. 'Well, that's what you are, isn't it? Do you think I'm stupid? I can smell one of you lot a mile off. But I won't tell if you don't.'

Then she was gone, limping through the archway, and merging with the shadows.

Kate made no effort to see which way she had gone. She was gone and that was all that mattered as far as she was concerned. She then quickly revisited the kitchen, replaced her key on its hook and went straight back to her room, where she propped herself on the edge of her bed, lost in thought. Her head was spinning. How the hell had the woman sussed her out for what she was? Was it that obvious? If so, could Brent have guessed too, and was he just playing with her like a cat with a mouse? It was a scary thought. But then she dismissed it out of hand. There was no way he would have let things carry on as they were if he'd known she was a plant. He couldn't afford to with the Collector about to pay him a visit. She just hoped the discarded razor blade on the floor of the cellar and the broken lockpick left in the cellar doorway would be enough to convince him that his prisoner had freed herself, but she would have to be very careful with him when he discovered his loss, very careful indeed.

It was then that her thoughts turned to what she had just done and she felt a new sense of shocked disbelief. She had actually assisted an offender to escape. An offender who was possibly a very dangerous assassin. The woman could well be wanted all over the world for past hits and would almost certainly try to take out Brent at the first opportunity. Okay, so Brent was a ruthless killer himself, but did that make his murder any the more justifiable than the murder of the people he had taken out? Morally, she wasn't sure, but without a doubt, there was no difference as far as the law was concerned.

So, should she not have intervened at all then? Should she have let Brent commit torture and another cold-blooded killing instead? Of course not, but her armchair critics would be sure to say in any future investigation that she could and should have alerted Cole, even if that had meant blowing her cover and wrecking the whole operation. After all, Brent and his cohorts could have been nailed for attempted murder, illegal use of a firearm and kidnapping at the very least, which would have put them all behind bars just the same. But it was easy to criticise after the event. She had had to make a spur of the moment decision in an effort to save the life of someone who had already been shot and could have been about to die. Surely that outweighed everything else? 'I bloody well hope Cole sees it that way,' she muttered as she undressed and climbed into bed, but somehow she didn't think so.

* * *

The woman who had caused Kate so much aggravation got through the new hole she had cut in Brent's wire fence earlier without being challenged and, due to sheer dogged determination, she made it back to the old Land Rover where she had parked it behind a hedge in a nearby field. Despite the agonising gunshot wounds to her thigh, which had sapped so much of her physical strength and energy, she managed to drive back to the house she had rented on the edge of the village. The place itself was an unremarkable grey stone building, probably a former farmhouse. It had three good-sized bedrooms and a typically large quarry-tiled kitchen and backed on to open countryside. It was in need of substantial renovation and had a musty, unlived-in smell about it, which was probably why she had managed to rent the property so cheaply. With three bedrooms, it was much too large a place for her, but she had chosen it specifically, not just because it was reasonably proximate to Brent's home, but exactly *because* it was so rundown and unremarkable. She had chosen the battered old Land Rover Defender, which she now parked round the back, for the same reason. She had learned very quickly in her dubious business that it wasn't wise to be flash. It was more sensible to blend into your surroundings, then you were less likely to attract attention.

As a former major in the British Army's intelligence corps, Lisa Heddon or Midnight, as she was known to underworld clients needing her services, had adopted this strategy in "theatres" all over the world while working undercover and it had usually paid off. What had not paid off for her was what had finished that career and turned her into the ruthless assassin she had become.

Ironically it had had nothing to do with soldiering. Instead, it had been her response to the unwanted advances of a drunken matelot from a British warship in the port of Marseilles. He had tried to force himself on her after following her out into an alleyway from a dockside pub where she had been gathering intelligence on the circulation of illegal narcotics within the service. The confrontation had led to the matelot pulling a knife on her and during the struggle he had fallen on it and fatally injured himself. Although she had pleaded self-defence, the army had taken a very dim view of the situation and after her appearance in a civilian court, where she had been tried for murder, but acquitted through lack of evidence, a court martial had followed, bringing about an ignominious end to her career.

Bitterness had set in and, after several unsuccessful attempts to straighten out her life, she had turned to the shadowy work she knew best, making use of the skills she had learned in the military to pursue another much less honourable career as a contract killer. The only slightly redeemable feature in the catalogue of cold-blooded murders she had so far carried out was the fact that all had been mob hits. None of her targets were ordinary citizens some other party simply wanted out of the way for reasons of financial gain, revenge, pure hatred or any of the other base motives that motivated degenerates in societies throughout the world. Heddon had made sure that the person she had been contracted to kill was embedded in the criminal underworld and therefore, to her mind, no loss to anyone. Hers was a curious morality, but it was one she found she could live with, if a little uneasily at times, and the bonus, of course, was that it paid top dollars too!

Once back in the relative safety of her temporary home, Heddon gulped down double the quantity of painkillers recommended. Then, stripping off her clothes in the shower, she examined the bloodied puncture marks in her thigh. Guessing she would now have a few more scars to go with those she was already carrying from the host of violent encounters she had suffered throughout her time in the army as well as in her present "profession".

She estimated that three pellets had embedded themselves in her leg and if she was going to avoid blood poisoning, she had no choice but to get them out. Seeing a doctor or paying a visit to the nearest hospital was obviously out of the question. They would want to know how she had sustained the wounds and were bound to inform the police. No, this was a job she would have to do herself and do it right now.

She had a comprehensive medical kit in her car for emergencies and she fetched it, together with some strong disinfectant she found in a kitchen cupboard. Pulling the curtains across her downstairs bedroom window and turning on the light, she dragged her bedside cabinet to the end of the bed. Then collecting an Anglepoise lamp from a small writing desk in the corner, she placed it on top of the cabinet, directing the light on to the edge of the bed where she was sitting.

Then came the moment of truth. She had treated herself on the battlefield more than once, but she knew the shotgun pellets would be deep and it would take all her courage and endurance to dig them out. Selecting a small steel probe and a pair of tweezers from her medical kit, she gritted her teeth until she heard them crack, then bent over and inserted the probe into the first hole . . .

CHAPTER 16

Angry shouts. Thudding feet. A door slamming back against a wall. Torches grazing the window of Kate's bedroom that overlooked the walkway. She shot up in bed with her heart almost doing pirouettes.

'Bloody idiots!' she heard Brent's voice yell. 'How the hell could this have happened?'

There was a gruff reply she couldn't catch and then the voices faded and she heard the sound of several pounding feet.

Glancing at her watch, she saw that it was just after six in the morning.

Throwing off the bedclothes, she padded to the window, at once struck by the coolness of the air after the previous day's heat, which only lowered her spirits and added to her trepidation even more. Peering through the slats of the blind, she was greeted by a grey misty light, but there was no sign of anyone. She didn't need to be told what the pandemonium had all been about. Brent had obviously just been told of the escape of his prisoner and he and his thugs were no doubt down in the cellar checking things out.

It was only a question of time before he began quizzing her, so she would have to be ready to withstand that perceptive stare. She didn't think it would happen immediately, though. She imagined he would want a search carried out first and she was right. A couple of minutes later he and his cohorts were back up to the walkway.

'Find her!' Brent shouted, his voice shaking with fury. 'She was bleeding. There's got to be a trail leading somewhere.'

She kept well away from her window. The last thing she needed was for him to see her guiltily peering out. But she realised that staying in her room while everything was going on outside would also be unwise. It would suggest she was hiding from scrutiny. What she had to do was to stick to her usual routine, as if nothing had happened. So she took a shower, pulled on her jeans and her sweater, and ventured out into the hallway, casting a quick glance up at the glass staircase as she passed by. The living room was deserted and, though breakfast was laid, Brent was not sitting in his usual place at the steel table.

The morning was even more gloomy than she had realised and the garden in front of her was swallowed up by vaporous clouds. There wasn't a sound to disturb the heavy stillness, which the mist seemed to have brought with it. She found that quite strange after the hullabaloo that had woken her up, but guessed Brent and his crew were still out looking for their escaped prisoner. That was okay by her. It gave her time to prepare herself for the inevitable face-to-face interrogation by Brent. But she nevertheless felt uneasy, as she pulled out her usual chair and sat down at the table, selecting a croissant from a large plate of them and pouring herself a glass of orange juice from a jug. She remained there for several minutes, sipping the juice and half-heartedly nibbling the croissant, as she watched the sun's determined efforts to burn its way through the mist. But no one appeared and she was on the point of returning to her room when Alfredo, the chef, arrived with a plate of bacon and eggs, which he set before her with a smile.

'Meester Lutterall, he busy for now,' he explained. 'He say he hope you not bored and to, er, relax, *si*? Sun come up soon and he see you later.'

She nodded. 'I'll be quite all right, Alfredo,' she replied. 'I'll probably read in my room.'

He raised his eyebrows. 'Read in room? But is soon beautiful day? Go swim. Drink. Lay in sun, eh?'

She smiled back. 'Maybe later,' she replied. 'When that sun actually comes out.'

'When it come out?' The little man looked astonished. Then simply raised both hands in a gesture of puzzlement and turned on his heel, back to his kitchen, muttering away to himself in his native tongue at the same time.

Kate was not in the mood for bacon and eggs, but she tucked into them to show willing, nevertheless; she had no wish to slight Alfredo and make an enemy of him. She was finishing the last mouthful when Brent finally arrived.

'Ah,' he said, pulling out his usual chair and sitting down, 'you are up then? Good night's sleep?'

He had reached for the coffee pot and his question was a little too casual, as if he was simply making polite conversation. Kate heard warning bells jangle in her head.

'Till this morning,' she said, forcing a laugh, 'when it sounded as if all hell had broken loose.'

He set the coffee pot back on the table without pouring any into his cup. He looked irritated, which was not surprising, as the coffee had to be cold by now.

'Yes, sorry about that,' he replied. 'Boys thought they had spotted that damned burglar in the grounds again. False alarm, though, it seems.'

He sat back with a nod of appreciation as Alfredo materialised at his elbow with a fresh pot of coffee and filled his cup.

'So,' he went on, as the little man tactfully withdrew, 'no bad dreams then?'

She shrugged. 'Slept like a log, as usual,' she lied.

His gaze was now fixed on her face as he sipped his coffee with both hands wrapped around the cup. 'No funny noises in the night?'

'Oh, I think I heard a screech owl at one point, but I soon drifted off again.'

He raised an eyebrow. 'A screech owl? That's very precise.'

She laughed again, conscious of the fact that there was a nervous edge to it. 'Oh, I grew up in the country. Heard a lot of owls in the woods there.'

'Indeed, so what is the difference between a screech owl and an ordinary owl? I am intrigued.'

Kate wasn't and inwardly she cursed her stupidity for trying to be clever. 'No idea,' she replied truthfully. 'As a child, I always called them that, but I suppose they all screech.'

He said nothing for a moment, then suddenly came in with the question he had no doubt been waiting to ask all the time.

'You didn't hear the sound of a shotgun at all?'

A skilled interrogator herself, Kate was used to being the person who asked the questions, but now on the receiving end, she found herself sadly lacking. As her brain fumbled for the right answer, she desperately tried to hold back the nervous swallow that was developing in her throat, knowing full well from her own experience that the jerk of a subject's Adam's apple was seen as one of the worst telltale signs of their guilt. How she managed it was a mystery even to herself, but seemingly through sheer willpower she resisted the urge to swallow and kept her cool, saying instead, 'Well, something woke me once in the early hours, I think, but I don't know what it was. A shotgun, you say? What? In the grounds here?'

A pause as he sipped more of his coffee. Then he said, 'Probably a poacher out in the fields. But I would have thought a country girl like you would have known what a shotgun sounded like.'

'I was in a deep sleep, so it probably didn't really register.'

'Then you didn't actually sleep like a log, as you said?'

'Well, I did, apart from being woken up by what you said was a twelve-bore.'

'I didn't say what bore it was. How do you know it was a twelve-bore? It could have been a four-ten.'

She took the bull by the horns and manufactured a frown. 'Sorry, but am I being given the third degree for some reason?'

He smiled again. 'I'm so sorry, I didn't mean to do that. I'm such a pedant. It's the devil in me. Please ignore my silly nonsense. The mist is clearing, the sun is nearly out, so let's enjoy the day. How about a swim? Then we can get on with your portrait. I'm really looking forward to that.'

Kate felt her stomach churn. *I'm bloody not*, she mused, but she returned his smile with a weak one of her own. 'A swim would be nice,' she prevaricated, keen to agree to anything that would put off the dreaded nude pose a bit longer.

He selected a croissant and cut it open. 'Excellent. Then shall we say we will meet at the pool in half an hour, eh?'

She nodded and she was about to climb to her feet, when Crosby appeared silently from the living room and whispered something in his ear.

His smile was immediately replaced by a look of pure malice. 'I understand our friendly policeman, PC Rheon, has called to see me,' he said, forcing his smile back with difficulty. 'For some reason he has asked to see us both.'

As Kate settled back in her chair again, Crosby went inside and a few minutes later he returned with Rheon in tow.

'Ah, PC Rheon,' Brent said, once again charm itself. 'To what do we owe this pleasure?'

It was a hammy, sarcastic invitation and Kate guessed it was intended as such, but the sarcasm seemed to pass right over Rheon's head, as he stood there, staring at them both, with his peaked cap in one hand.

'Do you own a shotgun, sir?' he asked.

Brent looked astonished. 'A shotgun? Good heavens, what on earth would I want with one of those?'

'What about your staff? Any of them own one?'

'I don't think anyone here has a licence. Would you like a cup of coffee, Officer?'

Rheon shook his head. 'No, thank you, sir. The thing is, one of your near neighbours reported hearing two blasts from a shotgun in the early hours of this morning and they reported it to our control room.'

Brent's face registered a look of bemusement. 'Can't help you, I'm afraid, Constable. It couldn't have come from my property. Probably a poacher out in the fields somewhere.'

'The lady was adamant the sound came from Smuggler's Reach. Quite worried about it, she was.'

He grunted and turned slightly to look at Kate. 'Did you hear anything like that, Mrs Lewis?' he asked.

'I'm sure Kate would have said if she'd heard anything,' Brent interjected before Kate could reply.

That seemed to annoy Rheon — as it would have done Kate if she had been in his shoes.

'I'm sure Mrs Lewis can answer for herself,' Rheon snapped.

'The answer is no, Constable,' Kate replied. 'I was fast asleep all night.'

Rheon grunted and frowned, unconvinced. 'Do you mind if I take a look around, Mr Lutterall?' he asked.

Brent's laugh was hard and without a hint of amusement. 'What would you be looking for, PC Rheon?' he asked. 'A body perhaps? No, I'm sorry, that is out of the question. I have nothing to hide here, but I think you are taking things to extremes.'

'If you have nothing to hide, why are you refusing?'

Brent's stare was now hawkish. 'Unless you have a warrant, Mr Rheon,' he said, 'the answer is an emphatic no. Now I think this conversation is over and I would like you to leave.'

Rheon glared at him, his mouth clamping shut. Then, when Crosby appeared behind him, as if by magic, he turned back towards the living room. But the next instant he swung round to face Brent again and pointed a finger at him. 'Something damned funny is going on at this house,' he said, 'and this isn't the last time you'll be hearing from me, Mr Lutterall.'

'Well now, that will give us all something to look forward to,' Brent replied with a sneer.

'And you, little missy,' Rheon said to Kate, 'I don't know what you're mixed up in here, but I'll find out, you can bet on it.'

Then brushing past Crosby, almost pushing him out of the way, he stormed back through the French doors into the living room and shortly afterwards there was the sound of a car pulling away with a swirl of gravel.

'Sorry about that, Kate,' Brent said. 'Most unpleasant. I'm afraid Mr Rheon is getting to be a bit of a nuisance . . . Now, why don't you go and get your swimming costume on and we'll have a mid-morning drink by the pool?'

* * *

Kate was relieved to get back to her room. She had found Brent's interrogation more than a little stressful and the arrival of Geraint Rheon had only added to it. She was not relishing a further awkward conversation about her own misdemeanours with Harry Cole either, but she knew she couldn't delay ringing him any longer. As usual, she was put through to him immediately and he went strangely silent when she briefed him on the latest events, this time remembering to turn on the shower again — for all the good she thought that really did.

'You should have contacted me immediately,' he said quietly.

She nodded, even though he couldn't see her. 'I know,' she said, 'but everything happened so quickly and I had to make my mind up on the hoof.'

'Do you know who the woman was?'

'She was hardly going to tell me that, was she? She said to call her Midnight. But she seemed to be a professional. As I told you, she was carrying a Glock 17 originally and she looked like she knew how to use it. She also appeared to have everything in her haversack someone in her profession would need, including the lockpicks.'

'Midnight, eh? Did she say who hired her?'

'We didn't really have time for lengthy discussions.'

He exhaled sharply. Mentally Kate could almost feel the coldness of his breath. 'Well, there's nothing we can do about her now. She's out there somewhere and, hopefully, too injured to do anything else. But I shall have to speak to Mr Norris about what we do next. According to your last info, the rendezvous with the Collector is only a day away and I want us to be there the very moment the stones change hands.'

'What are we going to do about PC Rheon? He could be a problem if he takes it into his head to barge into the place again in the middle of everything.'

There was a thoughtful grunt. 'We'll just have to keep our eyes on him. If we did anything else, it could only make him even more of a pain.'

'And Hayden? Any news on him?'

A rasping chuckle. 'What, good old Hayden? Seems he's going to be chucked out of the nick today and, from what I've heard, he's so embarrassed about his night in the pokey that he's unlikely to stray from behind the curtains of the bungalow for a few days, which suits us admirably.'

She made a face, but said nothing more on the subject. 'And me? What do you want me to do now?'

'I think you've probably done enough already,' he said sarcastically. 'Just keep your head down and your eyes and ears wide open, and don't go rescuing anyone else. I can't ring you on future plans this end, as I won't know who could be listening, so I suggest you make a point of calling me again tonight, by which time Mr Norris and I should have something organised.'

He emitted another short laugh. 'Oh, by the way, how's the modelling going?'

'Sod off!' she replied.

* * *

Lisa Heddon came round for the second time and groggily pulled herself up on to the bed from the floor where she had passed out, which, according to her watch, had been over an hour ago. There was a large pool of blood soaking into the frayed, patched carpet where she had collapsed and blood had soaked through the duvet on the bed too. But she allowed herself a weak smile. The cereal dish she had borrowed from the kitchen contained three small, spherical lead pellets and as far as she could tell, that was the lot. Digging them out of her leg had been sheer agony, and one had been a lot deeper than the rest and had caused her the most pain. With the amount of blood that was there, it looked like a transfusion was imminently essential, but she was not about to panic. She knew from past experience that blood loss often looked worse than it actually was because of the way it spread. At least none of the pellets had pierced an artery, so she could be grateful for that. By rights, the wounds needed stitching, but that was out of the question. Instead, after cleaning them with strong disinfectant, she applied special wound closure strips, which were not really intended for the kind of injuries she had sustained, but they would do until she could get proper medical help from the bent physician she had used before in Manchester. At least they helped to reduce the leaks from the nasty little holes boring into her flesh and the bandage she wound round her leg afterwards completed the job to her satisfaction.

Finally, she treated herself to a quadruple malt whisky and climbed in under the soiled duvet for a much-needed rest. She hadn't found the diamonds yet, but she had no intention of reneging on her contract, despite what had happened to her. After all, as with any business, she had a reputation to maintain. So, if Jeremy Brent thought he had frightened her off and that she was out of the picture now, he had a big, bad shock coming to him. With that thought in her head, and a couple of doses of a powerful sedative from her medical kit inside her, she went straight off to sleep.

CHAPTER 17

Kate didn't feel embarrassed anymore. Brent had already had an eyeful of her and she was more or less resigned to giving him the whole package in his studio later on. For the present, she sat on the edge of the swimming pool in her borrowed bikini, a G & T in her hand, courtesy of Adam Crosby on behalf of a still absent Brent, who had sent word that he had last-minute business to attend to but would join her when he could.

As she sat there, the hot sun now out with a vengeance and roasting her back, she found her thoughts focusing on Hayden and the state he must be in after being arrested and dumped in a cell for the night. He had made no attempt to ring her on her mobile and she wasn't surprised. Knowing him so well, she guessed he would be in one of his self-pitying sulks, angry at the world in general and at her in particular. She couldn't blame him either. She had treated him abysmally, even if she had kidded herself it was for the right reasons. Why should he trust her ever again? She wouldn't if the situation had been reversed.

Suddenly feeling the telltale prickling of her skin from the sun, she turned in another direction. She had enough problems at the moment. Sunstroke was the last thing she needed. In an effort to cool off, she put her glass down and, going to the edge of the pool, opted to lower herself gently into the still fairly cold water rather than diving in after her last wardrobe malfunction. She swam to the end of the pool and was standing up for a second to adjust her bikini top when she caught sight of movement in the tall hedge bordering the edge of the pool, as if someone were on the other side and trying to part the close-knit branches to peer through.

She strode across to the hedge, as the branches abruptly closed up, and jerked them apart again. She came face to face with none other than PC Geraint Rheon.

'Well, well, *Officer*,' she sneered, 'had a good enough look, have you? Funny, I never pictured you as a peeping Tom.'

He made no effort to back away, but glared at her angrily, his face reddening. 'I'm not interested in watching you prance about half naked, Mrs Lewis,' he threw back at her. 'But I *am* interested in what is going on at this house, as I said a short time ago. I'm sure it is connected with the attempted break-in at your cottage and the torching of that Met police officer in the caravan, and I also believe you're mixed up in it somehow.'

'Mixed up in what exactly?'

He gave a self-satisfied smirk. 'I'm not sure yet. But to start with, you don't strike me as the type to associate with the likes of Graham Lutterall and the rest of his dodgy-looking crew, like that thug of a chauffeur.'

'Thug? That's almost slanderous. I can't see anything wrong with any of them.'

'Can't you? Then you're either a liar or are totally naïve. I can smell a villain a mile off, Mrs Lewis, and this lot are definitely in that category. But it's funny how I end up being blocked by the powers that be and told to keep my nose out of things every time I try to make any inquiries. Why do you think that is?'

'No idea. I suspect that you may be suffering from some kind of paranoia.'

'Is that so? Well maybe I am and maybe I'm not. But there's a bad smell attached to this house, and the way my superiors are so keen on stifling any inquiries I want to make suggests that someone in high places is particularly keen on keeping everything under wraps — for whatever dubious reason that might be.'

Kate felt her stomach muscles tighten again. His barely concealed inference that some sort of criminal conspiracy involving the hierarchy of his own force might be at play was one suspicion she had not expected him to arrive at and it threw her for a moment. If pursued by him, that line had the potential for driving a giant wrecking ball through the whole undercover operation, but if she were to dismiss the idea too strongly, it could suggest by implication that she was being overly defensive because she herself knew there really was something in what he had alleged, which could be equally destructive.

In the end, meeting his gaze as steadily as she could, she shrugged and said, 'And I suppose the Pope is an alien from Mars?'

What Rheon's response to that might have been, had he been given the chance to answer, will never be known, because Kate let the branches of the hedge spring back into place the second the drawling voice spoke from immediately behind her.

'Talking to yourself then, Kate?'

She turned quickly and forced a smile at Brent, who was standing a few feet away, clad in a pair of blue swimming trunks.

'Sorry, Graham,' she blurted, thinking on her feet, 'you must reckon I'm potty. But it was such a lovely little robin and so tame too. I think he must have a nest in the hedge.'

He walked past her and, pulling back some of the branches, peered into the hedge, as she had done.

Then he turned back to her with a shrug. 'No robin there now, it seems. Maybe he only talks to pretty young women in string bikinis? What were the pair of you talking about?'

Kate gave an uneasy, self-conscious laugh. 'Oh, you know, bird talk. Tweet-tweet and all that.'

Her attempt at humour failed to elicit a like-minded response. There was no reciprocating smile and he said nothing at first, just stared at her thoughtfully for a second or two. Then he simply waved a hand towards the two canvas chairs standing on the edge of the pool.

'Let's sit for a few minutes, shall we?' he said. 'Adam should be out with the champers shortly.' He frowned. 'And I think you should cover up a bit now, as you seem to have caught a little too much sun. We don't want that beautiful ivory skin to be damaged just as I am about to paint your portrait, do we?'

* * *

Kate sat on the edge of the bed in her room for a long time, going over and over in her mind what had happened by the pool. Brent had not raised the issue of her so-called chat with the robin again, but she sensed he had not been convinced by her explanation. Had he seen more than he had let on? Was he fully aware of the fact that Geraint Rheon had been on the other side of the hedge at the time? What if Jack Ferris, the gateman, had spotted the policeman on one of the cameras, peering through the hedge, and had passed on the information to his boss? Brent had received a call on his mobile soon after their champagne had been brought to the pool by Crosby and, whether she had imagined it or not, she thought Brent had thrown a keen glance in her direction as he'd listened to the voice at the other end. Following the call, his demeanour had changed. Prior to it, the conversation had been very casual, covering topics on the subject of art, music and fine wine, but then he had suddenly become more focused and interrogative, quizzing her on her background. How long she'd been married. How she had met Hayden. Where she had lived in Somerset before coming to Wales. What her previous job had been. Why she had chosen to move to Pembrokeshire. What the crime novel she had said she was writing was all about.

The quizzing had continued over lunch on the terrace, though in a more subtle way, as if he had been trying to trip her up, and she was conscious of the fact that she had hardly touched her food or her wine as a result, prompting him to ask her if she was unwell and suggesting a lie down, out of the heat of the day, might be a sensible idea before the portrait sitting at three, a suggestion she had seized upon with barely controlled relief.

She had thought she had given a good account of herself, but the mere fact that he had delved so deeply into things so soon after the episode with Rheon had started the alarm bells jangling in her head again. Not for the first time, she felt that time was running out for her and it would only take one further slip-up to give the whole game away and bring everything crashing down.

Glancing at her watch, she saw that it was a quarter to three. The butterflies in her stomach had already turned into full-size birds at the prospect of the rapidly approaching sitting, but she had no choice but to do what Brent had demanded. To make an excuse of a stomach upset or a headache would be the worst thing she could do at a time when Brent's doubts about her could be at a critical point.

Reluctantly she stripped and donned a towelling robe hanging on a hook in the ensuite bathroom. Then, slipping on a pair of sandals, she left the room and headed along the hallway towards the living room and the terrace. It was time and she felt sick!

* * *

Kate didn't make it to the studio. Brent was waiting for her in the living room. He was standing by the French doors and his stare had a hostile look about it. Her heart sank.

'Ah, Mrs Lewis,' he said with deliberate formality. 'Sit down, would you?'

She adopted a puzzled frown, which was not wholly manufactured, and propped herself on one of the armchairs.

'Something wrong, Graham?' she asked, conscious of an uneasy feeling beginning to develop. 'I was just on my way to your studio for my sitting.'

'That will have to wait,' he said tersely. 'Something quite concerning has just come to my notice.'

She tried to hide her fears with an offhand shrug. 'Concerning?' she echoed. 'To do with me?'

'Have I not been good to you?' he went on. 'I've welcomed you into my home, following your ruck with your husband, put you up in a guest room and shown you every courtesy, including unstinting hospitality.'

Kate couldn't hold back the swallow this time. 'Absolutely,' she agreed. 'You've been brilliant.'

'Then why have you chosen to betray my trust?'

'I-I'm sorry, I don't understand.'

'You must be aware that CCTV cameras have been installed around the rear garden as well as around the front. Jack Ferris advised me while we were at the pool this afternoon that he had picked up Constable Geraint Rheon on one of the cameras, peering through the boundary hedge from the field next door.'

Kate forced herself to stare him out. 'So, what has that got to do with me?' she asked, desperately hoping that the extent of the camera's focus was confined to the external side of the hedge and that it hadn't caught her in shot.

'I would have thought that was obvious,' Brent said. 'That wasn't some stupid robin you were talking to, was it? You were actually having a conversation with Rheon, weren't you? What I want to know is, what was it about? Me? This house? What?'

Kate went for broke. 'That's not true,' she lied. 'I had no idea Rheon was even there. Why would I want to talk to that man at all? He hasn't exactly been very sympathetic towards me since my break-in. In fact, he's become a bit of a nuisance.'

His eyes narrowed and he considered her answer for a few seconds. The pause gave Kate fresh hope. If he had had concrete evidence of her conversation with Rheon, surely he would have immediately said so?

'Listen,' she went on, deliberately sharpening her tone, 'I have nothing on under this robe and I'm getting quite cold sitting here. Do you want me to model for you or not?'

The moment of truth. Kate waited, her mouth once more drying up with the suspense. Then abruptly his face broke into a watery smile.

'I apologise if I have upset you,' he said, apparently not entirely satisfied with her reply but lacking any evidence to dispute what she had said, 'but you must admit, it was rather coincidental that the policeman was peering through the hedge at the same time as you were chatting to your, ah . . . blackbird, wasn't it?'

'No, Graham, it was a robin, not a blackbird.'

'Ah yes, a robin. Nice little fellows, aren't they? Anyway, let's forget this unfortunate business and adjourn to my studio without wasting any more time. Not still cold, are you?'

'No, I'm fine,' she said, thinking ruefully, *But I'm likely to be a damned sight colder in a minute or two.*

* * *

After having her cover almost compromised by Geraint Rheon, Kate was so relieved to have avoided a calamity — at least for the present — that for the first time since Brent had asked her to pose for him, doing the unthinkable seemed like no big deal. She surprised herself when they got to the studio by slipping out of her robe with little hesitation, returning his devouring gaze with a thin, cynical smile that registered more than a trace of contempt. He appeared not to notice, however, and instead instructed her to lie full length on her side, facing him, on a worn chaise longue he pulled out from a corner.

'Excellent!' he commented. 'Titian would have been beside himself to have had you as the model for his *Venus of Urbino.*'

Kate frowned, casting her mind back to her school days and the art classes she had attended with that creepy little teacher, Denis Moreton. He'd had an unhealthy fixation about nude art and she well remembered the painting Brent had referred to from one of Moreton's art books. Resenting Brent's air of superiority towards someone he obviously regarded as nothing more than an empty-headed bimbo, she couldn't resist a kickback.

'Thank you for the compliment,' she said, 'but somehow I don't think a garden shed, even in as beautiful a setting as this, would compare with Titian's renaissance palace as a backdrop.'

He threw her a curious glance. 'Wow! So, you know your art then?' he replied. 'I have to say, I'm impressed.'

Don't be, she thought, *it's the only painting I remember from those art classes, simply because it had been creepy Moreton's favourite.*

'I know a lot of things,' she said, then abruptly clamped her mouth shut as she saw his eyes narrow again, inwardly kicking herself for her own stupid arrogance in trying to rub his nose in it.

'I'm beginning to realise that only too well,' he said. 'You are something of an enigma, Kate Lewis, and I just hope I haven't got hold of a scorpion by the tail . . .'

The portrait sitting lasted a good three hours, with two breaks in between to allow Kate to ease her cramped muscles. On each occasion Brent provided her with a glass of white wine and petit fours, delivered, as usual, by the soft-footed Adam Crosby. Kate made sure she had pulled on her robe before Crosby put in an appearance. But on his second visit she sensed the man's lazy, blue eyes sliding towards her and lingering just a little bit more than was absolutely necessary. She had never liked the man. There was something weird about him, just like Denis Moreton. Something almost feline in the way he suddenly appeared on those soft-soled shoes of his, without a sound, and withdrew in much the same way. That last sly look he had given her this time really bothered her. What could have been behind it? Was it just the usual man thing? A horny desire for an attractive young woman, perhaps, after seeing this one half naked in the pool? Hardly, if as Cole had claimed, he was gay. In which case, could it have been her imagination or did it have more sinister connotations? Was Crosby in possession of information about her that he had yet to pass on to Brent and was relishing the prospect of telling him when the portrait sitting was over for the day? Had her cover already been blown and was she about to suffer the consequences?

Her uneasiness only increased the longer she lay there on the chaise longue, until she could hardly contain herself. But then something happened to take her mind off what she could be facing in the next hour or so and forced her to concentrate on what was happening to her in the present.

And what happened came almost as much of a shock. Brent had become increasingly restless after Crosby had left, saying little and throwing quick, intense glances at her over the top of his easel. Finally, he came round from behind the easel and said, 'I think your long auburn hair would look better pulled around to the front.'

Before she could comment, he went behind the chaise longue and told her to lean forward. She did so and the next instant she felt his hands tug on her hair, which had become trapped between the back of the chaise longue and her body, lifting it over her shoulder and across her chest. In doing so, his hand brushed over her left breast, lingering over the nipple in the process, and she felt his breath on the back of her neck.

'*No!*' she shouted and erupted from the chaise longue so quickly that her head caught him on the side of his face, sending him stumbling backwards. There was a loud tearing sound as he crashed into the wall and, turning on him furiously, she saw that, in trying to regain his balance, he had put his foot through the canvas of one of his smaller nude paintings, ripping it open.

'You stupid bloody bitch!' he snarled and there was real venom in his eyes now. 'Look what you've done.'

'What *I've* done?' she said breathlessly. 'I thought you said if I modelled for you, it would be just a business arrangement and nothing more? So what was all that about?'

She had snatched her robe from the floor and was angrily pulling it on. As she did so, her gaze strayed to the ruined framed portrait, which had been standing in front of several others stacked against the wall. It was only about eighteen inches square and mounted in a thick block frame, designed to be exhibited on a free-standing basis rather than wall-hung. Not only was there a long tear in the canvas, but the corner of the frame had split open and, even from where she stood, she could see that there was something protruding from it. She bent down to have a closer look and saw that it appeared to be a small package, wrapped in some sort of black sticky tape. But she never got the chance to examine it further. Even as she bent down, Brent literally cannoned into her, sending her sprawling to the floor on her back.

'Leave it!' he shouted, all colour seeming to have drained from his face. 'You've done enough damage.'

Shaking from the experience, Kate rolled over on to her knees and levered herself up off the floor with both hands. There were tears of shock in her eyes as she pulled her robe around her and tied the belt securely. Then, without giving him another glance, she threw the studio door open and ran back barefoot across the lawn to the house.

When she got to her room, she sat on the edge of her bed, taking deep, controlled breaths for several seconds to calm herself down. Her tears had been genuine. Brent's lingering touch on her body had certainly upset her and his unprecedented violence in response to her reaction had given her quite a fright. But it had all been worth it and, as she quickly dried her eyes with the sleeve of her robe, she could not resist a grim smile of satisfaction. Through his own lack of self-control, Brent had unwittingly revealed the answer to the very question that had been plaguing her ever since she had arrived at Smuggler's Reach. The small package she had spotted protruding from the broken picture frame, and his violent reaction to her curiosity in it, had been a dead giveaway. Instinctively, she knew she had found where he had hidden the diamonds. The only frustrating thing was that there was nothing much she could do about it and now he would simply find somewhere else to hide them. Nevertheless, she quickly called Cole and passed on the information.

'Good work,' he said. 'So at least we can now assume he does have the stones. But do you think he knew you saw the package?'

Kate gave a short cynical laugh. 'I expect I'll find out if he did pretty damn soon,' she replied. 'Hopefully, he won't think it meant anything to me if he still sees me as a dumb bit of skirt.'

'And if he doesn't?'

'Then I'm in the shit big time!'

'Do you want us to pull you off? Is that it?'

'What and miss all the fun? Don't be silly.'

'Well. I've spoken to Mr Norris and everything is ready for the big day tomorrow. And this will be the difficult bit for you. We need to know when the Collector arrives and the diamonds are produced for inspection. This part is crucial for us to make any prosecution stick. So, you need to be on the ball.'

'Aren't I always?' she retorted and she was the one who cut off this time, and for one very good reason. Brent's voice was calling to her through her bedroom door.

CHAPTER 18

Brent's smile was back with a vengeance, and he shook his head regretfully. 'Kate, I'm so sorry. I don't know what came over me. I behaved like a cretin.'

'Yes, you did,' she agreed, 'and you really frightened me.'

He sat on the bed beside her and must have seen her flinch and pull away from him slightly, but he said nothing about it and instead, did his best to placate her.

'I feel awful about it,' he went on, 'you must believe me. But you have such a beautiful body and I just got carried away.'

Kate wanted to throw up at the obsequious, insincere compliment, but let him carry on.

'The thing is, I have been without a partner for so long and your presence here has made me realise just how much I have missed the company of an intelligent, beautiful woman.'

She dipped her head just in case the contempt welling up inside her was evident in her expression. Then, desperate to suss out whether or not he knew she had spotted the package in the broken picture frame, she risked provoking another interrogation from him by actually highlighting the issue. 'Even if I accept that,' she said, 'it still doesn't excuse the way you turned on me when that picture was damaged and knocked me over. It was because of what you did that it happened and it wasn't my fault that you put your foot through the thing. I only bent down to look at it to see the extent of the damage and you behaved like a madman.'

He listened, nodding quietly, then held up both hands in a deprecating gesture.

'What can I say? The fact is that that particular canvas had a very special significance for me. You see, the young model in question died in a nasty cliff accident shortly after she had finished her last sitting. All so dreadfully tragic.'

I bet it was, Kate thought to herself. *Did you get good old Frank to do the business for you because you had forced yourself on her and she needed to be shut up?*

He sighed. 'But what is done cannot be undone. The damage to the portrait is irreparable and it will have to be thrown away, but I hold myself totally responsible for what happened and I don't attribute any blame whatsoever to you.' He stood up. 'Now, can we put the whole sorry affair behind us and carry on as before? I promise that there will be absolutely no repeat of my previous bad behaviour.'

The manner in which he brought the conversation to such an abrupt close, without any reference to the package, suggested he was not aware that Kate had seen it and she felt an immediate sense of relief in that respect. But she also knew that it was vital for her to drop her manufactured animosity towards him and restore the status quo or there was a very real danger that she could overplay her hand. In other circumstances, of course, she would have rejected his apology out of hand and told him to "go forth and multiply" before packing her bags and leaving. But these weren't "other" circumstances and leaving at this stage would have defeated the whole purpose of her being in the house in the first place. So instead, she gave a slow, reluctant nod, which carried just the right amount of grudging acceptance.

'One more chance, Graham, that's all,' she said. 'But if it happens again . . .'

He shook his head firmly. 'Cross my heart and all that,' he said, making the appropriate physical gesture with his right forefinger.

Then he headed for the door, turning briefly with his hand on the handle to say, 'Dinner at eight then?'

I can't bloody wait, she mused.

* * *

Lisa Heddon felt like death warmed up when she awoke. She was hot, her body wet with perspiration, and she had a violent headache. She guessed she was running a temperature, which was hardly surprising after what had happened to her. But true to form and her army training, she remained calm and dragged herself upright against the pillows, staring bleary-eyed at her watch. It registered eight p.m. She had slept most of the day away.

Checking the thick bandage she had wound around her left thigh the night before, she was pleased to find no obvious signs of leakage from the wounds she had sustained. But she was acutely conscious of a nociceptive, sharp throbbing pain in her leg accompanied by a vertigo type sickness and loss of balance when she carefully eased her legs over the edge of the bed and tried to stand up. The burner phone lying on the bedside cabinet beside her rang as she was about to take another double dose of strong painkillers and she sat back against the headboard of the double bed again and waited for the five agreed rings before answering.

'Yes?' she said.

'You okay?' a thick, heavily accented voice queried.

'Why shouldn't I be?'

'Any news?'

'Not yet. Still looking.'

Silence for a moment. Then the caller said, 'We hear there's a new player in the game. Calls himself the Collector. Host is throwing the party at one thirty to two tomorrow, your time. Collector will be arriving by car. Be there.'

The caller was gone.

Heddon continued to sit there for quite a while after-wards, partially to give the painkillers time to work, but also to think about the message she had just received from the mafia contact who had hired her. So the exchange of the diamonds was due to take place the next day, was it? No more searching necessary then. They would be there on a plate for the taking. It sounded good, but there were a lot of unknowns to consider and unknowns could be potentially fatal.

For instance, where was the Collector coming from? Would he be alone or have armed protection with him? Allegedly the exchange was to take place at Smuggler's Reach itself, but whereabouts on the property? Hardly in full view on the terrace. That would be much too public, to say the least. So the study then? Or maybe, if, as she thought likely, there would be more than just Brent and the Collector pres-ent, the long conference room she had checked out that first night? Either could pose a problem since both rooms only had one way in and one way out, so she would have to think carefully about tactics. Then there was another consideration. Herself. With a dodgy, injured leg and her current off-colour state, would she be able to do the business *and* get away again safely afterwards?

Her gaze strayed to the holdall in the corner and she reflected on the assortment of lethal kit it contained. The lightweight Ruger sniper's rifle with its telescopic sights and effective firing range of 850 yards, would have been ideal for a simple hit from a safe distance away. But though she had been contracted to take out Brent anyway, she needed to seize the diamonds first, so the rifle was of no use on this occasion. But there were other items in the bag that might come in handy. First she had to devise a flexible strategy.

She sighed and reached for the pistol she had pulled out of the same bag to replace the Glock 17 seized by Brent's cohorts before climbing into bed the previous night. In her line of work it wasn't wise to sleep without a gun close by, but unlike in popular novels and films where characters were routinely depicted concealing their weapons under pillows, she had placed hers in plain sight on the bedside cabinet next to her mobile to ensure it was much quicker to hand and avoided the risk of becoming entangled in the folds of the bed linen. She had learned the hard way over the years that you always kept your personal weapon within easy reach, not where you might have to fumble for it in an emergency, as that could mean the difference between life and death.

The piece itself was a M1911 Sig Sauer semi-automatic and, though she favoured the Glock that had been her constant companion for so long, this was a very reliable weapon and should do what was required of it if she needed the services of the powerful 9 mm. It was just that, like male tennis stars who refused to shave between matches if they were on a winning streak because they believed it could bring them bad luck, she was equally superstitious about changing her firearm in the middle of a contract. It was stupid, she knew that, but she still couldn't help feeling uneasy — even more acutely now, when she was physically and mentally under par with her injured leg and what she suspected was a developing infection. But she had no choice but to see things through and fulfil her contract. The mafia were not known for their forgiveness of failure and in any event, in her business, reneging on a contract for whatever reason was tantamount to a death sentence.

Depositing a kiss on the pistol's cold metal, she managed a pale smile. 'Well, Mr Sig,' she murmured, 'it looks like we've got a party to go to tomorrow, but I don't think there'll be any champagne welcome for us.'

* * *

Kate once more found dinner a strain after all that had happened. The lamb shank and accompanying fresh vegetables were, as usual, cooked to perfection and the wine from Brent's cellar was an excellent Chianti. Alfredo was certainly a talented chef. Pity he happened to be a gangster as well, she thought, but such was life. Brent made a point of trying to lighten her mood after his earlier hollow-sounding apology. He avoided any reference to her portrait, but once more talked about art, this time concentrating on humorous anecdotes he had read about some of the great masters along the way.

She tried to laugh with him but found it a real effort and she was sure he must have picked up on her depressed mood, no doubt assuming it was all down to his reprehensible behaviour in the studio earlier. In fact, it had nothing to do with that. It was due entirely to her anxieties about the following day and how things might pan out when the Collector arrived. Somehow, she would first have to establish precisely where the meeting was taking place, which would be difficult enough. Then she would need to ensure she was in the right position to witness the exchange as it happened and immediately message Cole so he could launch his raid and seize the goods before either of the key players could get away. A very tall order and one with inherent risk to herself. For the first time since she had agreed to the undercover operation, it dawned on her how precarious the whole setup was and how hit and miss the result was likely to be. But it was much too late to try and back out now. She was in it to the end, whether she wanted to be or not.

The sudden appearance of Frank Delaney at the table shortly after dessert put paid to any further thoughts on the issue, however. Brent had always seemed to keep the big ugly ex-boxer at arm's length, despite his claim all those days ago to have rescued him from a doss house out of the goodness of his heart. To see him now lurch into sight from the walkway and approach Brent directly was an unprecedented development and it immediately aroused Kate's curiosity.

Brent, for his part, seemed almost relieved to see him and, dabbing the corners of his mouth with his napkin, he motioned him to one side, and stood up.

'My apologies, Kate,' he said smoothly, 'I need to have a quick word with Frank.'

She gave an understanding nod and, grasping Delaney by the arm, Brent led him away a few paces, engaging him a in low-toned conversation.

Trying hard not to show any interest in what was going on, Kate nevertheless pricked up her ears as she made a pretence of continuing eating her cheese and biscuits.

'Found the place,' she heard Delaney growl in an attempted whisper, which failed dismally.

Out of the corner of her eye she saw Brent glance quickly in her direction and shake his head irritably, as if warning him to lower his voice. Then she heard Brent say something like, 'Just do it right,' to which Delaney replied in his best conspiratorial tone, 'Won't be a problem, boss.'

'Little job I asked Frank to do,' Brent explained as Delaney lumbered away again and he sat back down at the table 'He's not the brightest of characters, but he's a very reliable chap, provided you give him chapter and verse on everything you want him to do. Now, seeing as you've finished your cheese and biscuits, how about a nice brandy?'

* * *

PC Geraint Rheon lived in an old Welsh cottage on the outskirts of Lamphey, on the edge of the Pembrokeshire National Park. The cottage was over 200 years old and though it had an attractive beamed living room with an inglenook fireplace, it was damp and draughty. Rheon didn't mind that one bit. He had lived there all his life, having inherited the place from his parents, and he had brought his childhood sweetheart, Karen, there as his wife thirty-two years ago. Karen had been dead now for ten years, but Rheon still lived on in the cottage, adamant that he would only ever leave in a box.

The property had just a small kitchen garden at the front, but it backed on to a couple of fields which Rheon owned. Not that he did anything with them, apart from regularly mowing the rough grass with the tractor he kept in his barn, but he liked the open space and the wildlife that inhabited the copse in the top corner of one of them.

After a lengthy period of mixed duty shifts and a lot of overtime to cover absences through the sickness of colleagues, he was looking forward to Saturday, his only day off for the week. As a result, he was up at first light to check over his tractor and fuel it in readiness for mowing the back field before the sun got too hot later.

Lighting his pipe, he donned his gumboots and headed across the field to the barn, enjoying the fresh, sweet smell of the late spring air as he went, and he was totally unaware of the eyes that followed him from the side of the cottage or the heavy figure that strode after him once he had hauled the heavy barn doors open and gone inside.

He was bending over the tractor, checking one of the rear wheels, when he heard a shuffling sound behind him and, pivoting round on one knee, he saw the big, heavyset figure standing there looking down at him. The man was holding a can of petrol out towards him in one hand and the brass screw-top in the other, as if to make sure he could see them.

'Mornin', Occifer,' the stranger said, a broad grin spreading across his ugly, battered features. 'I got a message to give yer, but I don't fink yer gonna like it.'

As Rheon responded by grabbing the top of the wheel to pull himself back up on to his feet, his legs were suddenly kicked from under him, pitching him on to his stomach, and, even as he struggled to get up again, he was deluged in several litres of neat petrol. Then to his horror, he heard the rasp of a match . . .

CHAPTER 19

Kate awoke in the early hours of Saturday morning to the sound of sirens on the main road. 'Playing my tune again,' she murmured, half asleep, but thought nothing of it and promptly dozed off again. When she awoke a second time, it was much later than she had intended and, with an oath when she noted the time on her watch, she made straight for the shower.

Emerging after only twenty minutes, she sat on the corner of the bed and gave Cole another call as she hurriedly dried herself. The instant he answered she wished she hadn't.

'Bad news, Kate,' the policeman said and his tone was grim. 'Your PC Rheon?'

Kate felt her skin crawl, as a premonition hit her and she remembered the sirens that had woken her up. 'Rheon? What about him?'

'He's dead.'

She felt herself start to sway, dropped her towel and quickly grabbed the edge of the bed to steady herself.

'Dead?' she breathed. 'How-how can that be?'

'Fire in an old barn at the back of his cottage early hours of this morning. Neighbour reported it. Apparently Rheon had a couple of fields and kept a small tractor in the barn for when he needed to mow them. Fire service found a load of buckled petrol cans in the barn and one without a top by his body, close to the burned-out tractor. They also found the remains of a pipe under him. They reckon he'd been trying to fill the tractor's fuel tank with the lit pipe in his mouth, a spark ignited the petrol and whoosh! The whole lot went up.'

Kate thought of Brent's conversation with Delaney the previous evening and then, as if to nudge her thoughts along the same line, her subconscious threw up the comment Brent had made to her after Rheon's aggressive visit the day before. *Mr Rheon is getting to be a bit of a nuisance.*

'Oh, come on,' she said, 'why would he be filling up his tractor's tank that early in the morning? He could hardly have been about to mow his fields.'

'Seems he was off duty today, so he may have been getting the tractor ready. It gets light very early this time of year, don't forget, and a neighbour says he was always up with the birds.'

'This was no damned accident,' she said.

He grunted. 'Of course it wasn't,' he agreed. 'It was the inevitable consequence of leaning on Brent. It's a similar MO to Peter Foster's. Frank Delaney's paws are all over it. But it will take some proving and there won't be any prints.'

Kate's face had assumed the coldness of an ivory figurine's. 'Poor old Rheon,' she said. 'Right near his retirement too.'

'I know,' Cole said. 'But don't let this thing get to you. You have to remain calm and focused today if we are to put these swine where they belong.'

Kate's mind was far away, remembering the big, determined Welshman, with his unshakable moral compass, who had refused to give up on his suspicions and had paid for the commitment to uncovering the truth with his life.

'Do you hear me, Kate?' Cole snapped. 'No heroics or pre-emptive action. Stay focused and alert.'

She took a deep breath. 'Don't worry. I will stick to the plan, but I'm telling you now, even if things go pear-shaped, Brent is not going to walk away from this.'

'Don't do anything stupid,' he warned again. 'Or you'll be no different to that bloody assassin you helped escape.'

'Maybe she had the right idea,' she replied. 'Perhaps hers is the only way Brent will ever pay for what he's done.'

'That's dangerous talk, Kate. Just leave it to the courts, do you hear me? Your job is to concentrate on the job itself. Nothing more than that. Now, you said before that the Collector is arriving at around one thirty. Any further updates on that for me?'

'No,' she replied. 'But he could arrive earlier than that, as the ferry docks at twelve forty-six and it's only about fifteen minutes or so to here.'

'We'll know when he gets to you anyway. We've got the place under external surveillance, as you're aware. As soon as he turns up at the main gate, we'll be told.'

'How will you know it's him? You have no idea what sort of car he will be driving.'

'Yes, we do. Our source has told us it's a red Volvo XC90, though we don't yet have the number.'

'Well, thanks a bleeding bunch for letting me know.'

'I'm telling you now. Anything else?'

'Yes, the cameras. Jack Ferris, the gateman, monitors them from his bungalow at the main gate. How are your raid team going to get into the property when I phone you about the diamonds without him alerting Brent on his mobile before they can get anywhere near the house?'

'You leave that with us. We know all about Jack Ferris and the cameras and we've also got hold of local authority plans of the house, so we know exactly where everything is.'

'You *have* been busy.'

'You too, it would seem, in more ways than one, and you just have the very last task to complete, think on that.'

'I do — all the time — and it scares the hell out of me. So how about wishing me luck?'

He couldn't resist a final dig. 'You don't need luck, Kate. To repeat what you said your chief officers always say in such circumstances, we have every faith in you!!'

There was a chuckle and he was gone.

* * *

As Kate ended her conversation with Cole, a slim figure clad in army camouflage clothing parked their battered Land Rover in a field behind a four-foot hedge and got out. A quick look around and they pulled on a green, woollen hat and a camouflage face mask before grabbing a khaki haversack from the back of the vehicle and hoisting it up over their shoulders. Shortly afterwards the figure was heading across some rough land towards an ultra-modern house, which poked its roof above a line of tall trees. Lisa Heddon was about to join the party at Smuggler's Reach as an uninvited guest, just like the bad fairy in the tale of the *Sleeping Beauty*. But rather than a christening where everyone ended up sleeping for a hundred years, this particular event had the potential to ensure that some of the participants never woke up again . . .

* * *

To Kate's surprise, she received a call on her personal mobile within minutes of ending her conversation with Harry Cole. Grabbing the other phone, she glanced at the caller's ID and swore softly. Hayden. That was one additional complication she didn't need right now. She ignored the call altogether. But after a brief pause, he rang again and then, following a longer interval, a third time. It was obvious he was not going to give up. Shaking her head, she was about to switch the mobile off altogether, when the thought struck her that there was a risk he would get so frustrated by not being able to contact her that he would turn up at the main gate of the house, as he had before — perhaps just when the Collector was arriving.

She rang him back. 'What is it?' she said, deliberately hardening her voice.

'I thought I'd like to speak to my wife, if that's okay with Mr Damn Lutterall.'

'Well, you're speaking to her, so what do you want?'

'Want? I want you home.'

'But you threw me out.'

'Look, can we forget all that?' His voice partially broke. 'I-I can't manage without you.'

She released her breath in a hiss of exasperation. 'Listen, Hayden, I miss you too, and I *will* be coming back, but not quite yet. Give me today to think about it, then I will call you.'

'But why not come home now then? Is it because of *him*?'

'It's got nothing to do with Brent.'

'Brent? I thought you said his name was Lutterall? How many more of them are there in that place?'

Kate inwardly cursed her faux pas. She was so tense, so tired, that she wasn't thinking straight.

'Er, no, sorry. It *is* Lutterall. I was thinking of someone else.'

'What someone else?' He sounded indignant again, sod it! She had really put her foot in it.

'Oh, an artist whose oil painting Graham was trying to flog me. It was a landscape and pretty awful actually. Now listen, I want you to be patient. I said I will come home and I will, when I've got myself together, so trust me. But I don't want you to keep pressuring me. It puts me back every time. Just give me another twenty-four hours, that's all I want you to do.'

'Then you'll come home?'

She hesitated. 'Yes, then I'll come home.'

There was a loud sigh at the other end. 'So, twenty-four hours?'

She raised her eyes to the ceiling. 'Yes, Hayden, I *said* twenty-four hours. Now I've got to go.'

'Why have you got to go? What are you doing?'

'Hayden!' she snapped.

'Okay, okay, twenty-four hours.'

He rang off.

She sat there, breathing heavily. She felt she needed a cigarette, but she didn't smoke.

How could she have been so stupid as to come out with Brent's name. Hayden could be unpredictable. If he thought about her gaff long enough, then took it into his head to follow up on it, she could be in real trouble. She seemed to be falling apart. She really needed to get a grip on herself for the big moment in just a few hours.

The knock on the door was quite faint and she missed it at first. Then, pulling her robe more closely around her, she opened up.

Crosby stood there. 'Mr Brent wondered whether you would be joining him for breakfast, Mrs Lewis?' he said.

Kate glanced at her watch again. It was well after ten.

'Oh, I'm so sorry,' she said. 'My husband rang me and I completely lost track of time. I'll get some clothes on.'

He nodded and she saw him stare past her at the bed and frown slightly. 'Very good, Mrs Lewis.'

After he had gone, she turned back to the bed and felt her stomach sink for the umpteenth time since she had arrived at Smuggler's Reach. Both her personal mobile and the one given to her by Norris were lying on the unmade bed in clear view of the door. No wonder Crosby had looked puzzled. Two mobiles? He was bound to have asked himself why she needed more than one. What if he mentioned that to Brent? She was certainly cocking things up lately. As she hurriedly dressed in jeans and a long-sleeved shirt, she made a promise to herself. If she finally got out of this house in one piece and decided to rejoin the police, never again would she even contemplate undercover work as a specialism.

* * *

Lisa Heddon found the spot in the wire fence she was looking for. She had used it before and whoever had resealed it afterwards had not made a very good job of it. It was an ideal spot for her. Though there was a camera just feet away, it was blind to this entry point because of a large tree growing out of the hedge. She was surprised that, following her two previous break-ins, Brent had not done something about that, perhaps having the tree chopped down, but he'd probably thought it wasn't necessary as she was unlikely to come back after suffering the shotgun injuries she had. How wrong he was.

Pulling apart the wire mesh that had been used to repair the damage, she crawled through the hole, using her sound leg first and trailing the injured one behind her. It was a struggle, but she made it in the end and winced as she straightened the leg on the other side of the fence. She put the repair patch back in place as best she could afterwards, just in case one of Brent's goons decided to check it out again, then sat there for a few moments, gripping her calf tightly with both hands in an effort to reduce the pain that lanced through the thigh muscles. She had taken her usual quadruple dose of painkillers earlier, but it always took a while for them to have any effect and then it was only partially successful. Bloody hell!

She heard scrabbling in the undergrowth between the fence and the driveway close to where she was crouched and stiffened, her hand reaching for the Sig pistol in the holster at her hip. Silence, then more scrabbling and the culprit, a grey squirrel, emerged with something in its mouth, stared at her a second, then bolted back under cover. She breathed a relieved sigh and used a tree branch to help her back on to her feet.

Following the wooded strip along the edge of the driveway, she made it to the front of the house and once more sank down into the undergrowth right on the edge of the forecourt, completely invisible to anyone else in the vicinity in her camouflage clothes. Shaking the haversack off her back and placing it on the ground beside her, she thrust her hand inside and withdrew the pair of powerful military field glasses she had stolen from her army unit all that time ago before she was cashiered. Then she carefully manoeuvred herself into a comfortable, prone position on her stomach. Leaning on both elbows, she trained the field glasses on the house and adjusted the lenses until she was satisfied that they provided the best possible focus. After that, she set them down again beside her and stuffed some dark chocolate into her mouth to help stoke up her much depleted energy.

It was now ten forty-five. According to the information obtained by the mafia contact who had called her the day before, Brent's visitor was due to arrive at around one thirty, which meant actual kick-off could be any time after that. But she couldn't see things dragging on too long. A professional criminal like the Collector would want to be in and out as quickly as possible. So, even if there were to be lengthy haggling over the deal, everything was likely to be done and dusted by at least three thirty. Even earlier if the payout had already been agreed and this visit was just a formality to seal the deal and make the exchange. Whatever happened, her army training had equipped her with almost unlimited patience and she was prepared to lie there for as long as it took, despite the problems with her leg. In her head she heard the voice of one of her old army colleagues just before a raid murmuring to her over the radio. 'In position.' Yeah, well, now *she* was in position, as she had been so many times in the past.

* * *

Brent was sitting at the breakfast table on the terrace, fully dressed in casual clothes. His gaze quickly flicked up from his cup of coffee to study Kate as she arrived.

'I hope we didn't disturb your beauty sleep, my dear,' he said, tongue in cheek. 'But I wanted to have a word with you.'

Kate shook her head with a smile, but waited expectantly. She thought he might be about to make some reference to the death of Geraint Rheon, but wondered how he would broach the subject. In fact, he didn't mention it at all, probably so he could profess ignorance when it was eventually made public knowledge. He simply said, 'Just to let you know that there will be no studio sitting today. Tomorrow maybe, but not today. I have some people coming to see me at around one thirty. Business, I'm afraid. So I will be tied up all afternoon with them and, as I have some work to do this morning in connection with the visit, I regret that you will have to amuse yourself until later this evening.'

'That really isn't a problem,' Kate replied, making an effort to control the tremble in her wrist, as she reached for the coffee pot and thought about what was soon going to happen.

'Allow me,' he said and, rising to his feet, he picked up the pot and bent towards her to fill her cup. His face was quite close to hers and she felt that he hardly took his eyes off her as he poured.

'Why don't you go for a swim or relax by the pool while I am indisposed?' he added, sitting back down. 'You could always devote some time to your new book. Alfredo will serve lunch to you on the terrace here just the same, with a nice bottle of wine, of course, but I regret I will be unable to join you.'

Kate nodded and took a sip of her coffee, pleased that it had already lost much of its heat and was easy to drink. 'I fully understand,' she said. 'I'm just so grateful that you have put up with me for so long.'

He tutted. 'Not at all. I am just sorry I overreached myself yesterday at the sitting.'

'Best forgotten,' she said with a smile. 'Just a misunderstanding.'

He looked delighted. 'Very forgiving of you, my dear. Now, you make the most of yet another lovely day.' He half rose, then added what she guessed was far from being the afterthought he wanted to convey it as.

'Oh, one other thing, Kate. Please don't take this the wrong way, but I would be grateful if you could, er, stay away from the house itself this afternoon, from one o'clock, until my visitors have gone. We will be having sensitive negotiations and they are easily upset if they feel other people might overhear the deal we are discussing. By all means take a wander around the grounds, continue to enjoy the pool or just veg out on the terrace with a book. Okay?'

She shrugged. 'Absolutely fine. I'll see you at dinner then?'

He dabbed his mouth with his napkin. 'You certainly will and Alfredo will serve you lunch out here in the usual way at twelve thirty, as I said, even though I can't be with you. Anyway, enjoy your breakfast. I hope you like smoked salmon, but otherwise, there is also a choice of fruit, plus croissants, pain aux raisins and a fine selection of cheeses. Bon appétit, eh?'

Thinking about what had happened to Rheon, she could hardly credit how Brent could sanction someone's horrific murder and less than eight hours later, coolly sit down for breakfast and talk about smoked salmon and croissants. It beggared belief. But then, as he already had the blood of at least six other people on his hands, what difference would one more make to him? Obviously no more than it would to add a seventh to the list, she mused, and she just hoped seven would not prove to be her unlucky number.

CHAPTER 20

Following breakfast, Kate went for a stroll. After all, Brent had suggested it, so why not? But there was another reason, of course. She wanted to keep a periodic eye on the house, without making this too obvious. That way she could pick out any significant signs of activity, which might indicate where Brent's meeting with the Collector was going to take place.

She ran into Delaney a few yards beyond the forecourt. He seemed to be checking the strip of woodland lining the driveway on her left, maybe for any other signs of intrusion into the grounds.

'Well now, darlin',' he said, eyeing her suspiciously, 'what yer doin' wanderin' about out 'ere?'

'Graham suggested it,' she replied. 'He said I could go for a wander or use the pool, whatever I liked, provided I kept out of the house when his visitors arrived this afternoon.'

'Did 'e now? Then it must be okay then, mustn't it?'

Treating her to a broad wink, he said, 'You get back in that pool soon as yer can, though, gel. Very nice what I seen so far.'

With another of his raucous laughs, he then lumbered past her like the big ape that he was, heading back towards the house and leaving her with her skin crawling with revulsion at the very thought of him covertly watching her walking about the pool area in the string bikini. The man was as dangerous as Brent or Crosby, but in an altogether different, perverted sort of way and the prospect of ever finding herself left to his tender mercies was too terrifying to contemplate.

Trying to put the idea out of her mind, she ducked through a gap in the trees to her right and found herself in the ornamental garden she had spotted when she had first visited Smuggler's Reach. It was very beautiful, with wooden seats, a large lily pond and paths winding among flower beds full of wallflowers. To her left the garden ended at the side wall of the bungalow by the main gate. To her right, steps dropped down through a low wall to a couple of tennis courts, re-emerging the other side to disappear through an opening in tall, laurel hedging, which she guessed connected with the back garden alongside the house.

Standing in this idyllic spot, she once more found it difficult to mentally reconcile Brent's obvious love of nature and his appreciation of beauty in all its forms with the terrible things he had done and the monster he was capable of turning into at the drop of a hat. Like Robert Louis Stevenson's Dr Jekyll and Mr Hyde, the man was an enigma, but an enigma whose schizophrenic personality seemed to be shielding a lot more than one demon.

Feeling cold, despite the warmth of the sun, she decided to head back to the house, choosing to make her way through the garden, down the steps and round past the tennis courts to the gap in the hedge. She passed under a wrought-iron rose arch and found herself, as she had expected, following another path between the side of the house and some similar tall hedging to that enclosing the back garden. After a few yards, she could see the swimming pool ahead and, immediately beside her, a little gate accessing steps, which obviously led up on to the terrace.

She was about to open the gate when she heard the voices from above and for some reason stopped in her tracks to listen.

'All set then?' she heard Brent say and she caught the whiff of cigar smoke.

'Everyone knows what they've got to do, yes,' Crosby's quiet voice replied. 'Conference room's prepared and we've checked the fences and they're all secure. But I've got a feeling in my gut that something's wrong.'

'What do you mean?'

'I can't put my finger on it. It's just a feeling, but for a start, I'm not happy about the Lewis woman wandering about the grounds. Frank bumped into her walking along the driveway towards the main gate just now.'

'She can't do any harm and I did tell her she could take a stroll if she wanted to, but to keep clear of the house for the afternoon. Not much else I can do at this stage, unless you think I should gag her and tie her to her bed?' Brent chuckled. 'Mind you, it might be worth doing that later as a bit of foreplay.'

Crosby didn't sound amused. 'You know I've never been happy about her staying here. Even more so now, with what's going down this afternoon.'

'You worry too much. She's just a bit of tail. Rather naive and empty-headed, in my opinion, but hardly a problem.'

'Still . . .' Crosby began, apparently still not happy, but Brent cut him off with an irritable hiss. 'Okay, okay, I'll get rid of her once I've had my wicked way. Just keep an eye on her in the meantime. What about the chopper?'

'Out on the helipad, fuelled and ready, just in case.'

'Excellent. There shouldn't be any aggro from our Italian friends, but should they turn up, we must be prepared for a quick exit. Any more news on our bloody trespasser?'

'We've made discreet inquiries in the village, but no joy. She must be holed up somewhere outside. But she can't be in very good shape after her injuries. She's probably already bled to death.'

'Let's hope so, but I've got my own gut feeling too. That we haven't seen the last of that bitch. Tell everyone to keep their eyes open.'

Kate heard the scrape of a chair, a couple of coughs and then the familiar tap of Brent's shoes on the stone slabs, which quickly faded, as he must have gone back into the house through the French doors.

A bit of tail? Naïve? Empty-headed? Kate mused angrily, thinking of the phrases Brent had used to describe her. So that was his opinion of her, was it? Well, maybe he'd have to eat those words in a few hours, the bastard! At least she had found out where the crucial meeting was going to take place, and, as she well knew from her reconnoitre all those days ago, the conference room was at the front of the house, upstairs. So all she had to do was find a decent position somewhere to enable her to mount her own bit of static surveillance on the room.

Excited by her discovery, but sensible enough to appreciate that Crosby or Brent might clock her coming out of the passageway on to the rear lawn and sus that she had overheard the conversation between the two of them, she turned round and headed back along the path, intending to re-cross the ornamental garden, through the gap in the hedge and on to the driveway. But things didn't quite work according to plan. A thin woman with straggly blonde hair, dressed in shorts and a skimpy top, was standing on the other side of the rose arch when she emerged, a cigarette in her mouth, her arms folded over the shaft of a rake, and her hawk-like gaze fixed on Kate with naked hostility.

* * *

'So, you're the bit on the side, are yer, darlin'?' the woman with the rake said with a sneer, looking Kate up and down, smoke curling from between her over-painted lips. "Eard the boss had got himself a nice little red 'ead. Bedded yer yet, 'as 'e?'

Kate gave her a withering look. 'So, who might you be then?'

'Mandy Thomas is me name and I lives 'ere, don't I?'

'Well, Mandy Thomas, I don't know what you're talking about,' she retorted, feigning indignation, 'I'm just modelling for him.'

'Yeah, so I 'eard. The boys 'ave all got their eyes on yer, fer when the boss 'as finished wiv yer. Proper gang bang that'll be, I bet.'

Kate tried to keep up the pretence. 'Graham and I are just good friends. You have a dirty mind.'

Thomas emitted a harsh laugh. 'That right? Well, yer'll soon find out.' Her blue eyes narrowed, and she straightened up, dropping the cigarette on the ground and extinguishing it with one sandal-shod foot. 'So, what yer doin' creepin' about down there anyways?'

'I wasn't "creeping about" anywhere. Graham said I could take a stroll if I wanted to, so I was doing a bit of exploring. The garden here is so beautiful.'

Thomas softened a little, then sniffed and wiped her nose on the back of one hand. 'Yeah, thanks to me. I does it all, see, and cleans the big 'ouse once a week while me ovver 'alf sits on 'is arse.'

'Typical man,' Kate said with a smile.

Thomas grinned. 'Yer can say that again. Bleedin' tosser. 'e is, but good in bed, I'll give 'im that. 'Ere sit down fer a bit. I could do wiv some gel talk. Don't see many of 'em in this place.'

She indicated a bench seat a few feet away and turned towards it, dropping her rake on the ground. Kate nervously glanced at her watch while the woman's back was turned. This would have to happen now, wouldn't it? It was well after twelve. She desperately needed to get a message through to Cole to tell him where the meeting was due to take place, so that he could direct his teams to the right place when the Collector arrived. Every minute's delay could be crucial to the success of the operation. Furthermore, she was conscious of the fact that Alfredo would be expecting her to turn up for lunch at around twelve thirty and might tell Brent if she was not there. If someone were sent to find her, there was a real danger Thomas might mention to them where she had seen her snooping and it wouldn't take Brent long to put two and two together and realise she might have been eavesdropping on his conversation. Yet to refuse Thomas's invitation for a chat could also be risky if the woman were to take offence, which from the look of her, was a distinct possibility.

'From round 'ere, is yer?' Thomas asked as she sat down beside her.

Kate shook her head and accepted a cigarette from the proffered packet, even though she didn't normally smoke. 'Er, no, Somerset actually.'

Thomas produced a lighter and lit her cigarette for her. 'Never been there.' She sniffed again. 'Never been anywhere except the Smoke and 'ere. What did you do in Somerset then?'

'Oh, various jobs, but I'm hoping to be a professional novelist. That's why I came here.'

'What, writing books an' that?'

Kate nodded. 'Thrillers.'

Thomas laughed. 'I was in a book once.'

'Oh?'

'Yeah, centre page spread in a porno mag, though there weren't much readin' to be done there.'

Kate transferred her cigarette from her right to her left hand, so she could raise her arm and allow the long-sleeved shirt to slide back on her wrist and expose her watch. It was after twelve fifteen. She should be getting back to the house. She had concealed Cole's mobile under the pillow on her bed rather than risk carrying it around with her, but it meant that she had to get back to her room before the house became out of bounds to her from lunchtime.

'You married?' Thomas said suddenly after a pause.

Kate looked startled for a second. Her mind had been miles away. 'Yes, my husband is at home in our cottage here.'

'Mind you takin' your clothes off to pose, does he?'

'Yes, as it happens, he's pretty annoyed that I'm doing it.'

'Not surprised. Saw 'im jumpin' up and down t'other day outside the front gate. Looked proper narked, 'e did.'

Kate stubbed out her cigarette on the arm of the chair. She couldn't delay anymore.

'Look, it's been nice meeting you, but I really must go. Graham will be expecting me for lunch at twelve thirty.'

Thomas frowned and for a moment Kate thought she had blown it. But then she shrugged and also stood up, stretching. 'If yer gotta go, yer gotta go,' she said with a sudden grin. 'Me ol' man will want 'is nosh too, I reckon. Don't do anyfin' I wouldn't do, will yer?'

Then she was gone, her long tanned legs striding down the side of the tennis courts towards the bungalow on the other side of the ornamental garden where Kate could now see a half-open door.

Trying not to appear as though she were in a panic, Kate forced herself to walk at a much slower pace towards the other side of the tennis courts, then joined the yellow brick path and made her way back through the trees on to the driveway. She quickened her pace and got to the house just before half past twelve. The front door was unlocked and she went straight through and along to her bedroom.

Closing the door behind her, she grabbed Cole's phone from under her pillow and called him, her trembling, excited fingers stabbing clumsily at the keypad.

'It's the conference room at the front of the house,' she said when she was put through to him. 'That's where they're meeting.'

'Brilliant!' he said. 'I'll let everyone know. You okay?'

'I think so,' she replied.

But she wasn't and she had only just thrust the mobile back under the pillow when her bedroom door was suddenly thrown open and Crosby stepped into the room.

'What do you mean by barging in here?' she exclaimed, rising to her feet angrily. 'Don't you usually knock?'

'Not this time,' he said. 'Who were you talking to?'

'What? None of your bloody business.'

'That's where you're wrong and I'll ask you again, who were you talking to?'

She sensed the menace in his tone and swallowed. 'Hayden as a matter of fact,' she retorted, relieved that her personal mobile was lying on the bed beside her. 'Satisfied?'

'Give me your phone.'

She handed it to him and saw his mouth tighten. 'It's on standby. Put in your passcode.'

She did so and watched his fingers flick across the screen as he interrogated it. 'There's no record of any recent call here.'

'There wouldn't be. I was using WhatsApp and I always delete messages afterwards. I deleted this one before switching off.'

'You must have been pretty quick to do that. I'm afraid I don't believe you.'

She made a brave attempt at demonstrating her indignation. 'How dare you.'

He was unmoved and, striding to the bed, pulled both pillows off and threw them on the floor. Cole's phone gleamed almost mockingly back at her.

He picked it up. 'Is this the phone you were using?' he asked.

Kate was at a loss for an immediate answer and his smile was one of triumph. 'Exactly who are you, Mrs Lewis?' he asked. 'I'm sure we would all like to know.'

It was twelve thirty-three and Kate guessed that she would not be having any lunch today — if ever again.

CHAPTER 21

There was a palpable sense of tension in the bedroom and Kate now sat uneasily on the edge of the bed. Crosby had left her briefly to collect his boss and Brent looked none too happy at this new development. His face was once again cold and hard.

'It was only yesterday that we had our little chat about your questionable behaviour by the pool, Kate,' he said. 'Now here we are faced with another issue concerning what you may have been doing behind my back.'

Kate tried to look both hurt and nonplussed at the same time, but didn't have much confidence in it succeeding.

'I don't understand, Graham,' she replied. 'What am I supposed to have done this time?'

'You know very well what, Kate,' he said tersely. 'Why have you got two mobiles?'

She managed to manufacture a laugh. 'Heavens above, Graham, what is so terrible about that?'

'Just answer the question, will you?'

She shrugged, having just come up with what she thought was the plausible explanation she had been searching for.

'Well, the one on the bed here is mine and the one in your hand is Hayden's.' She forced a grin. 'I was a bit naughty when he practically threw me out and I pinched his

226

brand new phone, so he couldn't use it. Childish, I know, but he really annoyed me. I had just finished ringing him and winding him up about it when Adam rudely burst in on me.'

Brent didn't look convinced. 'How could you ring him on his mobile if you have it here?'

'I wasn't ringing him on his mobile. It was on the landline.'

'So open up his mobile for me now,' he said quietly.

She looked blank. 'How do you expect me to do that? I have absolutely no idea what his passcode is.'

He expressed surprise. 'You're married to the man and yet you don't even know the passcode on his phone?'

'Well, we're not joined at the hip. We might share the same bed, but we each have our own lives to lead. He belongs to vintage car clubs, for example. I am into writing and books.'

For a few moments he just stared at her, absently weighing the phone in his hand as he considered her answer. Then he nodded and smiled again at last. 'Of course. I must apologise for the rather rude interrogation, but I hope you will understand that I am rather sensitive to breaches of my privacy here and when Adam told me about the phones, the fact that you had two struck me as a bit of an incongruity in the light of your circumstances.'

She stopped herself from giving a sigh of relief just in time and smiled again. 'No problem,' she said. 'Let's just forget it ever happened.'

'That's very good of you,' he replied. 'So you won't mind if Adam hangs on to Hayden's phone for the present then? You can have it back when you decide you've had enough of us here and want to go home.'

She was nearly caught out by the sudden change in tack but recovered almost at the same moment. 'If that makes you feel happier,' she blurted.

His smile seemed practically carnivorous now. 'Oh it does, Kate,' he said. 'Very much so, in fact. And just to make me feel happier still, we are going to put you in the wine cellar for safekeeping until after the guest I am expecting has left.'

Kate visibly started. 'The wine cellar? You're going to lock me up? What on earth for?'

His sneering laugh was not pleasant. 'Think I'm stupid, Kate?' he asked. 'Your husband's mobile? Do me a favour. You don't think I believed that, do you? Any more than I believed your fanciful story about talking to a robin in the hedge, when I know you were having a much more meaningful conversation with the late Geraint Rheon?'

Her eyes widened convincingly at his use of the word "late", even though she knew about Rheon already. He obviously picked up on her feigned look of shock.

'Precisely, my dear. Poor old Rheon was becoming a real pain, so I sent Frank to make him aware of my feelings. Burned to a crisp, it seems. But then you shouldn't play with matches when there are cans of petrol nearby, should you?'

Kate felt a sense of doom. The fact that Brent had admitted to the murder was very bad news for her, because it meant that he no longer thought it necessary to keep up his former pretence of being a retired philanthropist with a bent towards portrait painting. Which also meant he had already decided to get rid of her as well.

She couldn't find anything else to say after that shock disclosure, but just stared at him.

'You see,' he went on, 'I've had my eye on you ever since Adam here caught sight of you listening to my private telephone call outside the pool changing-room hut. But I thought I'd give you a little more rope to hang yourself on.

'So maybe, *Mrs Lewis*, you'll now tell me who you are working for. Could it possibly be Old Bill? After all, you seemed to be having quite a nice chat with PC Rheon by that pool, didn't you? Or could it be my rivals from across the water? Which would perhaps explain why you decided to release their murderous assassin from my cellar. Oh yes, I know it was you who freed her after hearing the gunshots and seeing her being carried in. I mean, who wouldn't hear a shotgun blast in the middle of the night just a few yards from their bedroom window? According to Rheon, our nearest neighbour did and she lives nearly half a mile away. Furthermore, there was no way the bitch could have freed herself on her own, not unless she was a contortionist.'

'I-I really don't know what you're talking about,' Kate exclaimed, holding herself together with difficulty, as she felt the walls closing in on her. 'I am not working for anyone.'

He released a theatrically loud sigh. 'I thought you'd say that,' he said. 'But no matter. Frank will find out for me, I'm quite sure. I really would like to have been there when he gets started, but sadly, I have another commitment.'

Kate felt physically sick at his reference to the psychotic ex-boxer, knowing full well what he was capable of. But she tried not to think about him and what she had always sensed as his perverted sexual interest in her. Instead, she did her best to continue to project an image of confused innocence.

'But I haven't done anything, Graham,' she said desperately, shedding tears that were not entirely false. 'Why are you treating me like this?'

'Oh come on, Kate,' he said, 'You've no need to put on the act anymore. Just tell me the truth and it will all be over.'

'What-what act and what do you mean by all over?'

He sighed. 'Do you know, you have one of the most naturally beautiful bodies I have ever painted?' he said in a regretful tone that almost sounded genuine. 'You could have graced the walls of the best houses in the country. Instead, you chose the path to your own destruction.' He shook his head as the grotesque figure of Delaney appeared in the doorway.

'I think the lady has things to tell us, Frank,' he said, 'and she claims she doesn't know the passcode for this.' He slapped the mobile Cole had given Kate into his huge palm. 'I'm sure you can persuade her to be a bit more cooperative.'

Then glancing from Kate to the thug and back to her again, he emitted a cynical laugh. 'Beauty and the beast, eh?' he said. 'How very apt.'

* * *

It was pointless trying to struggle against a monster like Delaney. Especially with Brent and Crosby there to help him. Kate didn't try but allowed herself to be led out through the back door of the bedroom on to the walkway. But once she got to the door of the wine cellar and he bent down to unlock it, she saw her chance.

What she hoped to achieve by making a break for it, she hardly knew herself. Get clear of the slower moving man mountain and lose herself among the trees maybe, but then what? She would never have been able to get out of the grounds of the house. Coupled with which, minus both her mobiles, she had no means of calling for help anyway. But in situations where torture and certain death are on the cards, people tend not to consider things rationally. Desperation rules the day and, even with all her resilience and training, Kate was no different. She had just the one chance and she took it.

Before Delaney realised what was happening, she was, to use slang police speak, "on her toes" and streaking through the archway into the passage between the house and the garage block and heading across the forecourt towards the main driveway. To give Delaney his due, he showed surprising speed for someone of his bulk, but he was no match for athletic Kate.

But her flight was doomed to failure. Just yards from the house, she tripped and fell heavily. Before she could get up again, Delaney was there, hauling her to her feet with an angry snarl, the knuckles of one of his meat-hooks giving her a sideways blow to the back of the head, knocking her senseless.

When she finally came round, she was lying on the floor of the wine cellar, minus her shoes, and Delaney was propped on a stool a few feet away, the anorak he had been wearing lying on the floor beside him and the Glock pistol he had taken from the would-be assassin bulging from a shoulder holster.

'Do that again,' he said, 'an' I might forget what the boss told me to do an' wring yer neck like a bleedin' chicken.'

Kate grabbed the leg of the table behind her and pulled herself up into a sitting position.

Delaney stared at her fixedly and something in his expression warned her what was on his mind. She shrank further back against the table.

'Now we can get proper acquainted,' he said with a nasty grin and pulled the Glock out of the holster. Standing up, he laid the weapon on top of the stool and began unbuttoning his shirt. 'Take all your cloves off,' he ordered.

* * *

Lisa Heddon watched the whole drama being played out in front of her from her concealment among the trees. She saw Kate emerge at a run from the passageway and race across the forecourt, with Delaney in clumsy pursuit, and she watched her trip and fall. She gritted her teeth as the big man scooped her up and dealt her a deliberate blow to the head with his closed fist before carrying her back into the passageway and she heard what she guessed was the wine cellar door slam shut afterwards.

Angrily burying her face in the carpet of flattened undergrowth in which she was lying, she cursed Kate with a vengeance. Damn that bloody woman. What the hell had she done now? Just twenty minutes until the Collector was due to arrive and the interfering cow had poked her nose into things yet again. Plainly the dumbhead must have been rumbled. Otherwise, why would she have been running away? Also, it was pretty certain that she had been taken down into the wine cellar for interrogation and with that ugly, sadistic ape as her captor, it didn't require too much imagination to work out what form that interrogation was likely to take.

But so what? Kate whoever she was had got herself into the mess she was in and it was up to Kate to get herself out of it. Her plight had nothing to with Lisa Heddon. She had a much more important job to do than worrying about her and, even though the stupid, mixed-up bitch had previously saved her life, she had no intention of getting involved in her problems. She was here solely to fulfil her contract — nothing else.

But even as she came to that conclusion, she faltered and the next moment she was fiercely beating the ground with both closed fists in total frustration. *Come on, Lisa, you can't just leave her to get on with it*, the voice in her head cajoled. *You told her you owed her one. So now live up to the promise.*

'Shit, shit, shit!' she said aloud. 'I'm going soft.'

Rising slowly from her prone position, she left the cover of the trees and limped as quickly as she could around the edge of the forecourt and into the passageway. It was coming up to one thirty.

* * *

Frank Delaney was getting impatient. 'I told you to take all your cloves off, gel,' he repeated. 'Me an' you is goin' to 'ave some fun.'

Kate looked him up and down with undisguised contempt, making no move to comply. He had removed his own shirt and was tugging at the belt of his trousers. Suddenly she was no longer scared of him but furious at his arrogant self-confidence, and she was determined he wouldn't take her as easily as he seemed to think he could.

'I wouldn't allow an ugly pig like you to touch me, even if you were the last person on earth,' she threw back at him. 'You're disgusting and you smell as bad as you look.'

His grin faded. 'That so?' he retorted, and he advanced a couple of paces until he was towering over her. 'Well, we'll see abaht that, won't we?'

Kate threw up an arm in a futile attempt to ward him off. 'Your boss told you to find out what I know,' she blurted desperately. 'Not force yourself on me. He won't be very happy when he hears me screaming just as his special guest arrives.'

He shrugged. 'No one will 'ear you down 'ere wiv the door closed,' he said, bending over her. 'Anyways, boss won't care what I does to yer, long as I find out what 'e wants to know.'

Before she could do anything, he suddenly grabbed the front of her shirt and ripped it open. 'Go on, really scream,' he said. 'I'd like that.'

* * *

The big red Volvo approached the electronic gates at just after one thirty, flashing its headlights. Jack Ferris saw the car turn up on his monitor and verified that its registration number matched the one written on the piece of paper Brent had given him earlier, though he couldn't see anything of the occupants, as the windows were heavily tinted. Before pressing the button to open the gates, he called up Brent on his two-way radio, telling him his visitors had arrived, then watched as the powerful car drove through at speed. Normally he would have closed the gates afterwards, but this time he didn't and for one very good reason. The tall, hard-looking man in police uniform standing beside his swivel chair may have been smiling at him politely, but there was nothing polite about the business-like 9 mm Glock levelled at his left ear.

'Leave the gates open, Jack, there's a good chap,' the policeman said. 'Some more guests are about to join us.'

Where the policeman had come from, Ferris had no idea, but seeing on his monitor that one of the cameras behind the bungalow had blacked out, he guessed he must have got into the grounds by climbing over the fence or cutting through it. All he could hope for was that Mandy would have clocked the copper in time and raced ahead to warn Brent. But then his hopes were dashed as he heard Mandy's voice suddenly yell from the dining room behind him, 'Okay, okay, get off, bitch!'

As she shouted, Ferris saw, with a sinking feeling, teams of uniformed police officers, armed with what looked like submachine guns, pouring through the open gates and fanning out into the woodland on each side.

'Now, Jack,' the policeman standing beside him said, relieving him of his pistol from its shoulder holster with his other hand, 'we're all just going to sit here quietly like one big happy family. Maybe your good lady might even make us a nice cup of tea?'

* * *

The voice was cold and precise and it commanded obedience. 'Get up off her, you filthy animal.'

Delaney was shirtless and crouched on top of a futilely struggling Kate, hauling on her half-open jeans, his face flushed and his own trousers halfway down his backside. He jerked round with a curse at the interruption.

The Sig Sauer pistol in Lisa Heddon's black-gloved hand was fitted with a suppressor and it was pointing right at him.

Very slowly — even in his all-consuming lust, he was aware of the peril he was in — Delaney climbed to his feet, hoisting his trousers up and quickly fastening the belt, leaving Kate to roll away from him and out of the line of fire.

'Well, well,' he sneered, 'if it ain't the little bitch what I shot. 'Ow's the leg, sweet'eart? Still 'urt, do it?'

Kate watched him intently, fully aware of what he was up to. She knew his chat was just a blind. He could see Heddon was none too steady on her feet. She was swaying very slightly and her sound leg was bent at an unusual angle, as if to provide better support for the injured one. He had already surreptitiously moved a little way to his left towards the stool and he was obviously hoping she hadn't noticed the Glock lying on top of it. Counting on being able to get within reach of the weapon before she cottoned on.

'Noffink to say then, gel?' he mocked, moving another couple of steps. 'You got a nerve to come back 'ere after what I done to you.'

Kate opened her mouth to shout a warning, but she was a fraction too late, as at that exact moment Delaney went for the gun, once again demonstrating surprising speed and agility for such a big man. In a second the gun was in his paw, but that was as far as he got.

The assassin's face wore a contemptuous half smile as she fired coolly and unhurriedly. It was as if she had deliberately waited for him to commit himself before doing anything. The 9 mm Parabellum shells slammed into Delaney's body in a series of growling "phuts" — Kate counted four in total, with a slight pause between them — and she saw Delaney stumble under the impact of each one. Losing his grip on the Glock, which fell on to the concrete floor with a loud clatter, he clutched at the bloodied holes in his chest and belly from which the life force was pumping out of him like a fractured hose. Then his eyes glazed over and he dropped briefly to his knees before pitching on to his face. A single twitch of his body and he was still.

Kate was numb with the horror of it all. She just sat there, staring at Heddon blankly, as the assassin unscrewed the suppressor from the gun and holstered it. Then she limped over to where Delaney was lying and picked up the Glock from the floor beside him.

'Mine, I believe,' she said without emotion and threw Kate a critical look. 'We quits now then?' she said. 'Try and stay out of trouble from now on, will you?'

With a casual wave, she made her way slowly to the staircase and, taking the steps carefully, one at a time, disappeared through the door into the walkway, leaving the door wide open behind her.

* * *

The Collector was a large, very fat man with a full, ginger beard and thick sunglasses. He was dressed in a pale blue suit and brown brogues and carried an old-fashioned Malacca cane in one podgy, bejewelled hand. He was also wearing a white Panama hat, which when removed briefly by him to dab his perspiring brow with a handkerchief, revealed a balding freckled head with just a trace of ginger above the ears. He reminded Brent of a throwback from the Sidney Greenstreet–Bogart era of films set in the Middle East and he found him totally repellent.

He was accompanied by a couple of muscular, unsmiling heavies in dark suits, plus a fussy little man with sandy-coloured, close-cropped hair, an Adolf Hitler style moustache and thick rimless glasses, carrying a black briefcase. Brent guessed he was the so-called diamond expert.

The only case Brent was interested in, however, was the much bigger holdall chained to the wrist of one of the heavies and he ran his tongue along his upper lip as he glanced at it, knowing full well what it should contain in nice, tight, little bundles.

He was nevertheless his usual, outwardly courteous self and stepped forward when the main man got out of the car, his hand extended in greeting.

'Welcome, my friend,' he said. 'I have some refreshments for you and your party upstairs and perhaps you would like to freshen up after your journey?'

The Collector ignored the extended hand and his response was sharp, abrasive and to the point. 'I have no desire for refreshment or to freshen up,' he snapped in a rather effeminate, high-pitched voice. 'I do not intend staying here any longer than I have to. Let us just get down to business, shall we?'

There was more than a hint of venom in Brent's gaze and his smile looked as if it had been painted on. 'But of course,' he said. 'Please follow me.'

* * *

Back in her concealed position among the trees, Lisa Heddon had picked up on the gist of much of the conversation, noting with grim amusement Brent's reaction to the snub by the Collector. Then she watched as the whole party went into the house through the front door and, shortly afterwards, saw the blinds in the large conference room overlooking the forecourt close.

She looked at her watch. Two fifteen precisely. *Give them just a few minutes to get settled,* she mused, as the Collector seemed to be a man in a hurry. After that, maybe another few while the money was being counted and the stones checked over by the weedy-looking guy she assumed to be the diamond expert. She couldn't see the negotiations taking less time than that, and at least by then both the money and the stones should be on show, ready for her to gate-crash the party. She'd thought about taking that big fat holdall as well as the diamonds, because the amount of money she guessed was inside would have made a nice, hefty bonus, but she knew that doing that would have amounted to nothing more than plain greed and it wasn't feasible anyway. The holdall would be much too bulky to carry on a fast exit. *No, Lisa,* she told herself, *stick to the set brief. The diamonds and Brent's head. That and no more.*

Slipping the haversack off her shoulders again, she checked she had a full magazine in her favoured Glock and slipped it into her holster in place of the Sig, which she returned to the bag.

Easing her injured leg into a more comfortable position, she stretched it experimentally and winced. The job would certainly be no cakewalk in her present poor physical condition, she mused with a wry grin, but what else did she have to do in deepest Pembrokeshire on a nice sunny afternoon like this?

* * *

Kate continued to sit there for several more minutes, still in a state of shock, staring at Delaney's lifeless body, as if she couldn't tear her eyes away from the sight.

It was like being in the midst of a nightmare. She had just seen a man being executed right in front of her. Okay, so she had seen death in most of its forms in her time in the police service, but never before had she witnessed an actual cold-blooded murder like this. Because that was what it was.

Although, as a human being, Delaney had been the lowest kind of street scum and her own life would ultimately have been at stake if he had not been killed, his death was still murder and in a perverse sort of way, she felt herself party to the fatal shooting, since it had happened solely because of her.

Where her negative thoughts might eventually have taken her if they had been allowed to fester in her disordered state of mind, it was difficult to speculate, but at that point they were suddenly interrupted by the sound of a car's powerful engine somewhere outside, followed by doors slamming, which abruptly brought her back to the reality of the here and now.

Scrambling to her feet, she ran over to Delaney's coat lying beside the stool and grabbed Cole's mobile, which was sticking out of one of his pockets. Then, pulling her torn shirt around her as best she could, she raced up the stairs and through the open cellar door on to the walkway. Taking a big risk, she ran through the archway into the passageway and turned down the side of the house to the front to peer round the corner on to the forecourt.

A red Volvo XC90 was parked a few yards from the front door, but there was no one in it or nearby. Then she caught the sound of raised voices and stomping feet coming from inside the house. Brent and his visitors were obviously already making their way upstairs. Pulling Cole's mobile from her pocket, she inserted the passcode and quickly dialled the number.

'He's in the house *now*,' she said when Cole came on the line, and she was surprised that she was able to keep her voice so steady and matter of fact after what she had just been through. 'The Collector has arrived and his party must be upstairs in the conference room already, as there's no one in the parked Volvo.'

'How many of them are there?'

'No idea. I never saw them.'

'Why? Were you asleep?'

Kate bit her tongue. There was no way she was going to go into what had happened to her with Delaney and the assassin. There would be time enough for that when the business was all over. So she ignored his comment and said instead, 'But the female assassin is back, tooled up, and after the diamonds. The troops need to be careful. She's armed and dressed in camouflage gear . . .'

Cole cut her off. 'Thanks for the heads-up. Better late than never, I suppose.'

'You cheeky bastard,' she exclaimed, 'You have no idea . . .'

There was a soft chuckle. 'Joke, Kate, joke,' he retorted. 'Joke. We're on site now. Gateman has just been neutralised. With you soon.'

CHAPTER 22

Brent studied the Collector's face when he produced the small velvet pouch and carefully tipped the three uncut pink diamonds on to the soft cloth he had spread out on a small end section of the long table. The man's eyes seemed to burn with a kind of fanatical fervour, try as he might to conceal his excitement.

'My present from Angola,' Brent murmured.

'Hardly a present at the price you are asking,' the Collector breathed, obviously over-awed, nevertheless.

'No,' Brent replied smoothly, 'but each one is, as I promised you, over one hundred carats and, according to a valuation by one of my own experts, even in its uncut state, almost flawless, with a colour and clarity that would triple its value once it is cut and polished.'

'You say the stones are from Angola,' his guest queried. 'I have been dealing in diamonds for a very long time and I know for a fact that Angola does not produce many pink diamonds, mainly yellow or colourless stones. The best and biggest stone so far was, of course, the famous four-hundred-and-four-carat stone, but this was a D grade, colourless rough diamond, called the Fourth of February stone, recovered from that territory in 2016. . .'

It was a test and Brent knew it. 'But anomalies do occur,' he said. 'Only last year, the one-hundred-and-seventy carat Lulo Rose pink diamond was recovered from the Lulo mine in Angola and is said to be one of the largest pink diamonds ever found in around three hundred years.'

'Yes, but *you* will probably know that rough diamonds lose about half their weight during the process of cutting and polishing and even then, their value will depend on what we call the four "Cs" — clarity, colour and cut as well as weight or carat,' the little man sitting beside the Collector commented, and he began taking equipment, including a pair of long tweezers, a roll of soft cloth and what Brent recognised as a jeweller's loupe, from the briefcase he had opened up on the table top.

'Agreed,' Brent acknowledged, 'but even after that process, you would still have three very valuable diamonds. Not a bad investment, I would suggest.'

'Then why are you so keen to part with them if you think they have such inherent value?' the Collector resumed.

'Simply because I do not have access to the cutting and polishing skills required, which you do . . .'

'And because they are illegal blood diamonds no main-stream dealer would ever touch?'

Brent shrugged. 'I don't have a problem admitting that, which is why I have come to you.'

'Are you suggesting I am less than reputable? I could regard that as insulting.'

Suddenly the atmosphere in the room became tense. Out of the corner of his eye, Brent saw one of the heavies his guest had brought with him, who was standing in the corner opposite, slip his hand inside his jacket. Simultaneously Crosby, standing by the window, did the same thing.

Then abruptly the Collector emitted a high-pitched laugh. 'But of course, you are quite right. I am thoroughly disreputable. That's why I am so rich.'

Brent abruptly relaxed and laughed with him, if a little uneasily.

'Now,' the fat man said, 'let Joshua, my own expert, continue to examine these stones and then perhaps we can talk business, eh? Meanwhile, perhaps I *will* partake of the refreshments I see you have provided for us at the end of the room. I don't suppose you have some green tea, do you . . . ?'

* * *

Kate was in a dilemma. What to do now? Unarmed and on the second or third of however many of the nine lives she had left, she knew she would be stupid to try and do anything herself to spoil the party. Cole and his teams had evidently managed to infiltrate the grounds and were already on their way to the house, so she should leave it to them. Also, both Brent and the Collector were bound to have armed heavies with them in the conference room and she would only wind up in the early grave Brent had already planned for her if she poked her nose into that hornet's nest. Then she thought of the woman who called herself Midnight, a cold calculating killer who had not only saved Kate's life, but at the same time had calmly and deliberately gunned down Frank Delaney without a second's hesitation.

Where the hell had she gone? When was she likely to make her move? And what form would it take? Kate's anxieties were at fever pitch. The way sod's law tended to work, it was likely to be right slap bang in the middle of the police raid and heaven alone knew how that might end.

Remembering the camouflage clothing the assassin had been wearing, she scanned the trees and undergrowth lining the fence to her left. She was convinced the assassin would be hiding somewhere on that side of the forecourt, which was closest to the front door of the house and provided the best view of the conference room windows. But she was unable to pick her out from the matching vegetation, and in the end, she simply gave up. Like a ghost the professional killer had appeared and like a ghost she had disappeared again, but she was out there somewhere and it was a cast-iron certainty that she would reappear at some stage to fulfil her contract. Yet Kate was powerless to do anything about it. She had become little more than a passive observer now and she felt totally helpless and superfluous. But that was before she found herself with a more serious problem to worry about.

'Don't move, *signora*,' the soft voice ordered close behind her and something sharp was pressed into her back. 'This large filleting knife and I not like to slice open liver of much pretty lady.'

Kate instantly froze. Both the voice and the accent were easily recognisable. She had forgotten all about Alfredo Vitale. The little Sicilian chef must have been in the kitchen, no doubt preparing an evening meal that would not now be eaten by anyone, and had spotted her pass in front of the louvre doors. *Don't be fooled by him*, Cole had warned her. *He has pre-cons in Calabria for using his carving expertise on a lot more than roast meat.* But it was a bit late to consider that advice now.

* * *

Lisa Heddon had left her hiding place very soon after the Collector and his cohorts had gone into the house with Brent and just before Kate had left the cellar to check out the Volvo. Sticking to the very edge of the woodland, she had then crossed over at the entrance to the passageway between the house and the garage block and limped as quickly as her injured leg would allow past the front bedrooms before brazenly entering the house through the front door.

The hallway, as she'd expected, was deserted, but she didn't delay and painfully climbed the glass staircase to the upper level. She could hear the voices of Brent and his guests through the closed door as she passed by the conference room, but went straight past it to the adjacent storeroom.

Once inside, she removed her camouflage face mask. Then, shrugging off her haversack, she reached inside and took out several items of kit previously concealed behind a dummy panel in the Land Rover. They consisted of a respirator with tinted eyepieces, a pair of ear defenders and a small, steel, hexagon-shaped cylinder, with a series of holes in the sides and a ring-pull on top; all of which she placed on the floor in front of her. Taking her time to fit, first the respirator, then the ear defenders, she once more pulled on her haversack, checked to make sure her cocked and locked Glock was easily accessible, then picked up the cylinder, handling with respect what was in fact a lethal, military stun grenade. Sacrilegiously genuflecting, considering what she was about to do, she gave a grim smile and limped back out into the corridor. It was party time.

* * *

Brent had been getting very impatient as he sipped his coffee. The Collector's expert was taking what seemed like an inordinate amount of time to examine the three pink diamonds. He was so absorbed in watching him while the Collector tucked into the sandwiches on the table, that he failed to see the door open very slowly. The warning shout from Crosby was too late as something was lobbed into the room from the corridor outside.

The massive explosion that followed and the brilliant flash of light that accompanied it had a devastating effect on those inside the room, causing temporary blindness, loss of hearing and balance and resulting in total disorientation. Several found themselves on the floor, struggling to get up and the Collector was reduced to a child-like state, as he crawled around under the table on his hands and knees, moaning shrilly in a state of confusion, as Joshua, the diamond expert, rolled about the floor nearby, clutching at his ears.

Ironically, only Brent seemed less debilitated by the stun grenade's blast. Though briefly suffering from partial loss of vision, he was sufficiently compos mentis to be aware of the figure, dressed in camouflage clothing and a respirator, just feet away from him, snatching up what had to be the diamonds from the table and swinging round towards him. He saw the gun in Lisa Heddon's hand, but managed to throw himself to one side a fraction of a second before the Glock barked its message of death. She didn't get a second chance to fire, as a round from the pistol a recovering Crosby had suddenly hauled from his shoulder holster slammed into her lower back, smashing through her spinal cord.

Shuddering under the impact, she felt the diamonds she had packed back into the velvet pouch from the table slip from her fingers and fall on to the floor. Then, unable to feel her legs anymore, she fell to her knees and, after swaying for a second, pitched forward on her face. The party had certainly not turned out the way she had anticipated.

* * *

'I think you too nosey,' Alfredo Vitale accused Kate. 'That no good. How you get out of cellar? What happen to Frank, eh?'

'He had an accident,' she replied and there was a significant change of tone in her voice that he failed to pick up on.

'We go see, eh?' he said. 'You first.'

But Kate had other ideas. She was quite sure Vitale would be far from happy when he saw Frank lying on the cellar floor full of holes and, with his excitable Mediterranean temperament, there was no knowing how he would react. But in any case, she had no intention of going anywhere with him. Suddenly she was no longer scared, but very very angry. She had had enough of being pushed around, patronised and abused by everyone and that ended now. The quiet, submissive approach she had reluctantly adopted for the sake of the police undercover operation was totally alien to her normal way of doing things. The real Kate Lewis was a rebel. A tactless, obstinate, outspoken "doer", who had a reputation for putting backs up in high places and capitulating to no one, let alone a "short-arsed" Sicilian gangster like Vitale. She was actually on the point of making that fact plain with the risky recourse to one of the more aggressive, physical disabling techniques she had learned in her early police career all those years ago, when there was a dramatic intervention that changed the whole dynamics of the situation. Suddenly all hell broke loose upstairs, with a violent explosion. The party, it seemed, had taken a lively turn . . .

* * *

Alfredo Vitale was not a brave man. He was used to sneaking up behind people in his home country's mafia-controlled ghettos and knifing them before they realised what was happening. The detonation of the stun grenade right above his head completely unnerved him and, forgetting his prisoner, he instinctively turned away from Kate to stare in the direction of the sound which had briefly popped his own ears. That was fatal.

Kate spun round before he realised his mistake, bringing her knee up between his legs with vicious force. As he doubled up with a scream, dropping his knife and clutching at his nether regions, she brought the edge of one hand in an equally vicious cutting motion across his throat, reducing him to a choking, writhing wreck on the ground at her feet, just as several gunshots sounded from upstairs.

* * *

Brent was now on his feet, his vision and hearing rapidly returning after the blast from the stun grenade. The others in the room were also gradually recovering and Crosby was already by his side, helping him up. Outside, they could both hear the metallic chatter of police radios amid shouting and the sound of running feet. They had seconds to get away. Spotting the velvet pouch on the floor by his would-be assassin's body, Brent scooped it up with a feeling of relief, brutally kicking the Collector aside as he crawled out from under the table to try and reach for it.

'The chopper,' Brent shouted at Crosby and lurched drunkenly from the room, grabbing the door frame to steady himself as he went through, then jerking his own pistol out of his pocket on the other side. Crosby was right behind him, but even as they reached the top of the glass staircase, several uniformed police officers armed with Heckler & Koch MP5 submachine guns burst through the doorway into the downstairs hall.

'Armed police,' one shouted up at them. 'Drop your weapons now!'

'The gym,' Brent snarled at Crosby and instead of complying, both turned and headed back down the corridor, with the police officers starting up the staircase in pursuit.

The emergency exit doors flew open under Brent's charge, but unbeknown to them, they had no need to panic. Their pursuers had been forced to abandon the chase after finding themselves confronted by a much more pressing problem, as the Collector and his armed henchmen suddenly spilled out into the corridor in front of them.

* * *

The forecourt was now full of armed police officers in full tactical gear and, leaving the still groaning chef with one of them, Kate headed for the front door at a run, only to be restrained by another policeman as she made to go through the front door.

'Armed team inside,' he snapped. 'You have to stay outside.'

Kate glared at him. 'Do you know who I am?' she exclaimed.

'Yes, I do,' he said, 'and the answer is still no.'

Cursing him, she turned round and ran back along the front of the house to the entrance to the sideway, intending to go back in via the French doors off the terrace — and ran straight into Brent and Crosby at the foot of the emergency exit steps.

Before she could retreat, Crosby had her arm twisted up behind her back, the muzzle of his Walther pistol buried in her neck, as he pushed her ahead of him down the garden steps after Brent and across the lawn at a run. Kate guessed exactly where the pair were heading. It could only be the helicopter pad and unless Cole and his teams got their skates on, they would be airborne and on their way to Ireland or Europe with a useful hostage. As for her, she had no illusions as to where she would end up. No doubt a steep dive into the Atlantic Ocean.

* * *

'Well,' Brent said breathlessly, staring at Kate with a sneer on his face as he jerked open the door of the helicopter. 'It seems we will never finish that portrait of you now, will we, you little bitch? I'll ask you again, what are you? Old Bill, mafiosi, or just an empty-headed little cow who decided to turn snout?'

'Boss,' Crosby said uneasily, throwing a glance over his shoulder, 'we gotta go. Filth will be here any minute. Shall I pop her now?'

Brent shook his head. 'We'll take her with us,' he said. 'They won't touch us with her on board.'

'But then what?'

'We dump her in the sea from a great height. If the fall doesn't kill her, the sharks will.'

He nodded to Kate. 'Get in.'

'No,' she said defiantly.

'Put her in the back,' he ordered Crosby and climbed up into the cockpit.

Crosby grabbed her by the arm and instantly regretted it when she lashed out with her foot, catching him on the shin. With a snarl of pain, the thug slapped her hard across the face, with the back of his closed fist.

Kate's head snapped back and she dropped to the ground like a stone and lay still, her eyes closed, as the helicopter roared into life.

'I think I just broke her neck,' Crosby shouted above the din.

'She's faking it,' Brent shouted back from inside the cockpit. 'Put her in anyway.'

He glanced towards the gate in the hedge and saw the uniforms on the other side. 'Hurry, man. They're here.'

Crosby bent down and, grabbing Kate around the waist, attempted to lift her limp body into the back of the machine. That was a mistake. Kate suddenly came to life and delivered a bone-crushing headbutt to his nose.

As Crosby staggered backwards with an agonised cry, dropping her on the ground, he jerked his pistol from its holster and racked the slide. 'You bloody cow!' he snarled, ignoring Brent's warning shouts.

The barrel of his gun was just inches from Kate's head when the telltale infra-red dot appeared on the right lapel of his jacket. He never got to pull the trigger as two 9 mm Parabellum rounds from a police H & K slammed into his chest dropping him on the spot.

Even as he crumpled on to the concrete launchpad, pumping blood in all directions, the helicopter was already airborne and, knowing the police would not be allowed to fire on him because he didn't present a risk to life, Brent waved at the knot of helmeted officers trooping through the gate of the compound towards Kate and the dead minder.

He wore a broad grin as he left his house behind and headed out across the fields towards Freshwater East Bay. So he hadn't managed to sell his diamonds, but what did it matter? They were safely in his pocket, despite the efforts of the dead mafia woman to steal them and blow his brains out afterwards. He would soon find another buyer for them once he was settled in his other bolthole on the continent. There was nothing to stop him now.

Back in his old home, Lisa Heddon opened her eyes and turned her head with difficulty to check around her. The house was full of police officers, but someone called Cole had already declared her dead after removing her gas mask and ear defenders and carrying out a none too thorough examination. Consequently, the room had been left empty, as the raid teams loaded the Collector and his henchmen into police vehicles and waited for Forensics to arrive on the scene to go through the motions of collecting evidence. To be fair, they could afford to wait, since the dead were unlikely to be going anywhere in the meantime and that included Heddon's own "kill", Frank Delaney, whose corpse still lay stiff and cold in the wine cellar. Heddon knew that she would soon be dead like him, too. She had no illusions about that. She knew the signs from her experience on the battlefield. She had lost all feeling in the lower part of her body and a numbing paralysis was already creeping up her spine. Crosby's bullet had finished her. But she didn't care anymore. Death would be a welcome release from the tortured memories of all those she had killed over the years, memories that still haunted her conscience every hour of her existence. But before she slipped her mortal coil, there was one more task she had to do.

She had heard the gunshots, followed by the distinctive sound of the helicopter's engine and the rhythmic thud of its rotor blades as it took off. It told her that Brent must have escaped from the police with his diamonds and was now airborne, on his way to a new life. That realisation gave her the incentive to draw on the last ounce of strength she possessed to ensure he was given the most appropriate send-off possible.

She forced a last smile through gritted teeth as she pulled her "special" mobile phone out of her pocket and put in the passcode. Then, with her index finger poised over the keypad, she gave a bitter smile and said, 'See you in hell, Jeremy,' before punching in a number.

Way out beyond the yellow strip of Freshwater East beach, the signal from Heddon's phone connected with another "slave" mobile wired to a detonator and a package of powerful Semtex explosive she had attached to the underside of the helicopter's fuel tank in the hangar all those days ago. In an instant the IED activated and the helicopter exploded in a massive ball of flame, taking the remains of the machine with Brent and his three pink diamonds to the bottom of the ocean.

Walking into the conference room with a black body bag on a stretcher, several hours after the forensic pathologist and scenes of crime team had left, the men from the local undertakers bent over Heddon's corpse and slid it into the body bag they had brought with them.

'Funny, that,' one of them said as he zipped the bag up after a moment's hesitation. 'It's the first time I've ever seen a stiff with a smile on their face.'

His colleague grunted. 'Maybe she knows something we don't,' he said.

AFTER THE FACT

Kate Lewis put another log on the fire and cast a wry glance at Hayden slumped in the armchair on one side of the stone hearth. He was fast asleep and snoring loudly, as usual. Crossing to the French doors of their little one-bed cottage on the Somerset Levels, she stared out into the fading afternoon light. The mist was already rising from the sodden ground and creeping insidiously across marsh and moor towards them, beheading the willow trees marking the edge of the rhyne on the other side of the field behind the cottage. Soon the advancing white tide would engulf them completely, holding them fast in its silent, isolating grip.

Kate had seen it all before, of course, in her former life as a detective sergeant with the Avon and Somerset Police. But within herself she was still captivated by this remote, chilling environment. An environment so often populated in winter's smoky gloom by ghostly apparitions, which changed shape and substance at will, and will-o'-the-wisps that flickered enticingly out on the boggy marsh, producing elfin fires that rose and fell with a blue-green flame, as if in some sort of weird paranormal dance. The brooding atmosphere of this dark, almost primordial place was far removed from the bright, sunny climes of Pembrokeshire and the soft, hot sands and sparkling, blue sea of Freshwater East Bay they had left behind. Yet in a strange way, she was glad to be back to the home country she knew so well and even keener to resume the job she had been practically welded to for so many years.

It was eight months since the undercover operation in Pembrokeshire and the decision by both Hayden and herself to mothball Willow Cottage and return to their old life in Somerset. But at Kate's insistence, they had stayed on long enough to attend poor Geraint Rheon's funeral, which had been put back several months because of the necessary inquest into his death.

The funeral had been one of those wet, stormy days the south-west coast of Wales often experienced in the approach to autumn; the wind whipping through the crooked tombstones of a local church like a banshee and the sky low, leaden and threatening. As usual with the demise of a serving police officer, the ancient pews were jam-packed with uniformed colleagues, determined to pay their last respects to this dedicated old-style copper, though sadly, it seemed that the lonely widower had had no family, so no one else was there to mourn his passing. This got to Kate and she couldn't help dismally reflecting on the fact that it might so easily have been her remains in that wooden coffin with its shiny brass handles instead, and that had she and Hayden parted, she would have had no family to mourn her passing either.

This was a sobering thought, as she and Hayden had come perilously close to breaking up after everything that had happened at Smuggler's Reach. The fact that Kate had so shamelessly deceived him had been the most difficult thing of all for Hayden to forgive. It had taken a lot of time and effort by both of them to rebuild their relationship and their trust in each other. But the revelations about the murder of Jamie Foster's brother, Peter, and the near fatal consequences for Kate when her cover was blown, had helped the process along and had softened Hayden's stance a little, though Kate had had the good sense not to reveal her nude portrait sitting with Brent, which would have been just too much for him to take.

Kate felt they were now finally getting back to normal after many frank, late-night discussions and much soul-searching. But she knew they still faced a long, hard road ahead and Hayden had taken some convincing about re-applying for their old jobs at Highbridge police station, only capitulating when she had pointed out to him that it was all they had ever done and that they had no skills for any other career.

To be completely honest, she had feared that some of the errors of judgement she had made during her under-cover role might anyway turn out to be a bar to her rejoining the force, if not even lead to some form of criminal or civil legal action being taken against her. But in the final analysis, due to the influence wielded by both John Norris and Harry Cole, she was spared the intense scrutiny she had anticipated during the subsequent police inquiry into the case and at the coroner's inquests on each of the deaths that had occurred.

Not that the police operation had gone down as an unqualified success. No one would now be brought to justice for the series of ruthless murders that had been committed. Furthermore, neither Brent's body, nor the blood diamonds, which had caused it all, had been recovered. True, minor players in the conspiracy, including gateman Jack Ferris and his girlfriend, Mandy Thomas, as well as the Collector's two heavies, were facing prosecution for unlawful possession of prohibited firearms and the hapless chef, Alfredo Vitale, a charge of assault on Kate and eventual deportation as a result of an expired visa, but the Collector himself had escaped any form of punishment. With the help of a sharp, top-class lawyer, he had successfully challenged the police to prove he was guilty of anything other than accepting an innocent invitation to view some oil paintings offered for sale by a pro-fessional artist and as far as anyone knew, he was safely back in Ireland, free to negotiate more illegal diamond purchase deals. Such was the reality of justice.

As for Smuggler's Reach itself, it had been sold off anon-ymously to a local developer through a tight-lipped London estate agency and was due to be demolished to make way for affordable housing and a village shop. An ignominious end for a notorious property that would forever feature in the dark annals of criminal history.

At least it was all now over and life could return to some semblance of order. But at what price? Looking at herself in the bathroom mirror that morning, Kate had noticed how she had aged in the last twelve months. Her face was leaner and tighter, and her eyes seemed to have lost much of their former mischievous sparkle. Even her long auburn hair was no longer the rich coppery colour it had once been but looked dry and lustreless. Soon she would be looking for grey hairs instead of split ends, she mused cynically. It was ironic that she and Hayden had originally quit their jobs in the police to chill out in the peace and quiet of Pembrokeshire and recharge their batteries. Instead, they had ended up suffering more stress and trauma than if they had stayed put in Somerset.

Turning back into the room, she cast the still sleeping Hayden another glance and refilled her glass on the coffee table with the last of the bottle of red wine standing beside it. She had just raised it to her lips when she heard the bang on the front door, followed by the sound of a car driving away. Setting the glass back down, she frowned and looked at her watch. It was a bit late for the post, she thought.

Crossing the room to the front door, she opened it and peered out into the mist. There was no one there, but a large square package was standing against the corner of the porch. Mystified, as she knew neither Hayden nor herself had had time to order anything since returning home from Pembrokeshire, she took it back indoors into the kitchen and carefully laid it on the breakfast bar. Selecting a knife from the rack on the wall, she slit one side of the parcel open, then ripped back the brown paper and wad of corrugated cardboard packing, to stare with a sense of mind-numbing shock at what was inside. It was a one metre six inches by two metres six inches, unframed oil painting of a totally nude, young woman with a pale freckled body and long auburn

255

hair. Though unfinished, it carried enough intimate detail for Kate to know that she was staring at a familiar portrait of herself, and an unsigned note attached to the canvas with a paper clip, read:

Hi Kate, Pity this couldn't be finished, but there's always another day, isn't there?

* * *

The beach below the cliffs of Freshwater East was dotted with dog walkers, and a whole variety of different animals raced across the sand and through the gently lapping surf, barking with obvious excitement. The holiday season was now at an end and it was time for the local residents to meet up, chat and enjoy what was on their doorstep, now that the tourists had gone home.

Tommy Evans didn't actually live in Freshwater East, but his parents, Ron and Margaret, had decided that a day out by the sea from Haverfordwest and a picnic among the dunes would be a great way for their son to enjoy his sixth birthday. Despite the coldness of the winter air, it was dry and sunny and the tide was on the way out. Wrapped in a thick woollen sweater, a red plastic mac and matching wellington boots, he seemed even more excited than all the dogs put together, as he ran down the beach to try out his new boots in the sea under the watchful eye of his parents.

After picking up a few shells and some coloured stones and putting them in his plastic bucket, he spotted the shiny thing in the water within minutes and bent down to pick it up. 'Look what I've found, Daddy,' he shouted and turned quickly to run back to his father with his little bit of treasure clutched tightly in his hand. 'It's-it's a diamond.'

His father laughed and bent over him to study the glittering, slightly pinkish object thrust out in front of him.

'What is it?' Margaret asked, peering past her husband to see what her son had picked up. She made a grimace. 'It's only a bit of old glass, love,' she said. 'Throw it back and let's get something to eat.'

Tommy's mouth compressed into an obstinate line. 'It's treasure and I want to keep it,' he said.

Margaret looked at her husband inquiringly. 'He could cut himself on it,' she said, 'and you just don't know where it's been.'

Ron sighed. 'We'd better throw it back, son,' he said. 'Your mum's right. Just hang on to your shells.'

The little hand closed tightly over the find and Tommy released a tear. '*I* found it and it's *mine*,' he said determinedly.

Ron looked at Margaret and saw her shake her head.

'Sorry, old lad,' he said. 'Mum says no, so let's put it back, eh?'

'I want to take it home and keep it with my other treasures,' Tommy insisted and defiantly pushed it into one of his pockets.

Margaret laughed. 'Oh, okay,' she relented, 'let him keep his bit of glass if it makes him happy. Now, let's go and sit among the dunes and have our picnic, because I'm getting very cold.'

As they turned to walk back up the beach, Tommy beckoned his father, who bent his head towards him to listen to what he had to say.

'I think my diamond will make us rich, Daddy,' he said. 'You'll see.'

By the time they had all returned home, Tommy was out for the count and, as Margaret carefully took off his clothes before putting him to bed, his "glass" treasure from Freshwater East beach fell out of his pocket on to the floor.

'Diamond, indeed,' she said and, going downstairs to the kitchen, she dropped the Angolan 110 carat stone into the rubbish bin outside the back door, adding, 'chance would be a fine thing.'

THE END

THE JOFFE BOOKS STORY

We began in 2014 when Jasper agreed to publish his mum's much-rejected romance novel and it became a bestseller.

Since then we've grown into the largest independent publisher in the UK. We're extremely proud to publish some of the very best writers in the world, including Joy Ellis, Faith Martin, Caro Ramsay, Helen Forrester, Simon Brett and Robert Goddard. Everyone at Joffe Books loves reading and we never forget that it all begins with the magic of an author telling a story.

We are proud to publish talented first-time authors, as well as established writers whose books we love introducing to a new generation of readers.

We won Trade Publisher of the Year at the Independent Publishing Awards in 2023. We have been shortlisted for Independent Publisher of the Year at the British Book Awards for the last four years, and were shortlisted for the Diversity and Inclusivity Award at the 2022 Independent Publishing Awards. In 2023 we were shortlisted for Publisher of the Year at the RNA Industry Awards.

We built this company with your help, and we love to hear from you, so please email us about absolutely anything bookish at feedback@joffebooks.com

If you want to receive free books every Friday and hear about all our new releases, join our mailing list: www.joffebooks.com/contact

And when you tell your friends about us, just remember: it's pronounced Joffe as in coffee or toffee!